Blue Skies at the Beach House

Diamond Beach Book 5

MAGGIE MILLER

BLUE SKIES AT THE BEACH HOUSE: Diamond Beach, book 5
Copyright © 2023 Maggie Miller

All she wanted was one last summer at the beach house...

It's blue skies ahead as nearly everyone in the beach house is focused on the wedding that's about to take place.

With her old house now up for sale, Claire has agreed to do something she's never done before. Make the wedding cake. It's a big challenge, maybe too big, but she wants to prove to herself that she can do it. She also wants to impress Danny.

Roxie has her hands full with all of the wedding details, along with helping daughter, Trina, with odds and ends at the soon-to-be-open salon. She's glad to be busy but knows it's a temporary thing. More than anything, she wants to be needed. She just has to figure out how to find the right place for herself.

The wedding is a beautiful, beachside event that brings everyone together, but that doesn't mean everyone's happy to be there. Is trouble on the horizon for someone in the beach house?

Chapter One

Jules stood on the back porch, hands braced on the railing, and stared out at the blue skies streaked with bright morning sun and, beneath it, the sparkling water of the Gulf. Diamond Beach was such a beautiful place.

Toby, her dachshund, sat by her feet. She was still in her nightshirt, but it was early, and no one was looking in her direction. She inhaled the sweet, salty air and let the sound of the waves wash over her. It was a balm to the soul, and a great way to wake up, especially since she hadn't slept that well last night.

Didn't matter now. Today was a new day. A fresh start. A chance to improve on yesterday, which hadn't been bad at all until her ex-husband had called.

Lars had clearly been under the influence of

something. Whether he was drinking again or using drugs or both, she had no idea, but she'd spent enough years married to him to know when he wasn't sober.

The realization weighed heavy on her heart. Not just for herself or for Lars, but mostly for their sons, Fender and Cash. Cash in particular, because Lars had reached out to him last night, too.

She glanced at the spiral steps that led to the third floor where he was undoubtedly still sleeping. She had no plans to wake him up. Let him sleep as long as he wanted. It meant that much more time he didn't have to think about his father's threats.

In plain language, that's what Lars's promise last night to disown Cash had been. A threat. Probably one Lars wouldn't act on, but it was hard to say with that man. He was impulsive at the best of times. When he was using, it was worse.

Her prayer was that Lars would be sober today, would realize what he'd done, and that his next move would be to call Cash to apologize. And then his second call would be to a rehab facility.

Jules knew that probably wasn't going to happen. When Lars got off the program, he generally fell off pretty hard. He was on tour, too, which was typically when temptation was at its worst. He wouldn't dare leave in the middle of a tour, either. Not even for something as important as rehab.

She shook her head and sighed. This wasn't good. Cash was an adult and could deal with it, but that didn't mean he hadn't been hurt by what his father had said.

Toby let out a big sigh and lay down, resting his head on her bare foot. Jules looked at him. "I know, you want to go for a walk, don't you? You've waited long enough. I'll go change and we'll hit the beach, okay, baby?"

Toby let out another little sigh as if to say he'd believe it when it happened. Jules scooped him up and took him back inside with her, kissing his face as she went.

Margo, her mother, was in the kitchen making coffee. "You're up early."

Jules nodded. "Rough night. I'm going to change and take Toby out for his walk. Are you headed over to Conrad's?"

"Not today, although I am meeting him and his sister for lunch later."

"I didn't know his sister lives here."

"She doesn't," Margo said. "She's visiting." She smiled tightly. "And I'm already anticipating the day she goes home."

"Oh, boy," Jules said. "That good, huh?"

"According to Conrad, Dinah has never thought anyone was good enough for her brother. But you go take that sweet pup out for his walk. We can talk over breakfast."

"Works for me." Jules hustled to change and get Toby downstairs so he could do his business in a patch of the yard before they hit the beach.

Toby was more than ready, so it didn't take long. She cleaned up after him, tossed the bag in the trash, and they were off.

There were lots of other people out walking their dogs, so she kept his leash short. That also helped keep Toby from dashing into the water. Toby didn't always understand how much smaller he was than most other dogs. His love for Shiloh, the dog that belonged to Jesse Hamilton, Jules's new boyfriend, was proof of that.

Shiloh was a golden retriever who probably outweighed Toby by a minimum of fifty pounds, but Toby didn't let that stop him from playing with her. Jules was pretty sure Toby was madly in love with Shiloh. Thankfully, Shiloh returned his affections. Whenever the two of them were together, it was pretty much a guarantee that silliness and shenanigans would ensue.

She'd have to talk to Jesse today about a play date for the two dogs. She'd be seeing him for the day's rehearsal session at the studio inside the business he owned, the Dolphin Club. Thanks to meeting him on this very beach, Jesse and his club had become an important part of her life.

Without him, she'd most likely be back in Landry at her house, where she had a recording studio. But because he had one at his club, she'd been able to stay here in Diamond Beach with her family.

He'd also helped her by gathering the musicians and backup singers she needed to record her new song. *Dixie's Got Her Boots On* was going to be Jules's...not comeback, exactly, but hopefully her next big thing. Maybe even the biggest thing she'd ever done.

Everyone who'd heard the song seemed to think it was going to do amazing things for her career, her agent included.

All Jules could do was hope and pray they were right. She'd done well for herself over the years, earning a few awards and membership into the Grand Ole Opry, but she'd never had the kind of success most musicians dreamed about.

The kind of success Lars had.

Of course, Lars hadn't handled his fame and fortune so well. She sighed and watched a seagull that was eying Toby like he was Public Enemy Number One. A fairly reasonable assessment.

Jules tightened her grip on his leash as he barked enthusiastically at the glaring bird. "What are you going to do, Toby? Bark him to death?"

As per usual, the barking continued. She just laughed and kept a strong hold on the leash. In a few more minutes, she turned them around anyway. She desperately wanted coffee and a hot shower, or she might end up going back to bed.

That couldn't happen. Today would be the first time everyone who'd be playing and singing the new song would be together. They needed this rehearsal day. And then tonight, she hoped to run through a few songs with Cash and Sierra, his new girlfriend.

Sierra was currently playing keyboards and singing backup on the new song. The young woman was both exceptionally talented and sweet as pie. Jules could see why Cash was so smitten with her.

The two of them were going to sit in with her tomorrow at Miguel and Willie's wedding. Jules had already agreed to play for the ceremony, but the three of them were also going to do some music for the reception. Not the whole thing. Most of it would be a playlist the groom was working on with his son, Danny. Jules was just going to provide about an hour or so.

That and playing for the ceremony was her gift to the couple.

She smiled, thinking about the two of them getting married so late in life. It was inspiring, really, to think that love had no age limit. They seemed very happy together, too, even though they'd barely known each other two weeks.

No judgment from her. She understood the impulsiveness of love. And the weight of time pressing down.

From what she understood, the pair had picked out a lot and a house to be built on it. They had set in motion the plans for their future with no hesitation.

There was a lesson to be learned in that.

One Jules had trouble with sometimes. The thing with being fearless was that it required *no fear*. That was the hard part.

And while she could get on stage and sing and play in front of thousands of people, she wasn't sure she could ever say, "I do," again.

Maybe she'd feel differently after Saturday's nuptials, but she doubted it. Talking to Lars last night had been a real wake-up call. The reality was that a lot of relationships didn't last. And some went bad in ways that left scars.

Jules had been married twice and had the wounds to show for it.

She liked Jesse a lot. But there was no way the third time would be the charm for her. Even with a man that amazing. She just wasn't willing to risk her happiness again.

She took a deep breath. Was she losing out on more happiness by thinking that way?

Maybe. She guessed she'd never find out.

Chapter Two

Roxie wasn't ready to get out of bed, but she did anyway. Tomorrow was a big day. Tomorrow, her mother, Willie, was getting married. Which meant today was the last day to do everything that still needed to be done. That list wasn't *too* long, but it was long enough.

The real chaos would happen tomorrow morning when the florist, rental people, caterers, and photographer showed up.

Today, she was taking her mom and herself to get manicures and pedicures. Trina had already had her nails done recently, so she was good. Thankfully, she'd be doing their hair for the wedding tomorrow. One of the big perks of having a daughter who was an amazing stylist was in-house hair services.

Granted, once the salon was open, Trina would probably be too busy for them unless they made appointments, but Roxie wasn't going to be mad about that. She hoped Trina had more business than she could handle. Who didn't want their child to be massively successful?

She threw on her robe and went out to the kitchen to start the coffee. She yawned as she got it going. Did she have time for a powerwalk and some exercises? She glanced back toward the bedrooms. There didn't seem to be any movement from her mom or Trina, so maybe.

Besides the mani-pedis, Roxie wanted to check in with Claire to see if there was anything Roxie could do to help with the wedding cake. It was more than generous of Claire to offer to make the cake. It was unexpected, and truly kind. Roxie figured if she could help in some way, she would.

Baking wasn't really her thing, but she'd do whatever Claire needed her to do. Even wash dishes, which she *was* good at. No job was too small or menial if it meant her mom ended up with a dream wedding day. Claire's half-sister, Jules, was providing the music for the ceremony, something that would have cost a pretty penny if they'd been paying her, seeing as how Jules was a bona fide star and all.

Roxie went back to her room and put on her workout clothes, then slipped out through the rear sliding doors, went down the steps, past the pool, and out to the beach. Her plan was to work out fast and hard so she'd have the rest of the day to get everything done she needed to.

A fast, hard workout meant bursts of running in between powerwalking and, on the way back, some lunges. Those were a lot harder in the sand. She'd do some pushups and crunches in her room before she showered.

As soon as she got back, coffee would be her reward.

Her speedy workout took her about thirty minutes. She was happy with that. She was also pretty sandy and very sweaty. She left her shoes by the sliding doors and went in. The A/C felt good. Surprisingly, no one was up yet. She fixed a cup of coffee and went to her room to finish her workout and shower.

When she came out from the shower and returned to the living room wrapped in her robe, her hair in a towel, empty coffee cup in hand, her mom and Trina were already there, hanging out. Trina was fixing herself a cup of coffee.

"There you are," Willie said. "Slept in, huh?"

"Not hardly," Roxie said, laughing. "For your

information, I was up early. I've already worked out and showered. Who did you think made coffee?"

Willie looked over at Trina in the kitchen. "I thought Trina did that."

Trina shook her head. "Nope. I might have been up before you, Mimi, but the coffee was already made." She smiled at Roxie. "Thanks, Ma."

"Sure, honey." Roxie took a seat at the breakfast bar. "You're at the salon today?"

She nodded. "Most of the day, yep. I have a bunch of interviews lined up. Five of them are stylists, too, so I'm super excited about those." She grinned. "It's really coming together."

"I can't wait."

"Neither can I," Willie said. "You're going to be a big hit, my girl."

"I hope so, Mimi." Trina looked at her mom again. "You want some breakfast? I don't mind cooking."

Roxie shook her head. "I think I'm just going to do a protein shake."

Willie made a face. "Are you getting onto one of those diet-and-exercise kicks again? Look what that did to Richard Simmons! No one's seen that poor man in years." She leaned forward, her voice sinking into a low whisper. "It made him crazy, you know."

"Ma," Roxie said. "You shouldn't say that about people. And maybe he just wanted some time out of the spotlight. You ever think about that?"

Willie clucked her tongue. "He's probably as big as house by now. Poor man."

Roxie just sighed and rolled her eyes. Being in a relationship with Ethan had put her in such a permanent good mood that she wanted to take care of herself more than ever. Being with him hadn't quite made her forget about Paulina, however.

Nothing could do that. Paulina was the young woman who'd recently shown up at the front door of the Double Diamond, the beach house they were living in, with a baby on her hip and the shocking announcement that she was also Bryan Thompson's wife and the baby was Bryan's son.

A third wife *and* a third family. Unbelievable.

Roxie had fallen into an angry funk after Paulina had shown up. She'd felt betrayed in a much deeper way than when she'd found out that Bryan was married to Claire when he'd married Roxie. Paulina was younger and very pretty, and Roxie couldn't escape the feeling that she hadn't been enough for Bryan.

A man with two wives had found enough reason to take a third. How could that not affect her?

Thanks to Ethan, she'd found the strength to go see Paulina and have a talk with her. That had helped. Didn't mean Roxie wasn't still dealing with some feelings, but she'd seen some of herself in Paulina, who was currently facing the task of raising her infant son without a husband.

Roxie had been through much the same thing raising Trina. Bryan might have been alive, but he'd been absent more than he'd been around. It was something Roxie had always attributed to how much he worked in order to take care of them.

She knew better now. He'd been splitting his time between two other families. Claire and Kat. Paulina and Nico.

"You want more coffee, Ma?"

Roxie looked over to see Trina holding the pot. She nodded and pushed her cup toward her daughter. "Sure, I'll have some more."

Trina filled her cup. "You okay? You looked a little lost in thought there for a minute."

Roxie smiled and told a little white lie. "Just thinking about everything that has to be done for the big day tomorrow."

Trina nodded. "I feel bad that I'm going to be at the salon all day. Should I reschedule the interviews?"

"No!" Willie shouted. "Your mother and I will be just fine. There's not that much to do, is there?"

Roxie shook her head. "No. Everything is under control." She cut her eyes at Trina. "And you can't open that salon without employees, so those interviews come first."

"I know, but still," Trina said. "If there's anything I can do, you'll call me, right?"

"We will," Roxie said. "Promise. In fact, maybe we'll have you bring something home for dinner so we don't have to cook."

Trina nodded. "I can do that." She looked at her grandmother. "Mimi, what do you want for breakfast?"

Willie patted her stomach. "I'm not that hungry. How about just some toast with jam and a yogurt?"

"I can do that," Trina said. "Might just do some peanut butter toast for myself. I'm a little nervous about these interviews. Which I should be heading to shortly."

"Just remember," Willie said. "You're the boss. You have nothing to be nervous about!"

"I know," Trina said as she tucked slices of bread into the toaster.

Roxie sipped her coffee, then got up to make her protein shake. As she did, her phone rang in the pocket of her robe. She reached in and pulled it out, not recognizing the number on the screen.

She answered. "Hello?"

"Roxie Thompson?"

"Speaking."

"This is Thomas Plummer. The photographer who's doing your mom's ceremony?"

"Of course. Hello." A little chill went through her. She prayed nothing was wrong. She was counting on him to take the wedding photos tomorrow and finding a replacement at this late hour would be impossible.

"I just wanted to tell you in person that I've decided to take the unit I looked at yesterday. At your mom's shopping center? Ethan was great and reassured me that everything I need can be taken care of in a few weeks, so I'm ready to sign the paperwork."

Roxie exhaled. "That's fantastic. I can meet you today, if you'd like."

"You have to be busy with the wedding tomorrow. Why don't we just take care of it then, when there's a spare moment? If that's all right with you?"

"That would be fine." She smiled. "Thanks for calling. We'll see you tomorrow."

"Yes, you will."

She hung up and faced her mother. "Guess what?"

Willie looked stumped. "Is it about the wedding?"

"Nope. Might actually be better." Roxie laughed. "We just got our third tenant for the shopping center!"

"Hot dog," Willie said. "One more to go and we'll be fully occupied. Well done, Roxanne."

"Thanks, Ma." Her mother only called her by her full name when she meant business. Roxie grinned. Didn't matter how old she was, getting approval from her mom would always be a good thing.

Chapter Three

Claire shook her head at her family. "The kitchen is closed. If you want breakfast, you'll have to go out. I have a wedding cake to make and I'm starting now." She had the stand mixer out and ready to go, along with her measuring cups, measuring spoons, spatula, and all the necessary ingredients.

Her cake pans were spread out on the island, too, waiting to be greased and floured and lined with parchment circles. Claire was taking no chances that any of them would stick. Today was not the day for that kind of nonsense.

"No worries," Kat said. "I'm headed out anyway, because I'm picking up breakfast and taking it over to Alex's. I'll be back later if you need help."

Claire nodded. "Tell Alex I'm keeping him in my prayers."

"Will do. See you all later," Kat called over her shoulder as she went out the door and down the steps.

"Bye, Kat." Jules frowned from her spot at the breakfast bar, where she was drinking coffee. "You realize what it'll cost me to feed that boy upstairs if I have to take him out?"

Claire laughed. "Find a breakfast buffet."

Their mother, Margo, was leaning against the far counter, coffee mug clutched in both hands. She hmphed. "I understand you have a lot to do, Claire, but not allowing your family to eat is rather drastic, don't you think?"

"No, I don't think it is." As an afterthought, Claire got a few more packages of butter out, just in case she had to make extra buttercream. She'd gotten up at five a.m. to get the bulk of the butter out so it could come to room temperature for the cake *and* the pounds and pounds of buttercream she had to make. Two kinds, actually. "It's only one day. That doesn't seem like a lot to ask."

"Come on, Mom," Jules said as she slipped out of her chair. "I'll run upstairs and get Cash moving and we'll go grab something." She headed for the sliders and the circular stairs.

"Thanks," Claire said. But her mom didn't look like she was going anywhere.

Margo watched her daughter. "Don't you have to eat?"

Claire shook her head. "Not until I get the rest of these cakes in the oven. And this first batch of buttercream made. Until then, I'm just having coffee and one of those low-carb yogurts."

Her mother let out a long, exasperated sigh. "You're doing an awful lot of work, Claire. And they're not even family."

"No, they're not. But they're pretty close." Claire knew her mother was upset by the arrival of Conrad's sister. She'd said as much when she'd gotten home last night. For that reason, Claire gave her a pass.

That and she didn't have time for a long, drawn-out conversation about why she was making this cake. She'd committed to it. Now she just needed to do it.

Thankfully, her mother seemed to understand that was the end of the discussion and went back to the bedroom. Probably to get ready for breakfast out.

Claire looked at her list of things to do. She already had a few of the cake layers made. They were wrapped in plastic wrap and sitting in the freezer, but she needed to get the rest made and chilled before she could start putting the cake together with dowel rods and boards for the main layers, which was something she'd only seen done on YouTube videos so far. Hopefully, that went well, and the cake stayed upright.

If the cake fell over or collapsed before it was served, she'd probably die of mortal embarrassment. That could *not* happen.

Once the cake was structurally sound, she'd need to crumb-coat it and let that chill before it could be decorated.

And that was what she was most nervous about. She could make cakes. She made them all the time. But a wedding cake? That was a whole different level of decorating, something that wasn't exactly her area. She sighed. Why had she said yes to this?

There were a few reasons. One, she liked a challenge and she wanted to see if she could pull it off. Two, this would be the perfect gift for Willie and Miguel. And three, there was a part of her that really wanted to impress Danny with her skills.

Nothing stroked her fragile ego like his praise. It wasn't just because they were going to be business partners in the new bakery. She was falling for him, and words of encouragement from the man she cared about...those were like rare gems. And not something she'd ever gotten from Bryan.

She also wondered if making wedding cakes was something she might be able to add as a service at the bakery. Probably in a limited way. Like one a month or something. She didn't want to put too much of a load on herself, not when she would already have so much else to take care of. But if it was a way to bring in money and get the bakery's name out there, then it seemed silly not to at least consider it.

But she was getting ahead of herself. She had a lot of work to do before she'd know if this was a good idea or not.

While her family got ready to go out to eat, Claire got busy. The first thing she did was set the temperature so the oven could heat up. Then she greased and floured her pans before adding a circle of parchment paper to the bottom of each one.

With that done, she moved on to making the cake batter. She was doubling the recipe, which could sometimes be problematic in baking. There wasn't always an explanation for it, either. Baking was a science and if one little thing changed, it could affect the entire recipe.

She hoped that didn't happen. That would really set her back if it did.

She measured her sugar and butter into the bowl and started the mixer at medium speed, paddle attachment in place, to cream them together. A very important step, in her opinion, and one most people didn't take enough time with. Properly creamed sugar and butter should be lighter in color and have an airy texture. Without that, a cake's texture could turn dense or crumbly, neither of which would make for a pleasant end product.

She'd gotten the eggs out earlier, so they could come to room temperature as well. A portion of the whites would go into the Italian meringue butter-cream she was making, but the rest were for the cake. Now, with the mixer doing its thing, she cracked the necessary number of eggs into a bowl and started whisking them so they'd be ready to incorporate. It was an extra step to be sure she didn't break the emulsion happening in the mixer's bowl.

Jules came back down. "Cash is moving. My word, that boy sleeps like the dead. Where's Mom?"

"In the bedroom getting ready, I think."

"Okay. Toby should be fine until we get back."

"Don't worry about him. I'll keep an eye out."

"Thanks." Jules went into the bedroom she shared with their mother.

In a few more minutes, Margo came back out. She sat in her chair and scrolled through her phone while she waited for Jules and Cash.

Cash showed up next via the elevator. He looked a little sleepy, but that was usually how he looked in the morning. It took him a bit to wake up. "I hear you're kicking us out."

He was grinning, so Claire nodded. "That's right. I've had enough of you people in my kitchen."

He leaned his elbows on the counter along with the top half of his body. "Doesn't Kat own this house now?"

Claire laughed. "Good point. But she's already left to see Alex, so that makes me in charge by default."

"If you say so, Aunt Claire." He chuckled. "Hey, I think it's super cool you're making the wedding cake for those guys."

"Thank you."

"Me and Sierra are going to play and sing with my mom for the ceremony and reception."

"Is that right?" Claire glanced at him. "Well, I think *that's* super cool. I can't wait to meet her."

"She's really nice," Cash said, exactly like a man who was utterly charmed by the woman in question.

"She must be, or you wouldn't be spending time with her."

Jules came out, still dressed in shorts and a T-shirt, but this time a more presentable version. Her hair was in a ponytail that had been pulled through the back of a ballcap. "Everyone ready?"

Cash straightened to look at his mother. "Starved."

Margo got to her feet. "I'm hungry, too. Let's go."

Cash went over and pushed the call button. Soon they were all in the elevator waving goodbye to Claire.

The doors shut and silence descended. Claire took a breath. Now she could *really* get to work.

Chapter Four

As a little treat, Trina had stopped on the way to the salon and bought herself a mocha latte. She knew her grandmother was right about Trina being the boss. This was her salon. Thanks to her grandmother's generosity, of course. But it was her business to run.

She understood all of that. But it didn't keep her from feeling like she was playing pretend. It was a hard thing to shake. She kept thinking someone was going to point at her and call her out for being a fraud. It was a weird way to feel, and she was doing her best to push it down.

She parked and went into the salon. Ethan's truck was in the parking lot, but he wasn't in the shop. Probably down at the other end in the storefront that was going to be the bakery. That reminded her that she wanted to talk to Danny and Claire at the reception tomorrow to see if they were going to offer more than just regular coffee at the bakery. She was hoping for mocha lattes and maybe cappuccinos. Even an iced mocha would be great.

If they were going to offer those kinds of coffee drinks, she could promise them at least one sale a day.

A few of Ethan's guys were in the salon, working away on installing the new sinks and faucets that had come in. Every day, the salon got closer to being ready and despite Trina's doubts about herself, she was still very excited to open and get back to work. She might not have full confidence in herself as a boss, but she knew how to cut, color, and style hair like nobody's business.

Maybe that was what she needed to focus on: What she was good at. And stop worrying about the rest.

She waved to the guys who were working. "Morning."

They nodded back. "Morning, Miss Trina."

She walked over to look at the new sleek black sinks. "I've got interviews almost all day, but I'll be set up in the front of the shop, so I don't think I'll be in your way."

Doug, the guy who was sort of in charge when

Ethan wasn't around, stood up. "We won't be too noisy."

"Won't bother me even if you are," Trina said. "What you guys are doing needs to get done." She smiled. "It's looking so good in here."

Doug wiped a hand across his forehead. "My wife and sister are pretty excited about this place opening. They want to come and try it out."

"Awesome! I promise to take care of them personally. You just make sure they tell me who they are."

He nodded. "Thanks. I will."

She went back to the front of the store to the space that would be the client waiting area. She had a card table and two chairs set up, thanks to Ethan, who was lending her those things. She put her coffee down, then took her laptop out of her bag and set it on the table.

Her plan was to stay on top of the other work she had to do in between interviews. She also had her salon binder, a notebook, and several pens. It took about three seconds to organize all of that, so once she was done, she sat down and fired up her laptop.

She wanted to create a Grand Opening flyer that she could distribute to some of the other businesses in the area. Maybe she could even tack a few up on whatever community bulletin boards she could find.

Miles might know about that. He was pretty well-connected. Maybe they'd let her put one up at the firehouse. Although she wasn't sure how much traffic they got from regular folks.

She got her phone out of her purse, then hung her purse on the back of the chair. Her tote bag, she leaned against the table leg. Despite having been swept, the floor was a little dusty from all the activity going on inside, but it wasn't anything that couldn't be brushed off later.

She checked the time. Her first interview was due in about fifteen minutes. Enough time to start on the flyer.

The sign company had generously sent her the logo they'd created for the sign as a separate file. She'd already ordered business cards with it. Now, she added it to the header of the flyer she was working on.

The salon door opened, and Ethan came in. He grinned. "Morning, boss."

She laughed. "I am never going to get used to that."

"Yeah, you will," he said.

She sighed. "I don't know. I keep thinking any

second someone's going to figure out I'm a big fat fraud."

Concern etched his face. He sat down in the other chair. "That's not going to happen. But what you're experiencing is pretty common. It's called imposter syndrome."

She narrowed her eyes. "It has a name?"

He nodded. "Yep." He sat back. "How long have you been doing hair?"

"I was eighteen when I entered cosmetology school. I wasn't good at it then, but that's when I started and when I learned to do perms and color and all of that."

"Were you good when you graduated?"

She nodded, smiling. "Yeah, I was pretty good."

"How old were you then?"

"Twenty."

"And when you graduated, did you start to work right away?"

"Yes. Once I passed my licensing exam. Which I did on the first try."

"Good for you. And you're twenty-eight now?"

"Yep."

"So you've been professionally doing hair for eight years. That's a pretty long time to work in the same profession. Did you have a lot of repeat customers at your last salon?"

She smiled. She knew what he was doing, and she appreciated it. "I did. I was always booked."

"So you were popular." He nodded slowly. "Sounds to me like you knew what you were doing, and you were making your clients happy."

She laughed softly. "You're pretty good at the dad stuff, you know that?"

He shrugged. "Just being honest. Also, I saw your mom's new hair last night. She looks amazing. And she looked pretty good before. I'd say anyone who can improve on something that's already close to perfection isn't just good at what they do, they're *talented*. That's you, Trina. You are most definitely talented. You might be a little nervous about taking on a place like this by yourself, but I know your mom will be here to help you if you need it."

"Thank you." She'd needed to hear all of that. She just hadn't realized it until he'd said it. "And you're right, she will be. I just don't want to work her too much, you know?"

He leaned forward. "Can I tell you a little secret?"

"Sure."

"I think your mom is itching to be needed. She

would be happy to work whatever hours you want her to. At least for a bit."

"Really? I thought she was looking forward to having some time to herself."

He shook his head. "I might be wrong, but I don't think so. Seems to me she'd like very much to be busy. Especially helping you."

"I'll keep that in mind. Oh! I just remembered. The photographer is going to take the unit next to the bakery."

"Yeah? That's great. He certainly seemed to like it yesterday. Fortunately, what he needs to get open will be pretty easy to do. I bet we can have him in there in two to three weeks."

A car parked outside. Trina craned her neck to see it better through the window. "That might be my first interview."

Ethan got up. "I'll let you get to it, boss. I just wanted to check in with the crew before I head back to the bakery. Lots of equipment coming in today and I promised Danny I'd give him a hand. Call me if you need anything."

"I will. Thanks again."

He nodded. "Anytime." He went into the back of the store to see his guys.

Trina took a sip of her mocha latte, then stood.

She hoped she looked all right. She'd worn cuffed white capri jeans with a hot pink blouse, gold belt and gold wedge sandals. White pants in a work zone probably wasn't the smartest choice, but she planned on being very careful not to get dirty.

The door opened and a pretty thirty-something woman came in. She was in slim black pants with a black and white patterned blouse with puffy cap sleeves and red stiletto heels. Her hair was streaked with several shades of blond and cut in a modern shag style. She smiled at Trina. "Hi. I'm here for the interview for the stylist position. I'm Ginger Robinson."

Trina stuck her hand out. "Nice to meet you, Ginger. I'm Trina. Welcome to A Cut Above. Why don't you have a seat, and we'll get started." She already knew from studying the woman's resume that Ginger had tons of experience and a decent clientele that could potentially follow her to A Cut Above. She'd also trained as a color specialist, which was a real asset.

"Thanks. It's nice to meet you." Ginger took a look around. "This place is going to be fire when it's done. I can just tell. Diamond Beach needs a shop like this. Hip but classy, you know what I mean?"

"I do," Trina said.

"And I love the idea of working for a younger woman." Ginger grinned. "I've never worked for anyone around my own age before, but I find it very inspirational." She laughed. "I hope that's not being too gushy, but it's true. I am totally inspired by women who go after what they want. That's kind of what I'm trying to do with my life. Focus on my goals. Be the best I can be. Stay sharp. Stay inspired. Keep learning. You know what I mean. And I think working in a place like this would be amazing."

Trina smiled. "Thank you."

She liked Ginger already. Liked her positive attitude and her look. Trina took her seat to start the interview, but something told her she'd just found her first employee.

Chapter Five

As Kat drove to Alex's, the aromas of the food she'd picked up from Digger's Diner wafted through the car and made her mouth water. For Alex, she'd gotten blueberry pancakes, scrambled eggs, and bacon. For herself, a veggie omelet with home fries.

But the delicious scent of his pancakes was making her rethink her order. Maybe he'd let her steal a bite of those pancakes. He probably would. He was good like that.

She parked at his apartment complex, grabbed her purse and the bag of food, then headed up to the second floor where he lived. It was a small place. One bedroom, one bath, but plenty of room for a single guy who spent most of his time on the beach or at his job.

Although that wouldn't be the case now, while he was recovering. She wondered if being home so much was already getting to him.

He opened the door as she walked toward it, obviously watching for her. He grinned. "Hey, beautiful."

"Hello, yourself. Your hair looks great." It was shorter than it had been since she'd met him, but it really did look good. It would be easier for him to wash one-handed. She smiled. "And I can see the painkillers are working."

"For your information, I haven't taken any yet. I wanted to see how I'd feel without them."

"And?"

He shook his head. "All right but not great. I'm supposed to take them with food, so I'll do that after we eat."

She leaned in to kiss him. "Good thing breakfast is here then."

"Good thing." He was in bare feet, cut-off sweat-pants, and a short-sleeve button-down shirt but only his good arm was through the sleeve. The other side was just draped over his shoulder where that arm was in the sling.

That shoulder and part of his chest was mottled purple and yellow with bruising from being hit by the falling beam when he was working a fire. The marks looked incredibly painful, and Kat must have grimaced without realizing what she was doing.

"It looks worse than it feels, I swear."

"Sorry," she said. "I didn't mean to stare. It doesn't look good."

"I know."

She came inside and put the bag on the counter in his tiny galley kitchen and began to unpack the food she'd brought. "Are you sure you're going to feel good enough to come to the wedding tomorrow?"

"Totally. I'm looking forward to it. Anything to get out of this place and not have to think about how I have two weeks of doing nothing to get through."

She felt for him. Being inactive had to be driving him nuts. "You'll be able to catch up on all of your shows at least."

He leaned against the counter near where she was working. "Yeah, but I was never that into television to begin with. I'm sure I'll find something to keep me occupied." He looked at the food she was getting out. "Those pancakes will be a good start. Except if I eat them every day, I'll need new gear when I get back to work, because I won't fit in the old stuff."

She laughed. "How about after breakfast and

you've taken your pain pills, we go for a walk on the beach?"

"Yeah, that's probably a good idea."

"Go sit. I'll bring everything out. What do you want to drink?"

"I do have one good arm you know." He opened the fridge. "Miles and Trina bought me all kinds of stuff yesterday. I've got some Sunny D in here. You want some?"

"Sure. Thank you." If he wanted to help, she wasn't going to tell him no. Feeling like an invalid couldn't be fun for him.

He got the big bottle out, took two mismatched glasses down from a cabinet, then filled them, and put the bottle back in the fridge.

During that time, she took the food to his small dining table, along with silverware and paper towels for napkins.

He carried one glass out. She followed behind with the other one. They both took seats in front of their food.

"Thanks for bringing the food and yourself over," he said. "It's really nice to see you."

"It's good to see you, too. I'm sorry I couldn't be around to help yesterday. I'm thankful Miles and Trina stepped up."

"I'm sorry I couldn't be there to help with the move like I promised." He used his fork to cut a wedge into his pancakes. "How did it go? Was it hard?"

"It was hard, and I'm a little sore from it. Thankfully, my mom called our pastor, and he got some men there to help us. Plus, the veterans charity that we donated most of our stuff to showed up with six guys. They worked like machines. It went better than I anticipated. Thanks to all of those people, plus my cousin, Cash, we were able to get it done. The Realtor we're listing the house with is going to take care of the cosmetic stuff like carpet cleaning and painting, so we should have the house on the market pretty soon."

Alex smiled. "Good. I'm glad. I love that you're going to be here permanently."

"Me, too." She was so ready for it. So ready to move forward.

"Excited about starting the new job?"

She nodded, a bite of omelet waiting on her fork. "Excited and nervous, but mostly excited. It's the beginning of a whole new chapter of my life, you know?"

"I do know."

"And I've already decided that after I get a couple

paychecks under my belt, I'm going to buy myself a surfboard. Hopefully with your help."

He grinned. "Yeah? I would love to help you pick one out."

"Cool. I can't wait to get back out into the water with you."

"Same here. That was a fun day, huh?"

She nodded. "It was one of the best days I've ever had. I owe you a lot for helping me do that. It really made me see I'm capable of so much more than I think I am."

"*You* did it. I was just the pep talk you needed."

She shook her head in amazement that this kind, cool, amazing guy was now her boyfriend. "I am so glad you harassed me on the beach that day about the sandcastle-building contest."

He laughed out loud. "What? Harassed? Is that how you tell it?"

She giggled. "I mean, it is *sort* of what happened."

"Oh, man, kick a guy when he's down, why don't you?"

She stuck her foot out and rubbed her toes against his calf while she smiled at him. "How are your pancakes?"

"Worth whatever weight I gain."

A new thought occurred to her. "Hey. You're going to need help getting ready for the wedding tomorrow, aren't you?"

"Yeah, but Miles is picking me up and he's already said he'd help me with my shirt. That's all I can't do by myself."

"Okay, that's good. He's such a good guy, isn't he?"

"One of the best. And he's crazy about Trina, although he feels bad that Liz is giving her such a hard time."

"Liz, his ex?" Kat frowned. They'd run into her when they'd all been out to eat at a place called Coconuts. "How is she bothering Trina?"

Alex told her how Miles and Trina had run into Liz at the grocery store and the confrontation that had ensued.

Kat blinked in astonishment. "I had no idea. Trina didn't say anything to me. But that's kind of how she is. She doesn't like to make a fuss about stuff like that. But it had to be upsetting."

"No doubt," Alex said. "Hopefully, that was the end of it. I like Trina. Not only did she cut my hair yesterday and help Miles get me groceries, but she made me a casserole and packaged it up so that all I have to do is stick the container in the microwave."

"I guess I need to step it up, huh?" Kat had heard

about all Trina had done, but seeing the look of appreciation on Alex's face made her feel like she wasn't doing her full job as a girlfriend. It was hard not to feel like she should have done something more.

Alex shook his head. "It isn't a competition, you know. You were moving an entire house. You were a little busy. With a job I was supposed to be helping you with."

"Yeah, I know. I'm really glad Trina was able to do that for you. But I still feel like I should have done more."

"Babe. You sat with me at the hospital and you're here now. It's all good, I swear." He reached out and took her hand. "You're going to hang out with me a little today, aren't you?"

"As long as you want me for."

"Cool." He stabbed another bite of pancakes, syrup dripping off it in golden strings. "I don't think there's much we can do besides walk on the beach and maybe watch a movie, but I'm still happy for the company."

"There's got to be something we can do." She looked around. "What needs to be done? Anything?"

"I have some laundry, but that's no way to spend the day."

"Why not?" Kat shrugged. "Better to have someone to hang out with at the laundromat than be there alone, don't you think?"

He narrowed his gaze. "You really want to help me do laundry?"

"Sure." She sipped her juice. "Besides, how easy will that be for you to do with one arm and no help?"

He sighed. "I see your point. I hate that you came over here just to end up doing chores, though."

She ate some homefries. "That's what I'm here to do. Besides spend time with you, obviously. I'm here to help you do whatever you need to. Think of me as your home health care for the day."

He laughed. "If you insist."

"I do." She helped herself to a bite of his pancakes before they were all gone. "And honestly, I don't care what we're doing, so long as we're together."

"Yeah." He nodded. "I feel that way, too. Maybe you can help me pick out my clothes for tomorrow? Not that I have a lot to choose from when it comes to fancier stuff."

"I'd love to." A walk on the beach, some chores, time together – it sounded like a perfect day to her.

It was a little like playing house. Something that

was getting easier and easier for Kat to picture as practicing for her future with Alex.

Chapter Six

Willie wasn't in the mood to get dressed up today and she picked her outfit accordingly. She'd be plenty fancy tomorrow all day. She put on a terrycloth set of loose capri pants and a short-sleeve zipper jacket, under which she wore her new Dunes West T-shirt.

Sadly, it had no crystals or rhinestones, and she hadn't had a chance to jazz it up herself yet. She already had plans to talk to the boutique where she'd bought it about improving the quality of their merchandise. Plain was so boring.

Roxie drove them to the nail place, stopping on the way to pick up some coffees. Willie got an iced oatmeal cookie latte. Roxie got a plain iced coffee with just a splash of heavy cream and fake sugar.

The girl was definitely on a health kick. Willie didn't mind. Better for Roxie to take care of herself than to not care at all. It was Ethan's influence, of course. Willie understood that. Her daughter wasn't much different from Willie.

For them, the affection of a good man made it easier to put yourself first. Funny how that worked. Willie was glad for Roxie. She deserved a nice guy after that bum Bryan. To think he'd actually had a third wife and another kid. He must have really considered himself a Casanova, the jerk.

It hurt her heart to think how that had to have affected Roxie.

Willie used her straw to poke at the ice in her drink and looked over at her daughter. "How are you doing?"

Roxie kept her eyes on the road. "I'm good, Ma. How are you doing? Tomorrow's the big day! Excited?"

"Like you wouldn't believe, but that's not what I'm talking about. I meant, how are you doing with Bryan and Wife Number Three."

"Oh." Roxie turned into the shopping center where the nail place was. "I'm doing better since I went to see her. It's not going to be easy for her to raise that baby on her own. I'm glad she's got her mom with her. That will help."

"So will the six hundred thousand she got from Bryan's life insurance."

Roxie laughed a little. "That, too."

"You're not mad about that?"

Roxie shrugged as she pulled into a parking spot. "No. Not really. Not anymore. How can I be? That money is going to help take care of Bryan's son. I can't begrudge a baby something like that. Besides, I'm not exactly hurting for money. I did still get three hundred thousand."

"Yeah, I guess." Willie aggressively sipped her drink. "I still think he's a louse for all his running around."

Roxie threw the car into Park. "On that we can agree. Bryan was certainly not the man I thought he was." She grabbed her purse. "Ready to get your nails done?"

"Yes. I want blue and lavender to match my dress and my roses. Then, afterwards, lunch is on me at Dunes West so I can show you the lot where our house is going to go, and you can see the development. You're going to love it." Willie was excited and proud to show off the piece of land where she and Miguel were going to be living.

"I'm sure I will. I can't wait to see it, Ma."

They got out and headed inside. They were a few

minutes early for their appointment, but that was good, because Willie needed the time to find just the right shades of blue and lavender. She had a small swatch of the fabric from her dress with her and she held it up to the bottles on display.

She shook her head at all the selections. "Roxie, help me. There are too many to choose from."

Her daughter came over. "Ooh, you're right. And they're all so pretty." She looked for a few moments, then tapped a finger on one particular bottle that held a slightly iridescent lavender with tiny flecks of holographic glitter in it. "I like that one."

"So do I," Willie said. It had been one of her top three right away.

"I wonder what's it called?" Roxie mused.

"You look. My reading glasses are in my purse."

Roxie picked the bottle up to read the label on the bottom and immediately smiled. "I think it's meant to be, Ma. It's called *San Juan Nights*. San Juan's the capital of Puerto Rico."

Willie gasped. Puerto Rico was Miguel's home country and where they were going for a month-long honeymoon as soon as Trina's salon was open. "You're right. I have to have that one. I'll do that on my toes. Help me find a blue for my fingernails."

They found just the right shade, called *Crystal Blue Persuasion*.

Roxie picked out a soft subtle pink for her fingers and toes, a shade called *Blushing Bride*.

Willie cut her eyes at the bottle. "It's a very pretty color, but that's not your usual at all. You normally go for something brighter and sparklier."

Roxie shrugged. "It's your day, Ma. I don't need to stand out."

"That's sweet of you, but you're already wearing sequins. What's the real reason?"

Roxie laughed. "I don't know. New man, new hair, new me? What can I say. Maybe my tastes are changing as I get older."

Willie nodded. "It does happen."

They were directed to side-by-side pedicure chairs for the first round of beautification. Willie was glad they were next to each other, because she had something she wanted to talk to Roxie about. Once they had their feet in the water soaking, she leaned over. "Have you heard about this woman bothering Trina?"

Roxie frowned. "No. Who are you talking about? What woman?"

"She's the ex-girlfriend of the guy Trina's seeing. Miles. She accosted Trina in the grocery store."

"Accosted?" Roxie didn't appear to like the sound of that. "Did she hurt Trina? Why didn't Trina say anything?"

"You know how Trina is. She doesn't like to talk bad about people. Even people who deserve it."

"How do you know about this woman?"

"Trina told me the other night." Willie kept her voice down. There weren't many other people in the nail salon, but she wanted to be cautious all the same. "Her name is Liz Stewart. I wrote it down in my phone. I was going to ask Miguel if he knew her parents. Supposedly, they have money. I thought they might be members of the Chamber of Commerce."

Roxie nodded. "Maybe. But what good will that do?"

"I'll go have a word with them, that's what."

Roxie made a face. "Ma, I don't think Trina would want you to do that."

"Probably not, but I wasn't going to tell her."

"And you're telling me because...?"

"Because if I can track these people down, I want you to go with me. You are her mother."

"I don't think talking to them is a good idea."

"Well, I do. Trina's not a fighter. She needs us to defend her."

Roxie sighed. "You're right that Trina isn't a fighter. It's not her way. But she's an adult, Ma. We've got to let her handle her battles however she chooses. Now, if she asks us to step in, that's different. But until then, I think we should keep out of it."

Willie frowned. "She's my only granddaughter and the person I love most in the world outside of you and Miguel. I can't just sit by and let her be maligned."

"Maligned?" Roxie's brows pulled together. "Has this woman actually said something about Trina? Or the salon?"

"Not yet." Willie crossed her arms. "But what if she does? What if she starts a rumor about Trina? Or bad-mouths the salon? Or gives the place bad reviews online? People do that these days, you know."

"I know." Roxie exhaled. "And that wouldn't be good. But it also hasn't happened yet. I don't think we should poke the hornet's nest until there's a reason to."

"Hmph." Willie had never been one to back down from confrontation. Or from starting a confrontation. "I just don't like it."

"I don't either." Roxie put her hand on Willie's arm. "Listen, why don't you talk to Miguel and see what you can find out about these people. Just for information purposes. And then we can discuss it some more. Or just file it away in case something does happen."

Frustrated, Willie sighed loudly, causing the young woman doing her nails to look up in the midst of cuticle trimming.

"Everything all right, ma'am?"

"Yes." Willie nodded and smiled reassuringly. "Everything's fine."

But everything wasn't fine. Willie was worried that this Liz was going to cause trouble for Trina or the salon or both, and that Trina, in her usual way, would just take it and not defend herself.

Willie didn't want Trina getting hurt. She might be an adult, but she was still Willie's granddaughter and Willie's need to defend that sweet child was strong.

She was definitely going to talk to Miguel about the Stewarts. Then she might just go talk to them herself.

If Roxie didn't want to go, maybe she'd take Miguel. He was about to be Trina's step-grandfather, after all. Maybe he even knew the Stewarts. Miguel had been in Diamond Beach a long time. It was very possible he and the Stewarts were old friends.

Although, Willie pictured the Stewarts as being typical rich snobs and Miguel wasn't the kind of man who'd be friends with people like that.

She sighed again, a little softer this time. Was she about to open a can of worms? Or was she about to stop trouble in its tracks?

She had no idea. Some days, it would be really nice to be psychic.

Chapter Seven

"I don't like her," Margo said over her last cup of coffee. It had to be. Any more caffeine and she'd be too jittery to write. "Dinah isn't a likeable person, either, so I doubt I'm the only one who feels that way. And I have to say that Conrad did warn me about her."

"That's pretty telling," Jules said. She was just about done eating the breakfast skillet she'd ordered.

"I agree." Margo had chosen an egg white omelet with vegetables and ham, no cheese. With that, she'd had fruit as a side and dry toast on which she'd spread a thin layer of orange marmalade. Fat didn't agree with her when she was irritated about something. Dinah being that something.

Cash, on the other hand, had ordered the hungry man special, which was apparently three of everything the kitchen was capable of producing. His meal had come on three plates, as if underscoring just how much food it was.

Jules sipped her water. "I mean, who says that about their own sister? It was good of him to say something ahead of time, though."

Margo nodded. "It was. I must confess, if he hadn't, I might have felt a little betrayed. But he told me she wouldn't like me and had never approved of anyone he'd been in a relationship with." She snorted. "Honestly. Just because she's never married is no reason she should keep her brother from being involved with someone."

Cash paused briefly from shoveling pancakes into his face. "She ought to be afraid of you, Grandma."

"Thank you. I think."

He laughed. "Come on. You can be scary when you want to be. And maybe even when you don't want to."

"I am not scary," Margo said. Was that really what her grandson thought?

"Mom," Jules said with a little grin. "You are easily one of the most intimidating people I know. And you're my mother. Cash is right. If this Dinah isn't afraid of you, she might be a sociopath."

"What's a sociopath again?" Cash asked.

"Someone who exhibits antisocial behavior, and shows no thought for the feelings of others. Among other things," Margo said. "But that's not how Dinah is. She's not openly antisocial. In fact, she comes off as highly social but it's all a show. Everything she says is either a backhanded compliment or a poorly disguised putdown. At least to me it was."

Cash shook his head. "I'd actually pay money to see the two of you go head to head. I bet if it weren't for Conrad, you'd wipe the floor with her, Gram."

Margo knew it was wrong, but she was somewhat flattered by her grandson's assessment. "If it wasn't for Conrad, I wouldn't have to deal with the woman at all."

Jules scooped up the last bite of cheese-covered scrambled eggs, chopped vegetables, and sausage. "How have you been dealing with her?"

Margo sipped her coffee. "By not falling into any of her traps. By refusing to play the games she's trying to start. And by calling her out on her insinuations." She leaned forward. "The woman had the gall to ask if this thriller Conrad and I are writing is autobiographical for me, implying that perhaps I'd had a hand in becoming a widow twice over."

Jules's mouth fell open. "Seriously? Boy, that *is*

nervy."

"Dang," Cash said. "Maybe you *should* deck her, Grandma."

Margo pursed her lips. "I am not about to get into fisticuffs with another woman. One who is, I might add, a few years older than me, I believe."

"Still," Cash said. "That is really uncool."

"I'll say," Jules said. "I kind of want to meet this woman now."

"Would you like to come to lunch with me? I don't think Conrad would mind, seeing as how he's bringing Dinah."

Jules shook her head. "As fun as that might be, I can't. Sorry. We have a major rehearsal today."

"Of course. I don't know how I forgot that," Margo said. "I do hope it all goes well for you. I suppose we should be getting back." She glanced at Cash's trio of plates. They were remarkably bare of food. "I was hoping to do some work on this chapter we're rewriting anyway."

Jules got her credit card out as Margo was doing the same thing. She caught her daughter's gaze. "Why don't we split it?"

Jules glanced at her son. "Cash ate enough for three people."

Margo smiled. "I don't mind." She would have

paid double for the chance to share another meal with him. He was such a wonderful young man, and she loved spending time with him.

"Thanks, Grandma."

"You're welcome, sweetheart. I can't wait to hear how you sound on your mother's new record."

"And I can't wait to read your book," he said.

Jules waved at their server, who brought their check over. Margo added her credit card to it, as did Jules, and the server left again.

"You know, Grandma," Cash started. "This woman is probably jealous of you."

She gave him an odd look. "You think Dinah is jealous of me?"

He nodded. "It could be part of it. You said she's never been married. Meanwhile, you've been married twice and have two daughters and three grandkids. That seems like something to be jealous of to me."

She hadn't thought about that. "You might be right. But she made it clear she didn't like me from the very beginning."

Jules took another drink of her water. "Maybe she thinks you're going to take Conrad away from her. Give him a life that keeps him too busy to spend time with her. Like Cash said, you have family and bringing Conrad into it means all sorts of new demands on his time. Not in a bad way, obviously. But if he spends time with us, he's not spending it with her."

Margo sighed. "You might also be right, although she isn't normally around him anyway. Whatever the reason, she definitely doesn't want me involved with him. The good news is she's only here for the weekend and after that, Conrad is all mine again. He's already told her he won't be around tomorrow night because of the wedding."

The server returned with their checks and two pens.

Cash leaned in, elbows on the table. "Maybe you should invite her over. Tell Conrad to bring her to the wedding. I bet Willie and Miguel wouldn't mind one more."

Jules nodded. "That's not a bad idea. Show her that we're a fun group. We'll be super nice to her and—"

"No." Margo tucked her copy of the receipt away in her purse. "While I think that's a very nice offer, I wouldn't be comfortable with her there. What if she caused a scene? Or said something unkind to Willie? I would be mortified if I was the reason something ruined their day."

Jules made a face. "Yeah, I wouldn't feel great about that, either. Well, maybe things will turn a corner at lunch today."

"Perhaps." Margo wasn't convinced.

When they got home, Jules and Cash went off to get ready for their day in the studio. Margo got herself a glass of water and went to sit on the back deck with her laptop to read through the chapter she and Conrad had decided to rewrite. She turned the ceiling fans on to move the air, though there was a slight breeze coming off the water.

She and Conrad had realized that while the chapter was good, it was a little weak on tension. Upping the stakes was important and this chapter had the potential for more conflict. They had their killer—who was a doctor at the hospital where a body had just been discovered obviously murdered —leaving instead of staying, which would force her to talk to the police.

Having her talk to the police would give Margo and Conrad a chance to plant clues, raise suspicions or even have her appear innocent, although the reader knew better.

Margo narrowed her eyes at the screen. She and Conrad hadn't really discussed which of those they wanted to do. She could call him, of course, but he might be busy with Dinah.

Then again, maybe he'd want a break. She was about to pick up her phone and send him a text to see if he was available when another voice filtered down to her from the deck above. Cash's voice. And he sounded upset.

"Dad, I'm *not* coming."

Cash was speaking to his father, Lars. Lars Harrison was a rock musician and singer in a band that made more noise than music, in Margo's opinion.

Despite that, they were apparently very popular, something Margo would never understand if she lived to be five hundred.

Cash sounded frustrated and a little sad. "I don't care. You do what you have to do, but it's pretty obvious that you're not on the program anymore."

Margo looked up as if she could see through the ceiling. "Not on the program" made it sound like Lars was no longer sober. He'd had a lot of issues with substance abuse. It was one of the big reasons Jules had left him.

That and his incessant cheating. How some men could be so blind to what was right in front of them mystified her.

"Yeah, well, I hear it in your voice. The booze or the drugs or whatever. Really not cool, Dad. You promise—" Cash went silent. Then, "Hey, you know what? I'm an adult. I can make my own decisions and just like I've decided I'm not flying out there, I've decided I'm not listening to this."

A soft beep, most likely Cash ending the call, was the only other sound she heard. Then the sliding doors upstairs opened and closed again. Cash going back inside.

She felt bad for eavesdropping, though it hadn't been intentional, but she felt worse for her grandson. How awful to have a father who chose substances over sobriety, and at the expense of his relationship with his son.

It broke her heart.

It also made her realize that the nonsense with Dinah was petty and meaningless in contrast. Margo resolved right then to be nothing but nice to the woman at lunch. If Dinah didn't reciprocate, that was on her.

Conrad would see for himself what a horror his sister was then. And in two more days, Dinah would be gone, and Margo wouldn't have to worry about her anymore.

Wouldn't that be a relief?

Chapter Eight

*J*ules glanced at her son in the passenger seat of her Jeep. They were on their way to the Dolphin Club, but Cash had been oddly quiet since he'd come back downstairs. Not like him at all. "You okay?"

He nodded but said nothing. Just stared through the windshield like he was trying to see a thousand miles into the distance.

Obviously, he wasn't okay. Something had happened in the time he'd gone upstairs to get ready for the day and come back down to leave.

There were only two things she could think of that might have that effect on him.

"Sierra didn't break up with you, did she?"

That got him to look over. "What? No."

"Then you must have talked to your dad."

His heavy sigh was answer enough. "I don't want to talk about it."

She nodded. "Okay. I'm sorry that happened."

"Me, too. But it's not your fault."

"I know. Still sorry."

Cash turned his head to look out the side window and fell silent again.

She knew from firsthand experience that a bad mood was no way to head into the studio. She also understood that he didn't want to talk, just like she understood the headspace he was in. He was hurt and upset and probably angry.

So was she. It was one thing for Lars to fall off the wagon and ruin his own life. It was another for him to allow his addictions to ruin his son's.

Without saying a word, she reached over and took Cash's hand. For a moment, he did nothing. Then he gave it a squeeze.

"Why does he have to say things like he's going to disown me?" Cash shook his head, still looking out the window. "I would never say a thing like that to my kid, no matter how mad I was or what I was going through or what they'd done."

A lump formed in her throat. "I'm not making excuses for him when I say this, but it's the addiction talking. The drugs or alcohol or whatever's in his system. As hard as it might be to believe, your father really does love you."

Cash snorted. "I don't know how you can defend him."

"Because I've known your dad a lot longer than you have. I've had more time with him sober. I know there is a good man inside him. Even if he's trying to drown that man in bourbon and pills. I hate that he can't get control of his life. I really do. I hate it for him, and I hate it for you and your brother."

"I don't think Fen knows anything about this."

"Maybe not. I texted with him a few days ago and he didn't mention it."

Cash sat up and looked at her. "You think he could talk some sense into him? Dad always did like him better."

"That's not true."

"Yes, it is. It's okay. It's not like I need therapy to work out my feelings about it. Fen is Dad's favorite and I'm yours."

She laughed as she pulled into the parking lot at the Dolphin Club. "You always will be my sweet baby boy. Which is not to say that I don't love your brother, I do. But he definitely takes after your dad, and you definitely take after me."

"I'm going to call him."

She wasn't going to tell Cash no. It was his decision. But she didn't think there was much Fender could do about his father's current situation. When Lars was like this, he listened to no one.

She parked and turned the car off. "You want some privacy?"

"Nah, you can stay. In fact, I'll put it on speaker so we can both talk to him." Cash dialed.

Fender answered after two rings. "Hey, bro, what's up? How's it going?"

"It's going good," Cash said. "Just FYI, you're on speaker and Mom's with me."

"Hi, Mom."

"Hi, honey," Jules said. "You sound well."

"I am. No complaints."

"Listen," Cash said, the tone of his voice turning more serious. "Has Dad reached out to you recently?"

"No, why? Something going on?"

Cash sighed. "He's not currently sober."

Fen let out a curse. "Great. He call you or something?"

"Yes," Cash said. "He isn't happy that I'm here in Diamond Beach with Mom, I guess. Told me I needed to fly to Spain to be with him and the band or he'd disown me. He was really riled up about it, too."

"Sorry, bro. He doesn't really mean that. It's like he becomes someone else when he's high."

"Yeah, well, I thought I should give you a heads-up."

"You want me to call him? See if I can talk some sense into him?"

"I don't know," Cash hedged. "I didn't tell you this to put you in the middle of it. Just so you'd know what's going on."

"I appreciate that, but someone should say something. Did you talk to him, Mom?"

"For a bit," Jules said. "But he wasn't exactly being civil, so I cut the conversation short."

Fen let out a long sigh. "I hate when he gets like this. I really wish he could commit to his sobriety and stay that way."

"We all do," Jules said. "If you call him, maybe you shouldn't say anything to him about talking to us. Just let him tell you what's going on."

"Yeah," Fen said. "That's probably a good idea. If I tell him we've talked, he'll say we're going behind his back. You know how he gets."

"All too well," Jules said.

"How's the music coming?"

Jules smiled. "We're about to head into the studio for rehearsals. Right now the plan is to record on Monday."

"That's awesome," Fen said. "I hope you shoot me a copy when it's done. I can't wait to hear it."

"I will, I promise," Jules said. "You have a good day, honey."

"You, too, Mom. And Cash?"

"Yeah?"

"If Dad calls you again, you let me know about it, all right? We can't let him think that's all right. If I have to, I'll fly to Spain and talk to him. I can't imagine the rest of the band is all that thrilled with him, either."

"I'll let you know," Cash said. "Love you, man."

"Love you, too, bro. Love you, Mom."

"Love you, honey."

Cash hung up. He looked at her. "At least he knows now."

"Yep. Ready to go in?"

He nodded, looking slightly better than he had at the beginning of the drive.

They grabbed their guitars and went inside, making their way to the recording studio.

Jesse was in the control room while the rest of

the musicians were in the studio, Sierra included. Cash went straight to her.

Jules lingered in the control room to speak to Jesse.

He greeted her with a kiss on the cheek. "Hey, there."

"Hi."

"No Toby today?"

"No. Claire's home all day finishing up the wedding cake, so she's looking after him."

Jesse stuck his index finger into the air. "That reminds me. Did she say anything to you about the pie deal?"

Jesse wanted to offer Claire's sour orange pies as a signature dessert at the club, but it was a deal that would ultimately be between him and Mrs. Butter's Bakery. "I did mention it to her, but she said she'd have to talk to Danny about it. Danny Rojas is the man she's opening the bakery with. That talk probably hasn't happened yet, considering his dad is the groom tomorrow."

Jesse laughed. "Yeah, I'm sure he's got other things on his mind. Well, maybe I can talk to them both at the reception."

Jules nodded. "I will happily introduce you. Claire really seemed interested."

"Great." He squinted. "You okay? You don't seem your normal self."

She gave him a quick smile and sighed. "I'm all right. My ex is causing some turmoil. Nothing we can't handle." She shifted her gaze to Cash. "I hate that it's impacting my son, though."

"I can understand that. If there's anything I can do, just say the word."

"Thanks. Fortunately, Lars and the band are in Spain right now, so it's not like he'll be showing up."

"Lars?" Jesse got an odd look on his face. "As in Lars Harrison, right?"

She nodded. "That's him."

"I forgot you were married to him." He looked at Cash. "And I never realized Cash was his son. No wonder the kid's so talented with parents like you two. I guess the apple doesn't fall far from the tree, huh?"

She watched her son, smiling now as he talked to Sierra. "I hope it falls farther than you think. Lars is currently dealing with some sobriety issues. I would be surprised if it doesn't make social media, the way he's going."

Jesse sucked air in between his teeth. "That's rough. You sure you're both all right to work today?"

She smiled for real this time, his concern touching. "Yes. It's nothing new to either of us. Just a big letdown that he's regressed after doing so well for so long. Getting to work is probably what we need most right now."

Jesse stretched his arm toward the glass that divided the two rooms. "Then let's make some music."

Jules had never been more ready.

Chapter Nine

*R*oxie followed her mom's directions to Dunes West, but she'd set her GPS, too. She'd never been to the community before, and she didn't want to accidentally end up in Alabama. She and directions weren't always friends.

She drove through the main entrance, which had an impressive sign, lots of big palm trees, and tons of flowers. It sort of reminded her of something you'd see in a movie or on a TV show. It was that fancy. "Wow. This looks nice, Ma."

"You ain't seen nothing yet," Willie said. "Wait until we get to The Preserve. Our lot is going to knock your socks off. Rob—he's our representative —told us it was the last of their estate lots, meaning it is bigger than most. A real premium spot and we got it."

Roxie smiled. She loved hearing the excitement

in her mom's voice. "Why don't we go see it first, then have lunch?"

Willie nodded enthusiastically. "Yeah, all right." She looked down at her toes, currently encased in her orthopedic sandals. "My polish should be dry enough to walk around. The lot's not cleared or anything yet, so there's weeds and dirt."

"We don't have to walk around."

"Yes, we do," Willie said. "I want you to see the water. Maybe there'll be dolphins again, but that's probably hoping for too much." She pointed. "I think that's where we turn. Yep, there's the sign."

Roxie turned as directed and pretty quickly came to a gate and a guard shack. Another sign announced they had arrived at The Preserve. The sign was smaller but just as fancy as the first one. Roxie came to a stop and lowered her window as the guard inside came out to greet them.

Willie leaned toward Roxie's open window, resting her arms on the console. "Hi, there. Willie Pasternak. Miguel Rojas and I just bought estate lot number five. This is my daughter, Roxanne. I want to take her to see it."

He went back into the guard house, looked at his computer, then stepped out and gave them a nod. "Go right ahead, Ms. Pasternak. Have a good day."

Willie stayed where she was, however. "Can you put my daughter on our permanent visitor list? Roxanne Thompson. Can you add her?"

"It's okay, Ma," Roxie said. "I don't mind checking in when I come over."

"Maybe not now, but you will. It's a pain in the butt," Willie said.

The guard came over to the car. He nodded at Roxie. "Ma'am, I'll need a copy of your driver's license to keep on file."

Roxie nodded. "No problem. Just a second." She didn't really want to dig into her wallet with her nails freshly painted, but that ship had sailed. She carefully worked her license out. "That address will be changing. I live in Diamond Beach now."

He nodded. "You can give me the new one when you get it."

He took the license into the office, returning a few minutes later. "There you go. You're all set now. You'll still have to check in at the guard house, because only residents get gate passes, but all you'll have to do is give your name."

"Thanks very much," Roxie said.

Willie sat back in her seat. "Maybe I can get you and Trina gate passes."

"It's not a big deal. It really isn't."

"For what we're paying for this house and lot, gate passes for my family should be part of the package." Willie pointed. "There! That's where our house is going to be."

Roxie parked alongside the vacant lot. A sign had been erected at the front. *Future home of Mr. and Mrs. Miguel Rojas.* "Wow, Ma. This is big. And right on the canal."

Willie grinned as she unbuckled her seatbelt. "I told you. Come on. Let's go look at the water."

Roxie got out and followed her mother carefully across the property. The lot was bigger than she'd expected, the houses on either side very nice. It was the kind of upscale community that she'd never imagined *any* of them might live in. Sure, the Double Diamond was nice, but there were much bigger places along the beach, too.

And while this place was an age-restricted retirement community, it wouldn't be too long before Roxie was that age herself.

They reached the water and Willie announced, "This is where our dock will be. We're going to get a boat, too. Won't that be fun?"

"It will be. Are you going to learn how to drive a boat?"

"No, but Miguel and Danny already know. Danny has a little sailboat. Miguel told me about it."

"A sailboat and a power boat are two different things." Roxie didn't want her mom or Miguel getting into trouble out on the water.

"Don't worry, they have a boating safety class here at the community center. Miguel and I already talked about taking it."

"Good." Roxie smiled. "This is incredible, Ma. I am so, *so* happy for you."

Willie smiled back. "It doesn't seem real a lot of the time. Not this place or Miguel or the shopping center or the salon for Trina. I keep thinking I'm going to wake up and find out it was all a dream."

"I hope that doesn't happen, but if it does, it's the best dream you've ever had."

Willie nodded. "I owe Zippy a huge debt that I'll never be able to repay."

Roxie stared out at sun glinting on the water. Sunsets here would probably be spectacular. "You could name your boat after him."

Willie laughed. "That's not a bad idea. Not sure if Miguel would go for naming the boat after one of my other husbands, though."

"Fair point." Roxie looked into the water directly below them. Little schools of silvery fish swam past. "When are they going to break ground?"

"Soon, I hope. Rob said it would be as soon as possible. Not entirely sure what that means, but if I don't see dirt being moved in the next two weeks, I may hire Ethan to run things from our end and keep the Dunes West people on their toes. I may do that anyway after the salon and the bakery are open."

Roxie laughed. "It sure is nice having him to rely on, isn't it?"

"It is." Willie narrowed her eyes. "How are things going between you two?"

"Really well. I'm going to church with him day after tomorrow."

"That's nice," Willie said. "He's a good man. Not like that bum you married."

Roxie tried to hold her tongue. She remained upset with Bryan for his marriage to Paulina, but at the same time, she didn't love hearing him run down. He was still the mother of her child. "Ma, don't speak ill of the dead. Even if they deserve it."

Willie just pursed her lips. "How about some lunch?"

"I'd love some."

"Good. I'm glad you're driving, too, because I might have a little gin and tonic at the restaurant."

"You sure? Tomorrow's a big day."

Willie headed back toward the car. "Just one. To take the edge off my wedding jitters."

As if. Roxie followed after her, rolling her eyes. "Ma, you've been married too many times to have jitters now."

Lunch was at a place called the Gulf Café. It was gorgeous inside. Roxie took it all in as the hostess seated them. The walls were painted with under-the-sea scenes and there were large aquariums all throughout the restaurant. At the back, the biggest one of all made up an entire wall. Their table was right across from it.

The pale blue light from the tank spilled over them, making Roxie feel like they were underwater, too. She took her seat, menu in hand, but her gaze was on the aquarium. Schools of flat, silver fish drifted past while smaller, more colorful groups darted through the coral formations. One large blue and yellow fish patrolled the tank like he was the boss.

It was magical.

"Okay," Roxie said. "I think I'm officially jealous of you living here."

Willie laughed. "You can visit anytime you like, you know. And maybe someday, you could move here, too. They have condos. You don't have to have a whole big house if that seems like too much." Her expression changed to something a little dreamier. "Or maybe you and Ethan would want a house."

"Ma, we're not at that place yet. Not everyone moves with the speed of light like you and Miguel, you know."

"I know," Willie said. "I also know that you're still grieving Bryan, even if he doesn't deserve it. But someday, you'll be at that place again. Don't you think?"

Roxie nodded. "Probably. And if there was ever a guy I'd want to be at that place with, it's Ethan. But I'm not going to rush things, either. We're taking things nice and easy. Just letting them happen."

"You're going to church with him on Sunday. That seems like a definite step forward."

"Sure, but it's not a step toward the altar. It's just a step. That's it." Roxie wasn't about to tell her mother that she'd be meeting Ethan's parents on Sunday.

Although, in light of their conversation, that did seem like a step toward something, didn't it?

Chapter Ten

The cakes were made, split, cooled, and then filled with the delicious pina colada filling Claire had made earlier. The layers were now chilling in the refrigerator, which was almost entirely taken up by those cakes. At least the three bowls of various shades of blue buttercream and the one bowl of white could stay out on the counter.

Claire would be so glad when she had a commercial kitchen to work out of. Working from home for a bake of this size wasn't easy.

Good thing there was plenty of counterspace at the beach house. Even so, most of it was occupied.

She was currently molding white chocolate shells and starfish to decorate the cake with. Tempering the chocolate had been a lot of work but she'd done it, paying close attention to the temperature of the melted chocolate, raising it then lowering it according to the YouTube video she'd watched.

Fortunately, the process had worked, and the chocolate was ready to mold. Tempering it meant it would come out with a shiny finish and a good mouth feel—important, since the decorations were, obviously, edible.

Using a small craft brush, she brushed the inside of her shell and starfish molds with the edible glitter, pearl powders, and powdered food coloring she'd bought at the crafts store. If this worked, her shells and starfish would be beautiful when they were released from the molds.

If it didn't work…she'd be doing a lot of piping.

Once these molds were filled and ready to set, she'd take the cakes out, crumb coat them, then they'd go back into the fridge to harden up.

The final assembly of the cake wouldn't be done until tomorrow right before the wedding, because there wasn't enough space in the refrigerator to store a cake that tall. Maybe if she took a shelf out, but that would create more work and necessitate having to find a new home for some of the other things already on the shelf.

It didn't seem worth the effort. She didn't love leaving the assembly until tomorrow, but it was probably safer. She was using dowels and plates to support the two smaller tiers, but having never done that before, she figured the less time the cake had to hold itself up, the better.

The big bottom layer would get a partial coating of Lorna Doone crumbs, crushed fine to look like sand. The rest of that tier and the two smaller ones would be iced in an ombre effect going from a white like the foam of the waves to pale blue, then deepening to a beautiful medium sea blue on the very top.

The two Barbie-sized Adirondack chairs she'd found at Michael's would be sitting on top to represent Willie and Miguel. She'd found two little wooden initials and she planned to rest the "M" in one chair and the "W" in the other.

The white chocolate shells and starfish would decorate the layers, along with some piped coral and some small dots that she hoped would look like bubbles.

She'd seen so many beautiful cakes online and had taken the prettiest elements from several of them. All she could do was hope her cake looked half as good as those when she was done. Molds filled with chocolate, she set them aside to cool. She hoped they came out as expected, shiny, sparkly, and unbroken.

She couldn't think about the alternative.

The white buttercream, which would be the crumb coat, was sitting on the counter, spreadable and ready to go. She got the cakes out and put the biggest one on her icing turntable. Then, using her big offset spatula, she began the process of crumb coating.

All that meant was she was giving them a thin layer of icing that would seal the cakes and keep the crumbs from breaking off and mucking up the top, pretty layer of icing.

She had three cakes to do but it didn't take long. The crumb coat didn't have to look good, just be functional. When she was done, the cakes all went back into the refrigerator so the icing could firm up.

She took a little break to have some lunch, which was just leftovers cobbled together from containers she no longer had room for in the fridge. Her phone buzzed about halfway through.

A text from Roxie. *Headed home soon. Do you need anything? I know you're working on the cake. I can run to the grocery store if you want.*

Claire smiled. That was sweet. *No, I'm good. Thank you for offering, though!*

How about actual help? I can come up when we get back.

Thanks again, but I'm good there, too. Claire was pleasantly surprised and touched by Roxie's offer. She hadn't expected it and even though she didn't need the help, it was a lovely gesture.

After she'd eaten, she checked on the chocolate. Still not hard enough to unmold. She thought about putting them in the fridge for a bit, too. Maybe while she had the cakes out? That was about the only time there'd be room for them to lay flat.

She cleaned up, handwashing some of the big things she'd used, then dried them and put them away. It was good to get that done. Made her feel like there was less on her to-do list, even though the dishes were only a small part of it.

Next, she gave each of the three shades of blue buttercream a good stir. They were all ready to go, as was her bowl of white buttercream. She'd been careful not to transfer crumbs into it when she was doing the crumb coat, because she was going to need that icing.

The white buttercream was her standard but very delicious recipe. The blue buttercream, because there was going to be so much of it and it had to hold up to being outside, was Italian meringue buttercream. A lot more work, but light and fluffy, with greater staying power.

She checked the time. Since the cakes had been in the refrigerator long enough, she was ready to move on to what she considered the trickiest part: Inserting the dowels that would hold up the other two layers. She wouldn't be stacking the layers until tomorrow, but the dowels were going in now.

They had to work. The top and middle layers might be smaller, but each cake was loaded with heavy filling and would be carrying a lot of buttercream icing as well as the chocolate decorations.

If the cake collapsed, all her work would be for naught. Worse still, Willie and Miguel wouldn't have a very happy memory of their day. Not to mention how embarrassing that would be for Claire. A collapsed cake wasn't much of a gift.

She'd watched numerous videos on how to put the supports in, how to measure them, how to place them, how to put the cake plate on to hold the next layer, but part of her wondered if she should go watch a few more.

Shaking her head at her hesitation, she knew that wouldn't help. She'd probably seen them all anyway. She started with the big bottom layer. She centered the cake plate that would hold the middle layer and used a toothpick to sketch around that plate. Then she carefully lifted the cake plate off.

The dowels had to go just inside the circle left on the crumb coat. She was putting eight in the bottom layer and six in the middle one.

Each dowel would have to be pushed all the way down, then lifted slightly and snipped so that when it was pressed back down, it was flush with the cake's surface. She got out her sharpest kitchen shears, the ones that could cut through small bones, and kept them at the ready.

She inserted the eight clear plastic dowels. They were hollow but durable, like very sturdy tubing. One by one, she pulled them back up and, using the faint line of icing around them as her guide, snipped them off and pushed them back down.

She did the next layer exactly the same. It seemed to be going well. She was tempted to put the cake plate on the bottom layer, then add the middle layer just to see how it looked, but then she'd have to take it off again. She wanted to handle the cakes as little as possible to reduce the chance of anything going wrong with them.

It was finally time to start decorating. First, she'd ice all three layers with the blue buttercream, slowly adding in small amounts of white as she went to create the ombre effect she was going for.

She took her time and worked carefully, using her small offset spatula. All the shades of blue were so pretty. It started with a deep marine blue that held just a touch of green and paled all the way to a frosty sea-glass aqua.

Stunning, in her estimation. Would Willie and Miguel think so, too? She knew they'd appreciate the work she'd done. But would they like the cake? That was all Claire wanted. For them to like what she'd done and be happy with it.

Layer by layer, she spread the blue in soft, rippling bands of icing to give it thc feeling of move-ment that water would have. The Italian meringue buttercream held the shapes she was creating beau-tifully and when she stepped back to look at the three tiers of cake, she couldn't help but smile.

They were *very* pretty. Even without all the shells, starfish, piped additions, and Lorna Doone sand.

She nodded. She was happy. Exhausted, her arms a little shaky from so much careful, concen-trated work, but happy.

With a lightened mood, she put the cakes back into the fridge to firm up. Her attention then went to the chocolate molds. They seemed plenty hard. She gently popped a shell out of the mold.

It was prettier than expected. With the way she'd painted the interior of the mold, the shell had come out a soft, tawny color with a slightly pearlized finish. Perfect. If they all came out this good, she'd be in great shape.

All she'd have to do was make one more full set of shells and starfish, then, in the morning, assemble the cake, add the decorations, sand, and finish the piping.

The most nerve-wracking part of it all would be moving the cake downstairs. Obviously, it would go in the elevator, but it was still going to take some careful maneuvering. She was counting on Danny and Cash to carry it.

The cake wouldn't be able to sit outside too long if the weather was really warm. A melted cake would be almost as bad as a collapsed one, and if the buttercream melted enough, a collapse might be inevitable.

But she wasn't going to think about that now. Instead, she came up with a new mantra. *The cake is going to be beautiful, it is going to taste delicious, and it is going to survive the trip downstairs.*

Anything else was unacceptable.

Chapter Eleven

Interviewing people was a lot more tiring than doing hair, Trina thought. Maybe that wasn't exactly true. Doing hair was pretty tiring but in a different way. Interviewing people was much more mentally exhausting. Doing hair was physically exhausting.

She'd found some great candidates. Some not as great, but that was to be expected. Three of the women she'd talked to seemed perfect. Ginger was one of them. She'd also talked to one young woman about being a general salon assistant.

Having someone who could do all the little jobs, like restocking stations, folding towels, sweeping up, getting clients drinks, wiping down sinks, making sure the bathroom was tidy, and running whatever errands needed doing would be invaluable. Especially if they got busy.

When, Trina reminded herself. *Not if. When.* They would get busy. She would do whatever it took to make that happen. Her mom would help, too. Her grandmother would hopefully be off in Puerto Rico, enjoying her honeymoon.

There were bound to be opening hiccups and Trina didn't want Mimi worrying about any of those.

With her purse strap over her shoulder and her tote bag in hand, Trina smiled as she left the shop to head for her car. Ethan's guys were still working in the salon, but they'd lock up when they were done. Probably not for a few hours yet. She hadn't seen Ethan again after he'd stopped in. He must be busy down at the bakery.

She glanced that way, but from a distance, it was hard to see if there was anything happening inside. It was exciting to know the whole place was coming alive, though. Soon it would be a bustling little shopping center with all kinds of activity.

Her new goal was to be doing a good, steady business by the time her grandmother got back from Puerto Rico. Mimi and Miguel were going for a whole month. That seemed like a pretty reasonable time period. Especially if she got that flyer finished and printed out.

Tomorrow was the wedding, the day after that

was Sunday, and Trina was thinking about going to church with her mom and Ethan. She had a lot to be thankful for, so why not?

But on Monday, her plan, after the last couple of interviews she had scheduled, was to put on a nice outfit and start visiting local businesses that could maybe help spread the word. Lady M's boutique would be one of her first stops. The woman who'd helped them with their dresses for the wedding had offered to put the salon's business cards in the store, so there was every reason to think she'd take a flyer.

But that was a good reminder that Trina needed to check on when her business cards were arriving.

There was so much to do. She smiled as she unlocked her car and got in. She liked being busy, she just didn't want to forget anything.

And even though tomorrow was the day of the wedding, Trina would be making calls in the morning to let the people she'd interviewed know the good—or bad—news about the job they'd applied for.

She started for home, sunglasses on, tunes playing, and thought about that. Telling someone they'd gotten the job seemed pretty easy. Telling them they hadn't...she'd never done that before. What was the best way to say a thing like that? She didn't want to upset anyone.

She'd had enough of that from Liz. Thankfully, she hadn't turned up at the salon today. Trina had been a little concerned she might after their run-in at the grocery store.

Maybe that confrontation had been what Liz needed to get it out of her system. Even though she'd been nasty to Trina, Trina still felt bad for her. That woman was clearly dealing with some issues.

Trina's stomach rumbled. She hadn't eaten lunch, figuring she'd just eat when she got home, even if it was a little later than usual. They hadn't texted to ask her to pick anything up, either. No big deal. She could always run out again if they wanted her to.

Maybe when she got home, she'd grab a quick bite, then lay by the pool for a bit. Unless her mom and Mimi needed her for something. It was very possible that there was wedding stuff to be done. Trina wasn't about to blow that off. She could lay out anytime.

She arrived a few minutes later and parked under the house. Her mom's car was there, so she and Mimi must be back from getting their nails done. Trina walked up the steps to the first floor, letting herself in with her key. "I'm home," she sang out.

"In the living room, Trina," her mom answered.

Trina went straight through. "How was the nail appointment?"

"Great," her mom said, wiggling her fingers to show off her new paint.

"Pretty," Trina said. "Very ladylike."

Her mom smiled and patted her hair as she fluttered her lashes. "That's who I am now."

Trina laughed. "Mimi, let me see yours."

Her grandmother stuck out her hands and feet.

"Oh, that's beautiful. I love those colors. They're perfect with your dress!"

Mimi nodded. "That's what I was going for. I took a little swatch of the fabric with me to be sure. Your mom helped me. Afterwards, we went to lunch in Dunes West, and I showed her our lot."

"Trina, you would have loved the place where we ate," her mom said. "The whole back wall of the restaurant was a huge fish tank."

"That sounds amazing." Trina put her stuff down on the breakfast bar, then went into the kitchen to see what she could find to eat.

"It was. They had other tanks, too, but the back wall was one giant aquarium."

"I promise," Mimi said. "I'll take you just as soon as I can."

"I can't wait." Trina pulled out some lunch meat and cheese, along with mayo, bread, lettuce, and pickles. "Just talking about food is making me hungrier. I haven't eaten yet."

Her mom got up from the couch. "I can make that for you if you want to go change."

"Well...is there any wedding stuff that needs to be done?"

Her mom looked at Willie, then shook her head. "I think we got it all done."

"Really?" Not the answer Trina had expected. "Wow. Okay. How about we get some pool time in then? Anyone up for that? After I eat, of course."

"I'd love to," her grandmother said. "But Miguel's expecting me soon. I promised I'd come over so we could go over a few house things and some details for the Puerto Rico trip. But you and your ma go." Then her grandmother frowned. "Hey, you didn't tell us how things went at the salon today."

Roxie held her hands up. "Hold that thought. You go put on your suit while I make your sandwich and then you can tell us everything while you eat."

"Deal," Trina said. "Thanks." Smiling, she took her purse and tote bag to her room and changed into her blue and white polka dot bikini. She tied a pink and white flowered sarong around her waist and went back out.

Her sandwich was sitting on the coffee table. Next to it was a small handful of chips, a pickle spear, and a can of diet soda. She grinned. "Thanks, Ma."

"You're welcome, honey. Got to take care of our working girl, don't we?"

Mimi nodded. "That's right. So? How did it go?"

Trina sat in front of her plate. "It went really well. I found three stylists and an assistant. I'm going to call them tomorrow morning and let them know the good news that they got the jobs."

Her mom sucked in a breath and clapped her hands. "Trina! That is wonderful!"

Trina nodded. "I'm really happy."

"I knew my girl could do it," Mimi said. "You're going to be the star hairdresser of Diamond Beach."

Trina laughed. "Thanks, Mimi. They're all such nice people. I can't believe they're going to be my crew at the salon." Then she sighed. "I feel bad about the people I have to call and tell bad news to, though. How am I going to do that?"

"You know," her mom said. "Sometimes I'd have to call the relatives of my patients and give them less than great news. It was never easy. But if you do it with empathy and kindness, no one can fault you for that."

"She's right," Mimi said. "Just be yourself. Tell them you loved meeting them, thank them for coming in, and then just be honest. Let them know there were other, more qualified applicants. And if they were close to getting the job, tell them to think about applying again in the future. You never know when you might need more employees."

Impressed, Trina blinked at her grandmother. "Mimi, when did you get so smart about such things?"

Her Mimi shrugged. "I'm marrying one of Diamond Beach's most successful businessmen tomorrow. Maybe he's rubbing off on me."

Trina laughed as her mom chuckled. "Well, I hope some of that rubs off on me, too."

"You know," Mimi said. "I'm sure Miguel would be happy to give you advice anytime you wanted it. Just because he already has grandchildren doesn't mean he won't have time for his new step-grand-daughter."

Trina exhaled as a new kind of happiness filled her. "I don't know why, but I never thought of him that way until just now." She put her hand to her heart. She hadn't had a grandfather in a long time. "You might be getting married, but I'm gaining a grandpa."

She glanced at her mom, who looked a little teary all of a sudden.

Trina smiled. "How cool is that?"

Her mom nodded and wiped at her eyes. "Very cool."

Trina looked at her grandmother again. "I'm so happy for you. But I might be just as happy for me, now, too."

Chapter Twelve

*L*unch had been postponed because Dinah had had a small emergency, according to Conrad. What that emergency was, Margo had no idea, but pushing lunch back nearly two hours seemed rude.

Her meager breakfast had only gone so far and now Margo was famished. Hunger pangs were not helping her mood, either. Regardless of when it took place, this meal with Dinah wasn't something she was looking forward to.

She arrived at the Hamilton Arms, the gorgeous old hotel that housed Brighton's Café, and left her car with the valet. She was in no mood to park a mile away and walk. She'd be a hot, sweaty mess by the time she arrived, which would only sour her mood further.

If that were possible.

She should have made up an excuse and begged off. She sighed in frustration and reminded herself she was doing this for Conrad.

She walked into the lobby, a nicely air-conditioned space that was as beautifully appointed as it should be for a hotel of this reputation. She took a breath and decided to seek out the ladies room to take a quick look at herself before she met up with them at the café.

The last thing she wanted was to appear unkempt in any way. Thankfully, since her trip to Landry to get more of her things, she had a much larger wardrobe to choose from.

As a result, she was wearing one of her best and most expensive dresses, a pale blue silk crepe de chine shirt dress by St. John printed with large, dark blue roses. With it, she carried another of her prized possessions, a tan, quilted Chanel handbag. It was quite old, but she'd taken excellent care of it. And Chanel was Chanel.

She went into the restroom and surveyed her appearance. She fixed a few strands of hair, then reapplied her lipstick, blotting it on a piece of paper towel.

The only good thing about the delay was she'd made excellent progress on rewriting the chapter.

After texting Conrad, he'd told her just to go in whatever direction felt right. She'd emailed him the results of her efforts. She was a little nervous to find out what he thought once he'd read her pages.

That wouldn't happen until much later. Probably not until this evening, when he was able to find a little time to himself.

Margo had no idea how occupied he was with Dinah, but Margo had a feeling Dinah wanted him as busy as possible so he wasn't available to Margo. Maybe she was wrong, but that just felt like something Dinah would do.

If Margo lingered any longer in the restroom, Dinah would accuse her of being late. She left and headed for Brighton's Café, where she was meeting them.

Maybe today would be nothing like what Margo was anticipating. Maybe Dinah had had a change of heart and realized that her brother deserved to be in whatever relationship made him happy. Maybe Dinah's emergency, whatever it was, had caused her to reconsider her actions. Such things did happen.

Not that Margo wished ill on the woman, but perhaps a small brush with her own mortality might be just the ticket.

Margo walked into the café and approached the

gentleman at the front. "Hello. I'm meeting two other people, a man and a woman. Conrad—"

"Conrad Ballard?" the man finished.

Margo nodded. "Yes, that's him."

"Right this way, ma'am. They're expecting you."

She hoped they hadn't been seated long. She'd find out soon enough.

The man led her to a nice table by the windows. Conrad stood as she approached, giving her a big smile. "There you are. You look lovely. As always."

"Thank you."

He leaned in and kissed her cheek, whispering into her ear, "Thank you for coming."

Obviously, he knew this wasn't something she was looking forward to. She put on a smile all the same, made easier by his understanding and appreciation.

Conrad and Dinah were seated on one side of the table, meaning Margo had no choice but to sit alone on the other.

A server, an older man with a handlebar mustache, showed up with a menu for her. "Good afternoon, ma'am. Can I get you something to drink while you look at the menu?"

"An Arnold Palmer, please."

"Right away. We do have two specials. First is a

Florida grouper sandwich with freshly made mango salsa. The fish can be fried or grilled. Then we have a sirloin steak salad with heirloom tomatoes and Cashel Blue crumble, which is a mild, buttery blue cheese. The steak, of course, is cooked to order."

"Thank you," Margo said.

"I'll be right back with your drink," the server said.

Margo set her menu aside. "That steak salad sounds marvelous." Red meat felt like exactly the kind of fortification she needed to face this next hour and a half or so.

Dinah made a face. "You're so brave to eat red meat. Aren't you worried about mad cow disease?"

Margo laughed, then realized the woman was serious. She ignored the question and went straight to the heart of the matter. "What was your emergency, if you don't mind me asking?"

Conrad sighed. "She broke a nail and had to have it repaired."

Margo's hands were on her lap. She clenched them into fists, causing her nails to dig into her palms. She fixed her gaze on Dinah. "You must be joking. A broken nail isn't an emergency."

Dinah glared at Margo. "When you care about your appearance it is." When Margo didn't respond to that, Dinah went on. "It was practically broken down to the quick. It was nearly bleeding. I had to have it taken care of. It could have gotten infected. Or worse."

"What would be worse?" Margo asked with all sincerity.

Conrad shook his head. "I told her to put a Band-Aid on it and take care of it later, but she wouldn't hear of it."

And, of course, Conrad hadn't put his foot down, because what Dinah wanted, Dinah got. Margo was starting to lose hope that the man across from her would ever be free to make his own decisions.

"There was blood, Connie," Dinah pouted.

Margo couldn't let it go. "You said it was nearly bleeding. Was it or not?"

Dinah pursed her lips. "It welled up a bit," she said with a dismissive twist of her shoulders. "Let's decide what we're eating, shall we? I'm starving."

"So am I," Margo said. "I'm not used to eating so late."

"My apologies," Conrad said. He glanced at Margo, his eyes pleading with her, but for what? To be kind to Dinah? To take pity on him? To just get through the meal?

She wasn't sure. She liked Conrad very much.

She was buying a house in his neighborhood, for crying out loud. But dealing with Dinah was just a bridge too far.

The server returned with Margo's drink. He asked, "Are we ready to order?"

Margo nodded.

Dinah stuck her finger into the air. "I might need another minute."

Conrad looked at her, his menu flat on the table. "Figure it out while Margo and I order. We've waited long enough to eat."

Margo just barely managed not to smile. Good for him. She looked up at the server. "I'll have that sirloin salad please."

"How would you like the steak cooked?"

"Medium-rare. Thank you."

"Good choice," he said. "And for you, sir?"

"I'll do the same thing, also medium-rare."

Dinah cut her eyes at him. "Your cholesterol."

"Is *fine*," he shot back.

Margo smiled, her doubts about Conrad receding further. Maybe he wasn't as cowed by his sister as she imagined.

With a deep sigh, Dinah shook her head at her menu. "I guess I'll do that shrimp salad. Are there any onions in that? I can't do onions."

"No, ma'am, no onions."

"All right, fine. And the dressing on the side, please."

"Very good." He took their menus and headed for the kitchen.

Margo decided to start over and, keeping her smile in place, she nodded at Dinah. "That shrimp salad is a good choice. It's excellent."

Dinah's brow furrowed. "You've had it before?"

"Yes."

"So you've eaten here before?"

"Yes." Margo gestured at Conrad. "With your brother, as a matter of fact."

He nodded, smiling. "That was a nice lunch, wasn't it?"

"It was," Margo agreed.

Dinah looked positively apoplectic. "You said this was a new place."

"It is, for you," Conrad answered. "But I've been here numerous times." He winked at Margo. "I bring all of my favorite women here."

Margo sipped her lemonade-iced tea blend and smiled. While Dinah simmered, Margo ignored her and spoke to Conrad. "I sent you the pages I worked on today. Hopefully, you'll get a chance to look at them later."

"I promise I will. I can't wait to see what you've done."

"Don't set your expectations too high. I definitely need your input."

"I look forward to the read."

Dinah sighed loudly and rolled her eyes. "Connie, isn't that book taking away from your real work at the *Gazette*?"

"Not in the slightest." He was still looking at Margo. "That reminds me. I talked with the editor about doing a piece on the bakery with that sour orange pie being the angle and he loved it. He wants an article and some photos."

"Really? That's wonderful," Margo said. Claire would be thrilled. The publicity for the bakery would definitely help get them off to a great start. Not that Margo was worried about the bakery doing well. Danny and Miguel obviously knew what they were doing when it came to business.

Dinah wrinkled her nose. "What's sour orange pie?"

"An old Florida classic," Margo answered.

"A lot like me," Conrad said.

Margo chuckled.

"Seriously," Dinah said. "What is it?"

Conrad looked at her. "A bit like key lime but honestly, I think it's better. Predates key lime, too."

She sniffed. "I've never heard of it."

"Well, it's fantastic," Conrad said. He reached across the table and took Margo's hand. "And Margo's daughter, Claire, is about to make it popular again."

"With your help," Margo said.

"Something I am thrilled to do."

Dinah looked fit to spit.

Margo just smiled. She was a little ashamed of herself for doubting Conrad's ability to be his own man. Clearly, he was just humoring his sister while she was here, but he was still very much Margo's boyfriend.

She couldn't have been happier she'd come to lunch.

Chapter Thirteen

"Thanks, sweetie." Willie accepted the glass of limeade Miguel handed her. They were in his living room instead of outside, because this wasn't a conversation she wanted to have where they might be overheard.

Despite what she'd told her girls, she wasn't here to talk about the trip to Puerto Rico. Not to start with, anyway.

He sat next to her on the couch, putting his own glass on the coffee table. "You're sure this is not bad luck for you to be here?"

"No, it's only when I'm actually in my wedding dress that you're not supposed to see me."

"All right. If you say so." He grinned and picked up his glass again. "Here's to our last hours as single people."

She smiled and clinked her glass against his.

"Cheers. Tomorrow, we start a whole new life together."

"I cannot wait, my love. I am so excited to take you to Puerto Rico and introduce you to my family there. They are going to love you."

"You think so?" Willie was under no illusions that she was everyone's cup of tea.

"Yes, of course. You are the woman who has brought me so much happiness. How could they not love you, too?"

She hoped he was right. "I look forward to meeting them and seeing your country. I like going to new places and trying new things. It's so much fun. And it'll be even more fun with a personal guide."

He nodded. "We will see all the sights and try all the best foods. You will fall in love with my country. You'll see."

"I can't wait." She sipped her limeade, which was tart and refreshing even without any rum in it, then set the glass down. "As you probably figured out, I'm here because I need your help with something."

His expression instantly turned serious. "Anything for you, my love. Just name it."

"I want you to keep this between us, all right?"

"Of course." He sat up a little straighter. "What's going on? Are you in some kind of trouble?"

"No, not me. But Trina might be."

His eyes widened.

"I'm hoping as connected as you are, you might be able to help. Not to mention, you're about to become her step-grandfather."

He nodded. "I will do whatever I can. Tell me what you want me to do."

"Well, here's the situation." Willie explained all about Liz Stewart, the young woman's connection to Miles, Trina's boyfriend, and the confrontation Trina had had with Liz at the salon and then the grocery store.

He shook his head as she finished. "I am so sorry for Trina. She's such a good girl. Sweet and kind and pure-hearted. No one should be treated like that, but especially not her."

"I agree. Do you know this woman's parents? Trina says they've been in Diamond Beach a long time and have money."

"Yes, I know them. Or I should say I know *of* them. I've met them maybe a couple times at different events, but it's been a few years. I don't go to those things as much as I used to."

"And do they have money?"

"They do. Her father owns the big insurance firm in town and her mother is one of the top-selling real estate agents, but they both came from money, as well. Granger Stewart, who would be Liz's grandfather, owned half of Diamond Beach. Some of it was sold off for big bucks, but the rest is still in the family."

He sighed. "What they earn off that land in the form of leases and rents...I'm not sure why any of them work, honestly."

"How about that." Willie sat back. "No wonder their daughter has such an entitled attitude. But why would she be looking for a job if her parents have all that money?"

"From what I remember of her parents, Edward and Grace, they are nice people. Genuine. Obviously wealthy, but not in your face about it. Not showoffs or braggarts. Maybe..." He thought for a moment. "Could they be trying to teach their daughter to be independent? Or perhaps they've cut her off for some reason."

Willie nodded. "Maybe. I'm glad to hear her parents aren't snobs. Gives me hope. Because Liz is currently being a giant pain in the rump roast."

He smiled. "If this Liz is causing problems for

Trina, I don't think her parents would like that very much."

"Well, I don't like it at all. I asked Trina how her day was today, and she didn't say anything about Liz, so I hope that means she left Trina alone. But my gut tells me just because she didn't show up at the salon today doesn't mean everything's hunky-dory between them, you know?"

Miguel nodded. "I know. I don't like to think of anyone upsetting Trina. Or you. You are all about to be my family. It's my job to watch out for you and protect you. If this Liz bothers Trina again, you tell me."

"I will." Willie scooted closer to him so she could rest her head on his shoulder. "Thank you. I feel better now."

"I am glad." He put his arm around her and kissed the top of her head. "Your nails look very beautiful."

She smiled. "You're not supposed to look at those."

"You said I could see you! How am I not supposed to see your fingernails, too?"

She laughed. "I'm teasing. It won't hurt if you see my fingernails." She sat up. "Is Danny taking you out tonight?"

Miguel's brows knit in confusion. "Why would he be taking me out?"

"You know, for a little last-night-as-a-single-man shindig. A bachelor party."

Miguel smiled. "I have not considered myself a bachelor in many, many years. I don't need a party to celebrate that. All I want to celebrate is marrying you tomorrow."

She kissed him. "I can already tell what a good husband you're going to be."

"I will be the best I can be, you have my word." He glanced toward the sliding glass doors. "Would you like to sit outside? I can light the firepit, if you like. Danny will be home soon. He's bringing Chinese food so no one has to cook. Will you stay? There is always more than we can eat."

"You sure he won't mind?"

"You are about to become his stepmother. He won't mind. Then, maybe after dinner, we can sit by the firepit and chat and have a little drink." Miguel splayed the fingers of his free hand. "Not too much. Just one. We want to be in good shape for tomorrow."

"I agree. Just one," she said. "Maybe like a little splash of rum in that limeade."

"We can do that," Miguel said.

Just then, the front door opened. A voice called out, "Hey, Dad, I'm home."

"Welcome home, Danny. Willie is here with me."

Danny came into the kitchen. "Hi, Willie. Are you staying for dinner?" He hefted two white plastic bags with the words "Hunan House" on them in red. "There's plenty."

Willie nodded. "I'd love to, thank you. Let me just text Roxie and Trina that I'm going to eat with you boys."

She got out her phone and was about to send them a group text, when she realized they might have been planning something for her. Not a bachelorette party, of course, but maybe...something?

She sent a different message than what she'd originally intended. *Is it all right with you two if I eat dinner with Miguel? Or do you need me to come back?*

If there was something planned, Roxie would invent a reason why they needed Willie to come home.

Roxie answered shortly. *Fine with me. Enjoy your dinner. See you when you get home.*

Then Trina chimed in. *Have fun, Mimi! We're in the pool.*

Willie looked up. "The girls are fine with me

staying. No surprise bachelorette party planned, apparently. Which is good! I didn't want one."

Danny let out a soft moan. "Dad, was I supposed to take you out for your last night as an unmarried man? With all the bakery stuff going on, I confess, it slipped my mind. I'm sorry. We can still do something if you want."

Miguel laughed. "There is nothing to be sorry for. I am very happy right here with the two of you."

"Okay," Danny said, smiling now. "I'm going to take a quick shower, then I'll get all the food set up on the table."

"Thank you, son."

As Danny went to his bedroom, Miguel took Willie's hand. "One more sleep and we will be married."

She nodded. "One more sleep." Although Willie was so excited about tomorrow, she wasn't sure she could sleep.

Life was such an amazing journey. She'd never thought she'd be this happy again, and yet, here she was, about to marry a wonderful man who cared for her and her family.

If that wasn't a blessing, she didn't know what was.

Chapter Fourteen

Kat drove home wishing she didn't have to leave Alex behind, but knowing she'd see him again tomorrow. They'd gotten a lot done, including a shedload of laundry. Not just clothes but Alex's sheets, too.

She'd figured if they were going to the laundromat, they might as well do it all. It had taken most of the day but now he wouldn't have to worry about it for a while. They'd entertained themselves while they were there.

They'd taken his tablet and watched a movie. When that was over, they'd played cards with a pack someone had left behind. It had been harder for him, what with only being able to use one hand, and the pack had been missing the two of hearts, but that hadn't stopped them.

For a bit, they'd just sat side by side and done

nothing but watch the clothes go around and talk about their hopes and dreams.

It had been easy and comfortable in a way she'd never experienced with Ray. In that moment, Kat had understood that that was how it was supposed to be. Not that she thought any relationship was going to be easy all the time. But there ought to be moments of it. Times when just being together was enough. When sharing each other's company was the only activity necessary.

It was like that with Alex a lot. Whether they were in a laundromat or walking on the beach, being together was all that was required.

Kind of amazing, considering she'd never even realized a relationship *could* be like that. Alex had changed her life in a lot of ways in a short amount of time. There was no telling what a year with him would bring.

She smiled. Maybe a proposal. One she already knew she'd say yes to.

She parked under the house, grabbed the groceries she'd bought after leaving Alex's, and got out of the car.

Roxie and Trina were in the pool, floating around with noodles under their arms to hold them up. Kat walked over. "How's the water?"

"It's great," Trina said. "You want to join us?"

Kat lifted her bag of groceries. "Can't. Need to make dinner. Thanks, though. All ready for the wedding tomorrow?"

Roxie nodded. "As much as we can be. I can't wait to see the cake your mom made."

Kat nodded. "Me, too. I better get these upstairs. Have a good night. See you guys tomorrow."

"You bet," Trina said.

Kat took the elevator up. She'd texted her mom before she'd come home, so she already knew that the work on the cake was done, and her mother was officially out of the kitchen until tomorrow.

Kat had offered to make dinner, which her mom had immediately accepted. Kat wasn't really *making* dinner, so much as she was putting all the premade ingredients together, but close enough.

She stepped off the elevator. Her mom was laying on the couch, television on to some home decorating show, a glass of wine within arm's reach on the coffee table. Toby was curled up by her feet, sleeping, though he lifted his head to look at her, then flopped back down. "Hey, there. Long day, huh?"

Her mom glanced back and nodded. "Long. And tiring. But good. I think even Toby is worn out."

"I didn't realize he was helping." Kat grinned. "Dinner won't take too long. I just have to put it all together." She went into the kitchen, setting her single bag of groceries on the counter. She took her purse into her room and tossed it onto the bed after taking her phone out and sticking it in the back pocket of her shorts.

"How's Alex doing?" her mom asked.

"He's all right," Kat answered as she came back out. "I can tell he's already a little frustrated with the inactivity but he's just going to have to get used to that."

"Is he in much pain?"

Kat unpacked the groceries. "A little. He doesn't want to take the pain meds they gave him, but I talked him into it today. He's incredibly bruised from where that beam hit him. I'm surprised he didn't end up with broken bones."

Her mom sucked air in through her teeth. "That poor man. Is he really well enough to come tomorrow?"

"He says he is." Kat walked over to her. "He also said he's really looking forward to getting out of the house, so I wasn't about to suggest he stay home. He says he needs the distraction, and I can see how that would be true. He's so used to being active, you know? Sitting around doing nothing is not what he's used to. Unless he's at the firehouse and then he's surrounded by the crew."

"It's good that you spent time with him today." Her mom lowered the volume on the television. "What did you get for dinner, by the way? Not that I care too much. I don't have to make it, so that's all that really matters."

"I'm making a chicken Caesar salad with cherry tomatoes and chopped bacon, because I needed something more than just lettuce. That okay?"

"Sounds heavenly." Her mom took a sip of her wine. "And it goes with what I'm drinking, so even better."

Kat smiled. "Just give me a few minutes. Are Aunt Jules and Cash home? Or Grandma?"

"Your grandmother's in her room writing. Aunt Jules and Cash are eating at the club before they come home, which should be soon."

"Okay." Kat walked over to the room her grandmother and aunt shared. She knocked. "Grandma? Do you want some chicken Caesar salad for dinner?"

"Just a minute," her grandmother called out. She opened the door. "That sounds lovely, thank you. I'm going to save my work and then I'm done for the day. I've worked more than enough."

"You've been at it all day," Claire said. "When you weren't at lunch, anyway."

Kat looked at her grandmother. "How was that lunch? Did you and Dinah end up scuffling in the middle of the dining room?"

Margo gave Kat a look. "We did not. It was fine. Dinah was Dinah and I don't think she's ever going to change, but neither Conrad nor I gave in to her nonsense, so hopefully she has a better understanding of how things are going to go."

Kat smiled. "Good. No one should stand in the way of your happiness. Or Conrad's."

"Thank you," her grandmother said. "That reminds me. Claire? Conrad is going to write an article on the bakery for the *Gazette*. The focus will be the sour orange pie and how you want to bring that back to the local consciousness. They want photos, too."

Claire sat up. "Really? That's amazing. Wow. That will do such good things for the bakery. Thanks, Mom."

"Thank Conrad. It was his doing."

Claire nodded. "I will, tomorrow."

"Congratulations, Mom," Kat said. "That is so cool! You and that pie deserve some recognition."

"Thanks." Her mom was all smiles and understandably so.

Kat pointed at the kitchen. "I'm going to get dinner made."

She went back to the kitchen and washed her hands, then got out the big salad bowl. She emptied the two bags of washed and cut Romaine lettuce into it, then dumped in the pint of cherry tomatoes she'd picked up.

Her next addition was two bags of precooked and sliced chicken breast. Over all of that, she drizzled the dressing, sending up the mouthwatering aroma of lemon and garlic. She'd gotten a jar of the good stuff from the refrigerated section.

The last addition was the bag of chunky bacon bits. The real stuff, not whatever those fake pieces were. She added about half of the bag.

Using the salad tongs, she tossed all of that together and finished it off with a healthy sprinkling of shredded Parmesan cheese and a few more pieces of bacon. She left the croutons off, because she knew her mom wouldn't want them, and her grandmother wouldn't care. Kat could have gone either way, but easy was better.

"All right," she said. "Dinner is served."

Her grandmother was just coming out of the bedroom. "That was fast."

"I'll say," Claire said. "Are we eating at the table?"

Kat shrugged. "Why don't we just fill our plates and sit in front of the TV? I know that's probably not what you want, though, is it, Grandma?"

Her grandmother shook her head. "It sounds just fine to me. Nothing wrong with being casual once in a while. I think I'll have a glass of that white wine, too."

"Really? Okay, then." Kat got out three shallow salad plates and set them next to the bowl, along with forks and napkins. "Let's eat."

Her mom and grandmother came over to help themselves. Kat got herself a glass of water while they were doing that. She got the wine out of the fridge, taking a moment to appreciate the gorgeous colors of the cakes in there.

But her mind was really on her grandmother. Was it Conrad's influence on her grandmother softening her up? Was it the more relaxed lifestyle of living at the beach? Or was Dinah having some kind of effect on her?

Kat didn't know, but she liked her grandmother's changing attitude.

Chapter Fifteen

Roxie looked at her fingers. "I'm wrinkling up. I think it's time for me to get out. Besides, we should eat something. Maybe you're not hungry, but I am."

"I won't be hungry for another hour or so maybe," Trina said. "But I didn't bring anything home, as you know. What have we got? Maybe one of those frozen lasagnas?"

Roxie paddled her way to the steps where hers and Trina's phones were sitting at the edge of the pool. "That would be perfect. It'll take an hour anyway. I'll stick it in the oven before I shower."

She got out, dried off, then picked up her phone and checked the screen. No new messages from her mom. She glanced over at the Rojas house.

The first floor was lit up, but she couldn't see

inside because of the angle. They must still be eating.

Hard to believe her mom was marrying into that family tomorrow. Not hard in a bad way. It had all just happened so fast. But obviously, her mom was happy, Miguel was happy, and they were meant to be.

Roxie was glad for them. Love at any age was a miraculous thing. Her mind turned to Ethan, and she smiled. No surprise there. He made her smile a lot.

Trina climbed out of the pool and went for her towel. "What are you all happy about?"

Roxie shook her head. "Just thinking about Ethan."

"I saw him today. He was working down at the bakery but he stopped into the salon to check on things. He's such a nice man. I'm glad you two are seeing each other. He'd make a great stepdad."

Roxie laughed. "Trina, we're not rushing into anything."

"You're going to church with him day after tomorrow."

"I am. But that's just spending time together. I should be going to church anyway. Might as well go with Ethan."

Trina wrapped her towel around herself. "Would you mind if I came with you?"

"No, that would be great."

"Okay, cool. Thanks. I don't want to be in the way or anything."

Roxie put her arm around her daughter. "You could never be in the way, honey."

"Well, you know. It's kind of a date, right?"

Roxie shook her head as she let Trina go and they got their flipflops on. "It's just us going to church. And probably out to lunch after."

"That sounds nice."

They took the steps up to the front door, which they'd left unlocked.

"You know," Roxie said. "It's just going to be the two of us pretty soon."

Trina nodded as she opened the door and went inside. "I know. It's sad for us, but happy for Mimi."

Roxie shivered as the A/C hit her skin. "It'll be strange not to have her around, but I can guarantee you're going to want to visit her and Miguel all the time when they get into their new house. Their lot on the water has amazing views. I can only imagine what the house is going to look like. And the community has so much to do. Shopping and restaurants and activities."

"Sounds perfect for them." Trina grinned. "I'm already looking forward to eating at the aquarium restaurant."

Roxie went into the kitchen and got a lasagna out of the freezer. She turned the oven on to warm up, then took the lasagna out of the box. "Listen, I got her and Miguel a stay tomorrow night in the Hamilton Arms' honeymoon suite. I figured since they're postponing their honeymoon until after the salon gets open, the least we could do is give them a special place to spend their first night together."

"Oh, I love that idea. That's so good, Ma!"

"It was Ethan's suggestion, so I can't take credit for it." Roxie smiled. "But I'm going to say it's from both of us. I just wanted you to know."

"You don't have to do that."

"I want to."

"Thanks."

"You're welcome. Now, go shower. We'll find a movie to watch while we eat. Or maybe there's a new episode of *Hater House*."

Trina laughed. "That is the worst reality-TV show ever."

"Why do you think I like it so much?"

Roxie stayed behind while Trina went to shower. As soon as the oven dinged that it was hot enough, she popped the lasagna in on a cookie sheet, set the timer, and went to her room to take a shower, too.

The hot water felt great after the A/C had made her chilly. She dried off and put on yoga pants and a T-shirt, then went back out to the living room. The aroma of meat, cheese, and sauce had begun to filter out of the oven, making her stomach rumble.

Trina was on the couch on her phone. The television was on, but just to the weather channel. She looked up. "I wanted to make sure it wasn't going to rain tomorrow."

Roxie grimaced. "That would not be good. I guess we could always move the ceremony to under the house, but it's going to be pretty crowded under there with the buffet, the tables, and the chairs. Maybe I should have ordered a tent."

"I don't think there's anything to worry about," Trina said. "They're showing clear skies and mild temperatures."

"Oh, good. That sounds perfect. I'm so glad."

Trina's phone chimed softly. She glanced at it, smiled, and started texting again.

"Let me guess," Roxie said. "Miles?"

"Yeah," Trina said softly. "I like him so much, Ma. I've never liked a guy the way I like him. And I've never really known a guy like him. He's so smart and thoughtful and interested in all kinds of things that a lot of guys his age just aren't. Plus, he's hot and goes to the gym."

Roxie laughed. "I think he has a broader world view because of his job. He interacts with all kinds of people, and most of them are not in a great place. He sees them when they're hurting. And that's made him empathetic to everyone, not just the people he sees on the job."

"That's a really good point. I hadn't thought about that."

Roxie got a diet soda out of the fridge and held it up. "Want one?"

"Only if it doesn't have caffeine. I need to sleep tonight."

"Me, too." Roxie grabbed two diet root beers and gave one to Trina. Then she checked the timer. "Lasagna has another twenty minutes."

"That's okay."

Roxie came over and sat down in her chair.

"Ma?"

Roxie popped open her root beer. "Yeah?"

"Would you marry Ethan? If he asked?"

Roxie narrowed her eyes. "Why do you want to know?"

Trina laughed. "No secret reason, I swear. Just

curious. All this wedding stuff has me thinking about it a lot."

Roxie nodded. "I see. The answer is yes, I would. If the timing was right and we were at that stage in our relationship. Absolutely."

Trina smiled. "Same with me and Miles." She set her phone down and opened her root beer, lifting it toward her mom. "Here's to whatever the future holds, huh?"

Roxie reached over to knock her soda can gently against Trina's. "I'll drink to that."

Chapter Sixteen

*J*ules was exhausted but happy. They'd had a long, productive day in the studio. Jesse had been kind enough to treat them all to dinner afterwards, so she and Cash were headed home with full stomachs.

"You know," Cash started. "If not for the wedding tomorrow, we could probably be recording the song. I think we're ready."

"I think we are, too, but I've already agreed to play at the wedding. Which I am going to have to practice for in the morning, since we're getting home later than I anticipated."

"Just come upstairs in the morning and we'll go over whatever songs you have picked out," Cash said.

"Thanks."

"At lunch, Sierra and I figured out a couple of songs we both know pretty well. She's going to bring her keyboard tomorrow, if that's okay with you? And she's willing to come early and practice with us. If you want."

"Yeah?" Jules smiled. "That would be great. I really like her. She might be the nicest girl you've ever dated."

"Are you just saying that because she's contributing to your new song?"

Jules laughed. "No. I'm saying that because I really like her, and she is genuinely a nice person. And also because you've dated some twits."

"Mom!"

"Well, you have. Angelina?"

Cash groaned. "You are never going to forget about her, are you?"

"A girl who thought country music had to be about farm animals or pickup trucks? No, I am not going to forget about her." Jules snickered.

"Do we have any ice cream at home?"

"Are you trying to change the subject?"

"Maybe, but it's still a valid question."

"I'm sure we do." She glanced over at him. "I really need you and Sierra to stay good. No ugly breakups, please."

"I know," he said. "Because of the tour."

She nodded. "If she comes with us, which I'd love for her to do, you guys are going to be together a lot. And I cannot have things imploding between you. Not only is the bus a very small space, but when you're on tour, it really helps if you can get along with the people you're with twenty-four-seven."

"The same thing is true about you and Jesse. If he's coming."

"He is. And we'll be fine. We've talked about it. And in case you haven't noticed, we've lived a little longer than you and Sierra. Our capabilities for handling things in a more mature manner probably exceed yours."

"I don't know about that."

"I just need to know that you two aren't going to break up halfway through the tour and make everyone else's life unbearable."

"We'll be fine." He grinned. "I like her a lot, Mom. And I'm pretty sure she likes me the same. Plus, she knows what a big opportunity this tour would be for her. She's not about to do anything to mess that up."

"I hope you're right." She really did. A breakup on a tour bus was bad news in all kinds of ways.

She pulled into the Double Diamond's driveway

and parked her Jeep next to Kat's car. "Let's go see if we can find you some ice cream. Toby probably needs to go out, too." She rolled her head around as they walked toward the elevator.

"I can take Toby out if you want." Cash pushed the call button. "You look tired."

"Because I am tired, but I don't mind taking him out. Get your ice cream."

"Okay."

The elevator arrived and they went upstairs. Jules's mom, along with Claire and Kat, were all watching TV. Toby was on the couch between Claire and Kat. He jumped down and trotted over to Jules as they got off the elevator.

"Hey, gang," Jules said. She crouched down to greet Toby. "Hi, baby. Mama missed you. I'm sorry I was gone so long. Do you want to go out?"

His tail wagged so hard his whole back end moved.

"Okay, let's get your leash." She stood up. "Everyone have a good day? Because we had a *great* day."

"Glad to hear it," Claire said. "I got most of the cake done. All that's left is to assemble it and finish the decorating."

"Well done, Claire. I can't wait to see it. Be right back. I'm going to take Toby out."

"And I," Cash announced, "am going to eat ice cream. Please tell me we have some."

Kat got up, laughing. "We do and now that you mention it, I might have a little bowl, too."

Jules left her purse on the chair next to the couch, grabbed her phone, then got Toby's leash and hooked him to it. "Come on, boy. Let's go pee-pee."

She took him back downstairs and he led her to his favorite patch of grass. While he sniffed around for the ultimate spot to relieve himself on, she pulled out her phone and texted Jesse.

Great day today. Thanks again for dinner. That was very nice.

Fantastic day. Can't wait to record. Also can't wait to see you tomorrow.

She smiled. *Same.*

I'm supposed to wear a tux, right?

She laughed. *That's right. And a top hat. Otherwise I'll look silly in my ball gown.*

He sent back some laughing face emojis. Then a heart.

She sent him a heart in return.

They'd be fine on the tour. She couldn't explain

how she knew that, but she just did. Jesse might be younger than her, but that hadn't mattered one bit so far. They were very well-suited.

And his appreciation for music, not just hers but any music, really, seemed to guarantee that he'd be on his best behavior during the tour.

Apparently unable to find satisfaction in his original site, Toby moved to a new patch of grass. She just shook her head, stuck her phone in her pocket, and walked with him. She'd been gone all day. She was happy to indulge him a bit.

"I don't know, Tobes. They all look like good places to pee to me. But then, what do I know? I go in the same place all the time."

Her phone vibrated in such a way that she knew she had a call coming in. Maybe Jesse had forgotten to tell her something. She pulled it out and looked at the screen, Her mood immediately dropped when she saw it *wasn't* Jesse.

It was Lars.

She hesitated, but he could be calling to apologize. If he wasn't, she didn't have to talk to him for long. She answered. "Hello?"

"Why are you turning my boys against me?"

She sighed at the softly slurred words. *Not* an

apology call. She wondered if this was because Fen had reached out to him. "I'm not, Lars. If they're upset with you because you're drinking and drugging again, that's on you. You need to own that. Might even be a good reason to get sober again, don't you think?"

"Don't tell me what to do."

She was about to hang up, then decided to hang on for one more question. "What knocked you off the wagon this time? I'm curious."

"Nothing knocked me off the wagon. I'm living my life. This is the dream. Rock and roll, baby."

She stared heavenward. He was really gone. "So you're happy, then? Upsetting your sons is all right with you?"

"My sons need to grow up. You need to stop coddling them."

"They're grown men, Lars. They can't get much more grown up. You, on the other hand, might want to think about your future. Drugs and alcohol have a way of cutting it short. Jimi Hendrix. Jim Morrison. Steve Clark. Amy Winehouse. Prince."

She'd picked the ones she knew he liked. The line had gone silent.

Then he sniffed. "I'm not going to end up like them."

"I hope you don't, Lars. For the sake of our sons, I hope you don't."

Another couple of beats of silence. Then a much more sober-sounding Lars spoke again. "Crystal left me."

She wasn't entirely sure who Crystal was. She could only assume a girlfriend and he had so many of those it was hard to keep track. "I'm sorry to hear that. Did you love her?"

"I don't know. Maybe. You're the only woman I ever really loved. Fly out to Spain to see me, Jules. We could have such a good time."

Toby, who'd done his business and then kicked grass over it, was looking up at her like he couldn't understand why they were still outside when there were people upstairs having ice cream.

She closed her eyes for a moment. "That's not going to happen, Lars. Not only are we not married anymore, but I'm—" She'd been about to say she was seeing someone. That wouldn't help his current mood, however. She knew him well enough to realize that. "I'm about to go on tour again. Gearing up for it, anyway."

"Good for you. You have a new album out?"

She started walking back to the elevator. "Soon. Listen, I'm going to let you go now. Please think about getting back into a program, all right? Have a good night. Take care of yourself."

She hung up before he could respond. If he called back, she wasn't going to answer. He might be the father of her children, but he was no longer her responsibility.

Chapter Seventeen

Margo looked at her grandchildren in the kitchen. "What kind of ice cream is there?"

Kat answered her. "Mint chocolate chip and Moose Tracks."

Margo knew Moose Tracks was chocolate and nuts, or so she thought. She didn't enjoy frozen nuts. They were havoc on her crowns. The tiny flecks of chocolate in the mint were much easier to deal with. "Would you please bring me a small bowl, just one scoop, of the mint?"

"You got it," Cash said with a mischievous grin. "One giant double scoop of mint, coming up." He winked at her.

She smiled back. She didn't often indulge in ice cream but after dealing with Dinah, she'd earned a reward. Kat brought her bowl over, a spoon stuck alongside the medium-sized scoop of mint chocolate chip. "Here you go, Grandma."

"Thank you."

Claire grinned at her. "A little treat for not killing Dinah?"

Margo chuckled. "Something like that."

The kids came back with their bowls. Cash's looked like it held a chocolate mountain. He'd added whipped cream and sprinkles, turning it into more of a sundae. Kat had gone with the mint, no whipped cream or sprinkles. He sat on the floor while Kat took her seat on the couch again.

Margo gestured with her spoon. "Cash, why don't you take the chair?"

"I'm fine on the floor. Plus, Mom needs a place to sit when she gets back with Toby."

Such a good son, he was. Margo took a bite of her ice cream, letting it melt slowly over her tongue. It was cool and delicious. Definitely a treat.

The elevator doors opened, and Jules rejoined them. She took Toby into the laundry room to clean his feet. He came scampering out a minute later, going straight to Cash and looking longingly at his bowl.

"No ice cream for you, Toby. Sorry." Cash shook his head. "Chocolate isn't good for dogs."

Jules came out of the laundry room with a dog biscuit in her hand. "Here, Toby. You forgot your cookie."

He looked at Cash's ice cream one more time, then reluctantly trotted over to Jules.

She laughed and sat down in the chair Cash had left for her. "Ice cream party, huh?"

"You want some, Mom? I can get it for you."

Jules held her hand up. "No, I'm good. Thanks, though. I'm saving myself for cake tomorrow."

"Speaking of," Kat said as she turned toward Claire. "Those cakes in the fridge are beautiful. Those colors are so good! Mom, I love them. I'm dying to see the finished thing all put together."

Claire smiled. "Me, too. Fingers crossed it ends up looking the way it does in my head. I'm glad you like the shades I picked. I think they're pretty good, too."

"Totally the colors of the Gulf," Kat said.

Margo spooned up another small bite. "You do beautiful work, Claire. I have no doubt the cake will be a showstopper."

"Thanks, Mom." Claire smiled.

"Have you ever done a wedding cake before?" Margo asked. "I can't remember that you have."

"No, which is why I've been so nervous about

this one." Claire blew out a breath. "Agreeing to make a wedding cake for the father of the man I'm going into the bakery business with might not have been my smartest move."

Margo actually agreed with that, but she wasn't going to say that out loud. Instead, she offered her daughter some reassurance. "You're worrying too much."

"I don't know," Claire said. "I think I'm worrying just about the right amount. It's not like I think Danny won't want to do business with me if the cake isn't so great, but I want to impress him, you know?"

Margo nodded. "I understand. But you've already impressed him. That's why he wants you as his business partner."

Jules bobbed her head in agreement. "Yep. What Mom said. You've made so much great stuff lately that even if the cake isn't as perfect as you want it, he's not going to care."

"Also, Mom?" Kat pointed at Claire with her spoon. "Mrs. Butter's Bakery isn't exactly a wedding cake destination. So who cares if you don't make a magazine-worthy cake? Willie and Miguel will appreciate it all the same because of the time and effort you put into it."

"Good point, Kat," Margo said.

Claire settled back against the cushions. "You're all right. Thanks. I was getting too much in my own head there, I think."

"If it helps," Cash said. "I'll eat it no matter what it looks like."

Claire snorted. "Thank you, Cash."

They watched a little television together, something Margo couldn't remember them doing as a family in some time. It was nice and a good reminder of how much she valued being near all of them. Having family around was wonderful.

So long as that family wasn't Dinah.

About halfway through the program, Margo's phone screen lit up with a new notification. A text from Conrad. She took a look.

Just read the new pages you sent. Great job. I love what you did. Made a few small changes and sent them back. Hope you like what I did. We make a great team.

She nodded. *I agree. Very pleased you liked my work. Can't wait to see your additions.*

Thanks again for coming to lunch.

You're welcome. How's Dinah?

Nothing for a few seconds, then, *She's in a mood, to be honest. Pouting that I'm leaving her for the wedding tomorrow.*

Margo rolled her eyes. That woman wanted everything to revolve around her.

Another text came in from Conrad. *I think she expected me to bring her along.*

That didn't surprise Margo. But she once again wondered if she should just tell him to bring her. Dinah would be outnumbered. What were the chances she'd do anything, other than make herself look foolish?

Margo hesitated, then typed, *I could ask Willie if she'd mind one extra guest. Not my place to assume.*

I couldn't ask you to do that.

You're not asking. I'm offering. Margo instantly questioned whether it was a good idea or not, but part of her couldn't imagine anyone would intentionally misbehave at a wedding where they were a guest.

You sure about this?

Not really, no. Margo added an "lol" so he'd know her mood was light. *But if it helps you out and makes your life easier...*

Up to you, Conrad texted. *It's completely your decision.*

No, it's Willie's decision. It's her wedding. Give me a few minutes, all right?

You're the best.

Margo smiled. *I know.*

She got up. "I need to run downstairs and talk to Willie for a moment. Be right back."

Claire and Jules gave her strange looks, but Margo wasn't divulging anything just yet. She headed for the steps, unlatched the baby gate, and went down a few. There were lights on and the distant sounds of another television.

She went down to the landing. "Hello? Willie? It's Margo. Do you have a moment?"

"Come on through, Margo," Willie called out. "We're in the living room. I just got in from Miguel's, so good timing."

Margo walked through. Willie, Trina, and Roxie were all there. The movie they'd been watching had been paused.

"Hi," Margo said. "Sorry to intrude. I have a large favor to ask you but at the same time, it's perfectly understandable if you say no. You won't hurt my feelings if that's your answer, either. What I'm asking is...a lot."

Willie narrowed her eyes. "Are you trying to ask me to help you hide a body?"

"What? No." Margo stared at the woman. She had to be drinking again.

Willie cackled with laughter. "I'm just kidding.

You're pretty savvy. I bet you could hide a body on your own just fine. What's the favor?"

Margo decided not to comment on Willie's assessment of her. She cleared her throat softly. "I wanted to know if you'd mind if my plus one also had a plus one. Conrad's sister, Dinah, is in town visiting him and he's going to be here tomorrow with me, and he just wondered—"

"Sure, bring her along," Willie said. "The more the merrier. It's a wedding, after all. It's supposed to be a party." She looked at Roxie. "There'll be enough food, right?"

Roxie nodded. "More than enough."

"There you go," Willie said. "All set."

Margo had honestly expected a no. "Oh. All right then. Thank you. I'll let Conrad know." She started to leave, then turned back around. "Maybe I should have explained that Dinah can be somewhat of a handful. She's particular. And very opinionated, if you know the type of person I mean."

Trina nodded. "I think I do. She sounds like Miles's ex. Kind of full of herself and can't understand why everyone else doesn't realize how great she is. Assumes she knows more than you, too."

Margo snorted. "That's a fair evaluation."

Willie's eyes stayed narrowed. "This Dinah, she

giving you trouble? Trying to get between you and that new boyfriend of yours?"

Margo sighed. How were these people so perceptive? "Yes, she is. Apparently, she's run off every woman he's ever been involved with."

"What the heck? Who does that?" Willie said. "This is his sister?"

"Yes," Margo said. "I'm not letting her get to me, but she's trying."

Willie waved a hand through the air. "Don't you worry about it. We'll keep an eye on her, won't we, girls? She acts up and we'll stifle that pretty darn quick." Willie shrugged. "Maybe she'll accidentally fall into the pool. You know how these wedding receptions can get when there's rum involved."

Roxie and Trina both nodded.

Margo laughed softly. "Thank you. I appreciate this very much."

"No problem," Willie said.

"Have a good night." Margo made her way back upstairs and sent Conrad a text that it was okay to bring Dinah along.

He was grateful, of course.

But as they were all turning in and getting ready for bed, she couldn't shake the nagging feeling that she'd just made a huge mistake.

Chapter Eighteen

Trina woke up early, something she was trying to get more in the habit of doing. It was a good habit and one she intended to continue. It meant she could get more done in the day and it made her feel like a responsible adult.

Which was a pretty cool feeling. Like she was growing up in a way that she never had before. Being with Miles made her feel that way, too. As if she was really getting her life on track.

She made coffee, then took her notebook and salon binder out to the back porch. Her plan was to read through all of her notes from the interviews yesterday, just to confirm the hiring decisions she'd made. She was also going to write out a little script to follow for turning people down. She figured that way she wouldn't get tongue-tied or say something she didn't mean.

While she worked on that, she'd drink her coffee, think things over, then at nine o'clock, she'd make her calls.

She was going to make the good ones first. She'd thought about saving them until last, but she just didn't want to.

Better to start the day out on a high. Then, if her calls to the people she wasn't hiring didn't go so well, she had Mimi's wedding preparations to look forward to.

She was finishing up her coffee when her mom came out. "Hey. Morning."

"Morning," her mom said. Roxie had a mug in hand and took a seat nearby. "Are you working?"

"Getting ready to make my hiring calls at nine."

"Oh. You want me to leave you alone?"

"Not yet." Trina smiled. "Excited about the day?"

Roxie nodded and sipped her coffee. "Excited and nervous. I just want it all to go perfectly."

"I'm sure it will. What time are the wedding people getting here?" The wedding wasn't until six so they could take advantage of the sunset for pictures.

"Since everything is going to be outside, not that early. About two hours ahead of time for the florist and an hour ahead for the caterers. But the place I'm getting the chairs and tables from, the party rental people, will be here around eleven. Thomas, the photographer, will be here at five."

"You need help with any of that?"

Roxie shook her head. "No, the suppliers are doing all the setup themselves. All I have to do is show them where everything goes."

"What time do you want me to do your hair?"

"Whenever you want. I don't need anything fancy. Maybe some soft curls." Roxie shrugged. "Your grandmother comes first."

Trina nodded. "Today, she's the queen. Are you going to let her sleep?"

"You bet I am."

They sat for a while, Trina reading through her notes and her mom drinking her coffee and staring out at the water. Then her mom got up. "I'm going to do a big scramble for us for breakfast. Ham and cheese with whatever veggies we have. You good with that?"

"Absolutely," Trina said. She looked at the time. Nearly nine. "I'll come in with you and get another cup of coffee, then I'll come back out and make my calls."

"Okay."

They went inside. Trina got her coffee and her

mom started assembling ingredients for the scramble. No sign of Mimi yet.

Trina went outside and looked at her phone. As she was staring at the screen, a message from Miles popped up.

Morning. Can't wait to see you tonight. Let me know if you need anything. I can always stop on the way.

She smiled. *Morning. I will definitely text if we need something. Thanks for helping get Alex, too.*

He sent her a thumbs-up emoji.

She took a breath and made her first call. It was to Ginger.

"Hello?"

"Ginger? It's Trina. From A Cut Above."

"Oh, hi! How are you?"

"I'm great. I hope you're having a good morning. I'm calling because I'd like to offer you a chair at the salon as a stylist."

"You would?" There was a small squeal of excitement. "Thank you! I am so thrilled you called. I've had my fingers crossed since yesterday."

Trina smiled. "Great. I'll have some paperwork for you next week and then it's just a matter of us getting open."

"You need help with anything over there, you

just call me, okay? If I'm free, I will come help, no problem."

"Thank you very much."

"Thank you! Woo!"

Trina laughed. "Bye now."

"Bye!"

Her next three calls went pretty much the same way. It was a good feeling to know she had some great people lined up for work. Even the girl she hired as the salon assistant had sounded thrilled.

Then it was time to call those she wasn't hiring. She set her phone down and drank some more coffee, although the caffeine probably wasn't going to help.

Reluctantly, she picked up her phone and dialed the first number. It was for a young man named Trent. He'd been very nice but also fresh out of cosmetology school and she wanted stylists with more experience.

"Hello?"

"Is this Trent Bingham?"

"Yes. Who's calling?"

"This is Trina Thompson from A Cut Above."

"Oh, cool. Maybe." He laughed nervously.

She almost sighed. "I wanted to thank you for coming in yesterday, Trent. I really enjoyed speaking with you. Unfortunately, there were a lot of highly qualified candidates, and the salon isn't going to have a place for you at this time. I would encourage you to keep us in mind for the future, however."

"Yeah, okay. I knew it was a longshot. Thanks."

"Don't be discouraged," Trina suddenly added. "You'll get there. Just takes time."

"Yeah. Thanks for calling. Bye."

He hung up, leaving Trina listening to dead air. She understood his disappointment. It had taken her a few shots to get hired at first and then she'd only gotten in as a shampoo girl. Two weeks later, though, one of the stylists had called in sick and she'd gotten a chance.

That chance had been all it took. The client had liked her work and her boss at the time had let her start taking walk-ins.

Still, she felt bad for Trent. She tucked his resume, such as it was, into a pocket in her binder.

She made the rest of her calls. They seemed to get easier as she went through them. Most people were pretty nice. Obviously disappointed, but that was to be expected.

When she was done, she felt a little worn out. Giving people bad news was hard.

She took a sip of her lukewarm coffee and

decided to go in. Maybe her mom needed help. That would be a good distraction.

She gathered up her stuff and went inside.

"How did it go?" her mom asked.

Trina shrugged. "The hiring calls were easy. Those were great. The other ones, not so much. But it's done."

Roxie nodded. "All part of being the boss."

"Yep. You need help with anything?"

Roxie looked around. There was a stack of toast on a plate already and the scramble appeared pretty much done. "Not really. I think we can eat, if you're ready. Your grandmother's up, I heard her. She should be out soon."

"Let me put my stuff in the bedroom."

"Okay."

Trina took a deep breath as she walked back to her space. She realized that what she was feeling wasn't just because the calls had been hard. That wasn't the heart of what was bothering her. The truth was, it was the idea that some people might not like her because she'd turned them down.

Then she realized something else. If she was going to be a good boss, she was going to have to get over worrying about whether or not people liked her. Some people never would. Liz was a perfect illustration of that.

Quite a revelation on her grandmother's wedding day. But then, if there was ever an example of someone who didn't care what other people thought, it was Mimi.

Trina smiled as she went back out for breakfast. Maybe she should get herself a bracelet that said What Would Mimi Do.

Chapter Nineteen

Claire took her cup of coffee outside. She needed a few moments of peace and calm to get her head together before she began the stressful work of layering the cake tiers and decorating them.

She needed caffeine and eventually breakfast, too, but the cake was at the forefront of her mind. She'd even dreamed about it. She snorted. It wasn't the first time she'd dreamed about baked goods, but it was the first time it had been more of a nightmare than something out of *Willy Wonka*.

She shook her head to get rid of the last little memory of the cake smashing to the ground. She'd be happy when the thing was done, and she could just relax and enjoy the evening. She sipped her coffee.

Music drifted down from the third floor. Jules

must have already gone upstairs to practice with Cash, because she was definitely hearing more than one guitar. There was singing, but she couldn't make out the words.

Didn't matter. She recognized the James Taylor tune. It sounded nice.

With a smile on her face, she closed her eyes and enjoyed the impromptu concert. Did Willie have any idea what an amazing gift it was to have Jules play at her wedding? Claire honestly wasn't sure. She didn't think Willie was ungrateful. Just that she might not really understand what an incredible singer and musician her sister was.

Claire guessed she would know by the end of the night, however.

She sighed contentedly, opened her eyes, and drank a little more coffee. She gazed out at the horizon. Before her, blue sky dotted with cotton candy clouds stretched in both directions as far as the eye could see. Willie and Miguel couldn't have asked for a nicer day.

Kat pushed the sliders open and stepped out, mug in hand. "Beautiful day for a wedding, huh?"

"I was just thinking that."

"Mind some company?"

"Not at all. How'd you sleep?"

"Like a well-fed baby." Kat grinned. She was dressed in gym shorts and a tank top, sneakers on her feet. "How about you? How are you feeling about the cake?"

"Like I can't wait for it to be done and off my plate. No pun intended."

"I'm sure. You want help with it?"

Claire was about to say no, then she smiled. "That's probably a good idea. You can help me line up the layers as I stack them."

"Be happy to." Kat sat next to her on the couch. "Should be a nice evening. I'm looking forward to it."

"Me, too. You doing anything? Other than the wedding?"

"Walk on the beach in about ten minutes. Are you up for that?"

Claire hadn't been planning on it. "I guess I should, considering I'm going to be eating some of that cake later."

Kat nodded. "I need to work off last night's ice cream. We don't have to go for as long as we usually do."

Claire shook her head. "I have time for half an hour. I don't want to put the cake together too early, because then it just has to sit. Of course, I don't want to do it too late, either, in case something goes wrong, and I have to figure out how to fix it."

"Nothing's going to go wrong," Kat said.

"From your mouth to God's ears."

Kat sipped her coffee. "Whatever help you need, I'm here. The only other thing I want to do is paint that surfboard clock for Alex. I haven't had the chance to, with him getting hurt and then the move and everything."

"Are you going to give it to him today?"

"Maybe. If it dries in time."

Claire finished the last mouthful of coffee and got to her feet. "All right. I'm going in to get dressed for our walk. See you back here in a few."

"I'm ready when you are."

Claire went in via the sliders that opened onto her bedroom, but walked through to the kitchen, put her cup next to the coffee maker so she could use it again later, then came back. She changed into Spandex capri leggings, a sports bra, and an oversized Diamond Beach T-shirt.

Now that she lived here, she probably shouldn't wear something so touristy, but she didn't care. She was only going to sweat in it.

She stuck her feet into her sneakers and slipped her phone into the pocket of her leggings.

She was grateful to Kat for getting her moving. Claire had no intention of walking when she woke up this morning, but she was already glad to be going. One missed day could easily turn into two missed days and so on. Not something she wanted. She was getting to a good place with taking care of herself. Keeping that up was important to her.

Especially since she was about to be working in a bakery around sweets and treats full-time. It wasn't that she planned to gorge herself, but she had to be able to taste-test the products to make sure the recipes were correct and the food was up to her standards.

She did *not* want to put back on the few pounds she'd already managed to lose. In fact, she would love to lose about ten more. Maybe twelve. Even if she accomplished that, she wouldn't be skinny.

But she didn't need to be. She just wanted to be healthy. She smiled. She wanted to be around for a long time. Long enough for Kat to make her a grandma, anyway.

She went back out to the porch. "All right, let's get moving."

"Yes, ma'am." Kat jumped up, leaving her coffee cup on the table.

They went downstairs using the spiral staircase and straight out to the beach.

"Man, it's a nice day," Kat said. "I know I've said it before, but I love living here." She sighed and tipped her face toward the sun. "Dad really screwed up in a lot of ways, but in a lot of ways, he also did some good."

Claire glanced at her daughter. "Does that mean you've come to terms with Paulina and Nico?"

Kat shrugged. "I kind of have to, don't I? He's my brother." She squinted against the sunlight. "I thought about how I'd feel if the situation were reversed. I know he's a baby but he's going to grow up. Would I want to find out at some point in my life that I had family who wanted nothing to do with me?"

She shook her head. "That would hurt. Nico doesn't deserve that. He had nothing to do with the circumstances that brought him into this world."

Claire smiled. "You make me proud, Kat. For all the animosity I have toward your father, neither Nico nor Paulina are to blame for what he did. We shouldn't shut them out because of his actions."

"Thanks, Mom. I know how hard it must be for you. Actually, I don't know. I've had no life experience that equates to what you're going through.

Finding out my father had two other families is nothing compared to what you, Roxie, and Paulina must be feeling. But I sympathize. I really do."

Claire grabbed her daughter's hand and gave it a squeeze, so grateful for how close they'd become. "I know you do. And I appreciate it."

She steered the conversation toward a lighter topic. "Are you going to be a client of Trina's when she gets the salon open?"

Kat nodded enthusiastically. "Yes. Especially because I'll be able to afford it now with my new job."

Claire laughed. "Good. I plan on being a regular, too. Not only do I want to support her, but there couldn't be a more convenient location."

"True," Kat said. "And we already know she does great hair. That makes me think...we should leave her reviews on Google when she gets open."

Claire cut her eyes at Kat. "You can leave reviews on Google?"

Kat shook her head. "I'll show you. You're going to want them for the bakery, too."

"You're right about that. Anything to help boost business."

They turned back toward the beach house in

another few minutes and picked up the pace as they finished their walk.

When they got back, they found Jules and Cash were still practicing upstairs, but Margo was sitting on the deck with her laptop and a cup of coffee, already dressed.

"Morning, Mom," Claire said. "I need to shower but then I can whip up some breakfast. Nothing fancy. Probably just eggs and whatever else I can scrounge up."

"Morning. Don't worry about me. I'm going to have a bowl of cereal and a yogurt in a bit. I know you need the kitchen."

Claire nodded. "I do, but there's plenty of time before I have to start working on the cake."

Kat looked at her. "What time do you want to start that?"

Claire thought. "How about after lunch?"

Kat nodded. "That definitely gives me time to paint that surfboard."

Margo frowned. "You're going to paint a surfboard?"

Kat grinned. "A surfboard clock. It's a craft project. Do you mind if I set up out here with you? After I shower and eat? I don't want to bother you. I'll be quiet, I promise."

"Be my guest," Margo said.

"That's our plan for the day, then." Claire went in to shower, but before she did, she looked through her wardrobe to see what she might wear to the wedding. A dress, obviously, and since it was an outdoor beach wedding, a sundress.

But which one? She had a lot more to choose from these days, thanks to shopping at Classic Closet.

The thrift shop was Roxie's secret to an extensive wardrobe without spending a ton of money, and she'd been kind enough to introduce Claire to it. Claire had then taken Jules and Kat. They'd had a great time and found some wonderful things.

Claire pushed some of the clothes aside to have a better look at her sundresses. One of those would have to be it. She just wasn't sure which one yet, although she was leaning toward the black floral.

Black was slimming and the dress, which she'd picked up for a song, was from the Tommy Bahama brand. It had to have been a hundred dollars or more brand new. She hadn't worn it yet and this really was the perfect occasion.

Plus, she had some cute, strappy black sandals that would go with the dress perfectly.

Decision made, she went into the bathroom and

turned on the shower. She'd actually forgotten about the cake for a few minutes. Now, however, it was back in her thoughts. She knew she shouldn't stress about it, and she was trying not to, but that wasn't so easy.

Kat's help was just what she needed, though. That would take some of the pressure off.

And it the cake didn't come together the way she'd imagined it, well, at least she knew it would taste good.

That was something, right?

Chapter Twenty

Willie had woken up feeling like today was the day she was going to win the lottery. She'd smiled as soon as her eyes opened. Of course she'd feel like that. She was getting married today. To one of the best men she'd ever met.

Miguel Humberto Rojas was about to be her husband.

The last one she'd ever have.

As she sat in her chair, drinking her coffee and eating the breakfast that her daughter had made, she thought about the men who'd come before him. All good men. All with their own faults and flaws, their own little quirks and peculiarities. She knew Miguel had them, too, but at the moment, she couldn't think of any.

She tried harder. Was he too attentive? Too

concerned that she was happy? Did he put her needs ahead of his own too often? Did he dote on her too much?

Were any of those things really faults? Not to her.

"You okay, Mimi?" Trina asked. "You've gone awfully quiet."

Willie nodded. "Just thinking about how blessed I've been to have had so many wonderful husbands. I've known the love of some great men, my girl. And today I'm about to marry another one. I guess the day has just made me a little introspective."

"You're allowed," Roxie said. "Only makes sense that a big day like today would get you thinking. It's made me think. Probably Trina, too."

Trina smiled. "Sure. Ever since Miles told me he wants kids, marriage has definitely been on my mind."

"Oh, Trina," Willie said. "I would so love to spoil some great-grandbabies."

"Ma," Roxie said. "Give the girl a chance to get engaged first, okay?"

Willie laughed and Trina's cheeks went a little pink. She looked at her grandmother. "I know you would, Mimi. But I'm not going to rush Miles, either."

"No, no," Willie said. "A man that age needs to

figure out for himself if he wants to be married and settle down. Has to be his idea or it'll never sit well with him. Take it from someone who knows."

"I believe you," Trina said. "How do you want your hair fixed today? I know you have that decorative clip from Lady M's to go in it, but any thoughts?"

Willie didn't mind that Trina had changed the subject. "Whatever you think looks good. I trust you with my hair, you know that."

Trina nodded. "I know you do. I just wasn't sure if there was something specific you had in mind."

"I want to look nice and have a good time. Once we say our vows, not much else matters." Willie grinned. "Do you think Miguel's nervous?"

"He might be," Roxie said. "He's about to marry you."

Trina giggled. "Ma, that's not nice."

"I didn't mean it in a bad way," Roxie explained. "But your Mimi is a handful." She looked at Willie. "Aren't you?"

"Heck, yes," Willie said. "But he knows that. I think it's one of the things he likes about me. I keep him on his toes. I make his life interesting."

Roxie nodded appreciatively. "You sure do that, Ma."

Trina reached out and took Willie's hand. "I'm

glad your house is going to take a while to build. I'm not ready for you to move out yet."

Willie could feel herself getting emotional. She smiled so she didn't cry. "There's a guest room at the new house with your name on it, Trina. You don't always have to stay over, but I expect you to visit on a regular basis. I know you'll be busy at the shop, but don't be too busy for me."

"Never, Mimi."

Willie nodded at her daughter. "Same goes for you, Roxanne."

"We'll be there, Ma. Probably me and Ethan."

Willie hesitated. "Are you trying to tell me something?"

Roxie shook her head, smiling. "Just that he and I are going to be together for a long while."

"Just marry him already, will you?"

Trina's eyes widened. "Mimi!"

"What?" Willie said. "You should both stop wasting time. If you love the men you're with, make it official."

Roxie looked at Trina. "Did you put vodka in her orange juice?"

"No!" Trina shifted her gaze back to Willie. "Mimi, did you add vodka to your orange juice?"

Willie narrowed her eyes, amused by her family. "I did not, but that's not a bad idea."

"Ma, I don't think—"

"Calm down, Roxie. I'm just teasing. I won't drink until the vows are said and we have our first toast as husband and wife."

"Good." Roxie got up. "I'm going to clean up the breakfast stuff, then get myself ready for the working portion of the day. Won't be long and the party rental people will be arriving. I'm not going to shower until that's done, because I'm sure I'm going to sweat."

"You're positive you don't need help with that, Ma?" Trina asked.

"No. Danny texted me earlier and said he'd come over, so I'll be fine. You have three heads of hair to do. I think that's more than enough for your contribution."

"Three?" Willie made a face. "Me, you, and who else?"

Roxie walked into the kitchen. "Herself, Ma."

Willie laughed. "Oh, yeah." She leaned toward Trina. "Your mother's right. That's already a lot of work for you."

"It's not that much," Trina said. "Although maybe

we should get you washed and set so you can airdry. I don't have a dryer for you to sit under."

"Fine by me. I'll go shower, then you can do whatever you want. Where do you want me to sit when I come out?"

Trina looked around. "The bar stools are really too tall. Maybe I'll get the chair from the vanity in my room and bring it out here."

"Or we can just do it in there, if that's easier," Willie offered.

"I don't have a TV in there for you to watch."

Willie shrugged. "I don't need a TV. I have my granddaughter to talk to."

Trina smiled. "Okay, Mimi. We'll do your hair in my bedroom."

Roxie put the last dish in the dishwasher and closed the door. "That works for me, too. Just set your beauty shop up in there and we'll come to you."

Trina laughed. "It'll be the satellite office of A Cut Above."

"There you go," Willie said. She loved that Trina was doing her hair for her on this very special day. She wouldn't have wanted it any other way. She went off to shower and wash her hair. "See you in a bit."

When she came back out dressed in her robe and slippers, her damp hair wrapped in a towel, she went straight to Trina's room and knocked on the open door. "You ready for your first customer?"

Trina was still setting a few things up. "Just about."

"Take your time. I'm going to get something to drink, then I'll be back. You want something?"

"No, I have my water. Thanks."

Willie went into the kitchen and grabbed a can of diet root beer from the fridge. She returned to Trina's room and settled into the vanity chair. She used a nail file from the vanity to open the can so she didn't damage her manicured nails, then took a long sip.

"Have you heard from Miguel this morning?"

"No and I probably won't," Willie said. "He got nervous just seeing my fingernails yesterday." She laughed. "I think he's probably going to err on the side of caution and not have any contact at all."

Trina smiled. "He's adorable. He really is."

"Maybe I'll text him. Just to say hi," Willie said. She dug her phone out of her pocket and opened up the texts. He was at the top of her list. She sent him a quick one. *Can't wait to see you. Love you.* Then hit Send.

Trina took the towel off Willie's head. "I think we're going to go for a little more fullness on top, then one side slicked back with the fancy clip. How's that sound?"

"Just fine, my girl." Her phone chimed, surprising her. Was Miguel really answering her? She looked at the screen and smiled.

This is Danny. My dad doesn't think he should reply in case it's bad luck, so I'm doing it for him. He says he loves you, too, and can't wait to see you as well.

Warm happiness spread through her. No matter what, Miguel wanted to make sure she knew how he felt.

She was definitely marrying the right man.

Chapter Twenty-one

*I*t took Kat longer than she thought it would to paint the surfboard clock for Alex. She'd snuck a picture of his board when she'd been over there yesterday, and she'd used that as her model for the painting. Her goal had been to recreate his board in miniature.

When she finished, it looked pretty close to her, but she had more paint on her hands than she did on the clock. It took her a bit to clean up her supplies, then clean up herself.

All the while, her grandmother had been writing. She'd pause briefly to stare off into space or at the screen, and she'd gotten up twice to refill her glass of water, but otherwise she'd had her fingers on the keyboard, typing away. It was something to see. Kat had the feeling that maybe her grandmother had really found her thing in life.

Kind of crazy to think it could happen at her age, but why not?

Kat left the surfboard on a piece of newspaper on the porch table so it could dry and carried all the rest of her stuff inside. From the kitchen, she glanced through her mom's bedroom door. Her mom was sitting on her bed with her laptop in front of her. Kat stuck her head in. "I'm going to shower."

Her mom looked up. "Don't forget that paint on your cheek."

Kat sighed. "Not again. I seem to get paint everywhere. You good?"

"Yep. Just looking at a few more cakes to be sure about décor placement."

Kat laughed. "Mom. You're overthinking this."

"I know." Her mother sighed and closed her laptop. "I just can't help myself. But you're right, enough is enough."

"After I shower, why don't we figure out lunch and then we can work on the cake?"

Her mom nodded. "Is the surfboard all painted then?"

"It is. It's as close to Alex's real one as I could get." Kat smiled. "I think he's going to like it."

Her mom looked through the sliders that led to the screened porch. "I can't believe your grandmother is still out there writing. She's really serious about this book."

Kat glanced in that direction, too. "I think it's pretty cool that she's found something that interests her so much at this stage of her life. It's almost as cool as you turning your hobby into a career."

Her mom smiled. "That *is* pretty cool."

"I just remembered. I need to wrap that frame I bought for Willie and Miguel. We have paper, right?"

"There should be some in the laundry room. Not sure what's in there will be wedding appropriate."

Kat shrugged. "I'll make it work. See you after I shower." She went off to her room. Her plan if there wasn't any wrapping paper that would work for a wedding was just to flip the paper over and use the white underside. With some bows and ribbons, it would be fine.

She showered and washed her hair, but she wasn't getting herself ready for the festivities just yet. She clipped her damp hair up and changed into shorts and a T-shirt. For the wedding, she'd wear a sundress. No idea which one, but she'd figure it out.

When she went into the kitchen, her mom was already in there, staring into the fridge that was currently a cake repository. "There's nothing to eat in here. I don't know what we're going to do for lunch."

"What do we have?"

"A loaf of regular bread, some low-carb wraps, half a head of lettuce, some sliced cheese, a jar of pickles, other assorted condiments...it's sad, frankly."

Kat went over to the pantry and opened it. An idea came to her. She glanced at her mom. "There's five of us, right?"

"Yes, but you might want to count Cash as two."

Kat smiled as she held on to the open pantry door. "Right. That's okay. How about tuna sandwiches and wraps? We have a lot of canned tuna."

"Do we?" Her mom came over to look. "And we have chips, for whoever wants them." She nodded. "That'll work. And if we portion it right, we won't have too much in the way of leftovers."

"But tomorrow," Kat said. "We really need to go grocery shopping."

"That's for sure. How about you text your aunt and cousin and tell them the lunch plan. Ask them to come down in ten minutes? And I'll go check with your grandmother."

"Will do." Kat pulled her phone out and sent the text as her mom went out to the porch.

Tuna sandwiches and chips in ten minutes. Be downstairs or go hungry. She added a smiley face.

Cash's answer was almost instantaneous. *I'm going to need two.*

Like that was even a question. Kat laughed. That guy could eat.

She got out the cans of tuna, then a big bowl to make the tuna salad in.

Her mom came in from the porch. "Your grandmother wants a low-carb wrap. So do I."

Kat nodded as she took the mayo out. "I'm just about to make the tuna salad."

"I'll get plates."

Together they got the wraps and sandwiches made and plated. They set out chips and pretzels from the pantry, as well as the jar of pickles with a fork in it so everyone could help themselves.

And everyone did. In a matter of minutes, Kat was at the table with her mom, grandmother, aunt, and cousin.

Cash's plate was piled high with sandwiches and chips. "Thanks, Kat and Aunt Claire. This is just what I needed."

Claire shot a look at Jules. "It's a good thing you did so well with music, otherwise I don't know how you'd have afforded to feed him."

"Hey," Cash said. "I don't eat that much."

Kat, along with her mom, aunt, and grandmother, all simultaneously said, "Yes, you do."

That got them laughing. Cash turned a little red,
which was probably the first time Kat had seen that
happen since his sixteenth birthday when he accidentally spit out his retainer while trying to blow out
his candles.

"All right, all right," he said. "I eat a lot. I can't
help it. I'm hungry a lot. And it takes a lot to fill me
up." As if underscoring his words, he ate the last bite
of his first sandwich. "Tell you what—how about I
make dinner some night this week? I'll shop for
everything and do all the cooking."

"For real?" Kat said.

"Yep." He grinned. "All I ask is that you guys
clean up."

Claire shrugged. "Seems like a pretty good deal
to me."

Aunt Jules smiled at her son like she was proud
of him. "I can't vouch for his cooking skills, but that's
very nice of you, honey."

"You're welcome," he said. "And if there's
wedding cake left over, we can have that for dessert."

Claire shook her head. "That traditionally goes
to the bride's family."

"Well, that's a dumb tradition." Cash made a

face. "You still need me to help carry that downstairs, Aunt Claire?"

She nodded. "I do. But that won't be until much later." Suddenly, she gasped. "Oh, no. I don't have a cake board."

"What's that?" Kat asked.

"A board sturdy enough to hold the assembled cake." Her mom looked pale and panicky.

"We'll find something," Kat said.

"You don't understand. That cake is going to be heavy. Maybe a hundred pounds. Maybe more. It needs to be a piece of plywood or...something like that."

Cash straightened. "I can run to the hardware store. Just tell me what size you need."

"Hang on," Kat said. "You need to work on the music for tonight, don't you?"

"Well, Sierra *is* coming over soon to practice..."

"Mom. Call Danny," Kat said. "I'm sure he could run to the hardware store. It is his dad who's getting married, after all."

"True. He might actually have a piece of plywood already. My phone is in the bedroom. Be right back." She got up and went off to make the call.

When she came back, she didn't look much happier. "Danny said he'll go but it would help to know the size of the cake table. Do we even have a cake table? I have no idea. I never said anything about needing one, so..." She groaned and shook her head.

Kat got up, done with her lunch anyway. "Sit down and finish your lunch. I'll find out."

She went downstairs and called out, "Trina?"

"In my room, Kat."

The smell of something floral wafted through the air. Trina's door was open. She stood behind her grandmother, who was sitting at Trina's vanity. Willie's eyes were closed as Trina sprayed the rollers in her hair with something.

"What is that?" Kat asked.

"A little extra setting spray. We want those curls nice and firm," Trina answered.

Kat nodded. "You're going to look beautiful, Willie. Happy wedding day."

Trina stopped spraying and Willie opened her eyes. She grinned. "Thank you, Kat. How are things upstairs?"

"My mom is about to start assembling the cake, which is why I'm down here. Do you know if we have a cake table?"

Willie shrugged and Trina bit her lip. She put the setting spray down. "My mom would know. Let me text her. She's downstairs right now with the party rental people."

While Trina texted, Kat waited. If there wasn't a cake table, what could they use? She wasn't sure they had anything sturdy enough.

Trina started nodding as she looked at her phone. "Yep, we have a cake table."

Kat exhaled. "That's great. What size is it?"

Trina texted again. A few seconds passed. She looked up. "My mom says it's thirty-by-thirty square."

"Thank you! That's exactly what I needed to know!" Kat ran back up the steps feeling very much like a crisis had been averted.

Her mom was standing by the kitchen island. "What did you find out?"

"There *is* a cake table. It's thirty-by-thirty square."

Her mom started texting. When she stopped, she let out a relieved sigh. "Danny says he has something that will work. It's bare plywood, though. That's not going to be very attractive. Maybe we can wrap it in something before the cake goes on?"

"Or," Kat said with a big grin. "I have a ton of white craft paint."

Chapter Twenty-two

As Roxie was directing the party rental people, Danny walked over from his house. He gave a nod. "Looking good."

She nodded. "I think so. I just want them both to be happy."

"They will be." He had a tape measure in his hand. "Which is the cake table? I want to measure it again before I figure out this cake board."

"Cake board?"

"It's the thing the cake goes on before it goes on the table. It's what Cash and I will be using to carry the cake down."

"Oh. Pretty important, then."

"If you want to have cake." He smiled.

She pointed to the small square table that was being set up at the end of the buffet. "That's the table right there. It will be getting draped in tablecloths."

"Okay. That shouldn't change the dimensions." He went over and measured it. "Yep, thirty by thirty. Figured it couldn't hurt to be sure. Thanks!"

Roxie nodded. "You're welcome."

"Back in a bit." He headed toward his house.

The party rental people were just about done setting up the tables and chairs. The existing dining table and chairs had been moved to behind the elevator and storage closet, so they weren't even visible.

Screens had been erected to block the reception area from where the cars were parked. A wooden dance floor had been put down, fitted together like a giant jigsaw puzzle. The two long tables had been set in an L shape along the dance floor. At the corner of those tables, a smaller round table had been set up. That was for Willie and Miguel.

The long buffet table was between the pool and the main reception area. At the end of it was the cake table.

The party rental people were still adding chairs and had begun covering the tables with white tablecloths, clipping them into place so the breeze wouldn't muss them. The chairs, which were the simple folding type, were getting slipcovers of white linen tied in the back with a bow.

With the flowers and the overhead string lights, it was going to be very romantic.

Roxie had also rented some potted palms, which were being spaced against the screens hiding the cars. She was glad she had now. That touch of green looked great against all the white. Her original plan was to keep everything white, since the roses her mom had picked out were hand-painted with shades of pale blue and lavender.

Roxie realized now that it was still a *lot* of white. Even for a wedding. Of course, the flowers weren't here yet. They'd help a lot. And her mom's dress was colorful. It would probably be fine.

No reason to stress. Other than she wanted everything to be perfect. But what daughter wouldn't want that for her mom on her wedding day?

Her phone rang. She answered it immediately, even though she didn't recognize the number. "Hello?"

"Roxanne?" A woman's voice, slightly breathless and edged in worry.

"Yes. Who's this?" Not a lot of people called her by her full name.

"Paulina. I'm sorry to call you but you said I could if I needed help and I need help."

Definitely not someone she'd expected to hear from. "This isn't really a great time—"

"Please. My mother fell and I need to go to the hospital. They think she's broken her arm and I don't have anyone to watch Nico."

Roxie took a breath. The panic in Paulina's voice was understandable now.

"Please," Paulina repeated. "The ambulance has already taken her. I can drop him off on my way. He's a good baby."

Roxie relented. "Okay, that's fine. You remember how to get here?"

"Yes. Thank you so much. I will be there shortly." She hung up.

Roxie sighed as she tucked the phone into her pocket. Maybe he'd sleep a lot. Or maybe he'd fuss and cry and make her wish she hadn't said yes. Today really wasn't a good day but how on Earth could she have said no?

"Ma'am?"

Roxie turned to see one of the party rental people holding an extension cord. "Yes?"

"We need a place to plug this in so we can run our steamer. Need to get the linens looking crisp."

"Right. Um..." She pointed toward the elevator. "On the front side there you'll find a GFI outlet."

"Thank you."

She nodded, still trying to figure out what she was going to do with a baby.

Paulina showed up ten minutes later. She walked around the screens, carrying Nico in his car carrier.

Roxie met her by the tables. "How's your mom doing?"

"I don't know. She was in a tremendous amount of pain and..." Paulina looked around at the tables and chairs. "You have something going on? A party?"

"You might say that," Roxie said. "My mother is getting married tonight."

Paulina's face twisted. "You can't watch Nico. It's too much."

Roxie put on a smile. Her mother might be getting married, but Paulina's mother was in the hospital. "We'll figure it out."

Paulina clung to the handle of Nico's car carrier. "You're sure?"

"Yes." Roxie held out her hands. "Give him to me."

Paulina hesitated, then handed him over. "I owe you a great deal. His things are in the car."

She went back and got them. A packed diaper bag, a tote with some toys and clothes, and a pack-and-play crib, folded up in a long rectangular carrying case with a handle. "I thought I should bring this in case..." She shook her head. "I tried to think of everything but could only think about my mother and what's going on with her. I hope you'll have what you need."

"We'll be fine." Roxie smiled down at Nico, his big brown eyes staring up at her. "Go on. Go be with your mom. I hope everything is all right."

Paulina nodded. "Thank you." She looked at her son. "Be a good boy, Nico. Mama will be back as soon as I can."

She took off, calling, "Thank you," over her shoulder one more time before she got in her car.

Roxie gazed down at Nico. He really was a beautiful child, something that was easier to admit because he didn't look like his father at all. If Nico had resembled Bryan, being around him might be harder. But since he favored his mother, it was simple for Roxie to let herself believe she was just helping a friend out.

Simple to think this baby was just a baby, and not a symbol of her husband's betrayal.

She shook her head. "None of that is your fault, is it, Nico?"

He grabbed at the air with his hands and cooed.

Her smile was genuine this time. He was an

innocent in all of this. "Why don't we take you upstairs, huh?"

She hoisted the diaper bag onto her shoulder, held the carrier in one hand, and the pack-and-play in the other. It was a lot, but she wanted to do it in one trip. She went over to the elevator, set Nico in his carrier down to push the button, then picked him back up.

Trina would probably be happy to see him.

The doors opened and she got on, setting both Nico and the pack-and-play down, this time to push the button for her floor.

When the doors opened again, she stepped out onto the first floor carrying everything Paulina had given her. She could hear voices in the living room. She went through.

Her mom and Trina stopped talking when Roxie walked in. She nodded at them. "Nice set on the hair, Trina. That's going to look great, Ma."

Willie was staring at Nico. "What in the Sam Hill are you doing with a baby?"

Roxie put the pack-and-play down, sighing. "Paulina's mom fell and broke her arm and had to go to the hospital. She didn't have anyone else to watch the baby. I couldn't bring myself to say no."

Trina was looking at Nico, grinning and waving at him.

Willie rolled her eyes. "We might be a little busy today."

"I know, I know, but what was I going to do? Tell her no when her mom's in the hospital?"

Willie made a face. "I guess not."

"I'm sorry," Roxie said. "I know the timing isn't good." She set the carrier on the coffee table in front of Trina.

Trina immediately unbuckled Nico and took him out. "Hello, there, baby brother. Do you remember me? I'm your sister." She bounced him on her lap. "You did the right thing, Ma. He'll be fine with us. I bet he won't be any trouble at all."

Roxie hoped not. She had no idea how long he was going to be here and she didn't want her act of kindness to be the reason her mom's big day got interrupted by a crying baby.

Chapter Twenty-three

Jules took a break as Sierra and Cash practiced a song together. They sounded great. All the same, she stepped outside and took a moment for herself in the sun. Her mind turned to the two issues lingering there. Lars and the need for a few more songs for the album.

Since the latter was easier to deal with, she focused on the songs. She liked to think of her albums as stories, which was what she was doing with this one. She'd already decided to title the album *Dixie's Got Her Boots On*, after the song she was about to record.

So it was Dixie's story she was telling. She thought about the path of a young woman's life and how it might go, from childhood to the teenage years, to becoming a young woman who would eventually marry and have children.

Dixie wouldn't have gone straight from the teenage years into marriage, though. She would have had some time between. Jules thought about her own life. About the wild oats she'd sown.

Dixie would have done that, too. She'd have had some fun times. Some girls nights out. Hmm. *Girls Night Out* made a great title for a song.

She went back inside. "You guys sound great. Keep practicing. I need to write for a bit."

Cash smiled. "Got an idea?"

Jules nodded. "I do." At least it felt like an idea. She held onto the thread that was beginning to unspool in her mind, the words that were starting to flow together. She grabbed her notebook, her pen, phone, and earbuds and went into the empty bedroom.

She put her earbuds in and played some white noise to help her focus and not hear Cash and Sierra practicing. Then she got to work.

She sat on the bed and wrote down everything in her head, whether it made sense or not. Minutes ticked by and she kept writing, rearranging the words, turning them into phrases that made sense.

Some of those phrases got rewritten, tweaked

until they were completely new. Didn't matter. Only the end result mattered.

She took a break to reread what she'd written, listening to the words to see what kind of musical ideas they gave her. She nodded as she read. This was a fun song. A girls night out was a fun time. It was all about connecting with your friends and enjoying their company. Flirting happened, for sure, but when she'd had those kinds of evenings, they never picked up boys.

They might have gotten some drinks bought for them, collected a few numbers, but they all went home the same way they'd come. Together.

She went back to writing, keeping that thought in her head. A new image of Dixie appeared. Maybe she'd been the leader of the pack. Maybe she'd been the wild child. Maybe she'd liked bad boys.

Jules sure understood that. Lars had definitely been a bad boy. So had her second husband, Trevor. Jules thought a moment. Was Jesse a bad boy? She made a face and shook her head. No way. He was a nice guy. Sure, he was involved in the music industry, but that hadn't turned him into a bad boy. Not yet, anyway. And hopefully never.

Bad boys were a bad habit, one she'd be happy to break.

She stared into space. That was actually another really good song title. *Bad Boys Are My Bad Habit.*

She flipped to a clean page and started the process all over again. Maybe Dixie's husband, the one who cheated on her, the one she ended up killing and going to jail for, maybe *he* was the bad boy she'd ultimately fallen for.

The story was coming together, and the words were flowing. Could she really have two new songs here?

She didn't want to stop and think about it, she just wanted to write. And write she did, filling pages with words, which she turned into lyrics.

It took her less than an hour to come up with two new songs. Amazing. She'd had inspiration like that before, but not in a long time. In fact, it had been years. When she'd first arrived in Diamond Beach, she'd thought her creative well had dried up.

Clearly not true. No idea what had gotten things going again. Maybe being around Cash and Sierra and all of their youthful energy. Whatever the reason, Jules was thrilled.

One more song, whatever that might be, and she'd have her album. These two still needed music, but that would come.

She took her earbuds out and rejoined Cash and

Sierra. They were working on a song Jules didn't recognize. It was sweet and soulful with an almost old-fashioned country vibe. She stood at the door, listening, and moving her head along with the rhythm.

When they finished, she clapped. "Very nice. What was that?"

Sierra answered. "Just something we were thinking about doing for the wedding."

"But what was it? I didn't recognize it."

Sierra blushed. "That's probably because I wrote it."

Jules lifted her brows. "You wrote that? What's it called?"

"*This Old Life Of Mine*."

"Can I hear it again from the beginning?"

"Sure," Sierra said. She looked at Cash. "From the top." She started to play the keyboard and he joined in.

Jules sat on the chair across from Cash and listened, absorbing the song and concentrating on the words. It was very good. It sounded like the reminiscing of someone in the twilight of their life, remembering all the good things that had happened to them, all the love and joy they'd experienced. It might not have been a perfect fit for Dixie's story, but it was beautiful and haunting in a way that stuck with Jules.

Not a lot of music did that these days.

When they finished, she smiled. "I like that a lot. In fact, I'd like to use it on my album. How'd you like to sell me the rights?"

Sierra's mouth came open and she stared at Jules. "You mean it?"

"I do."

Sierra shook her head. "You can have it."

Jules laughed. "No, that's not how this business works. I appreciate your generosity, but I can afford to pay you for the rights. My agent can handle the paperwork, if you'd like."

Sierra took a deep breath. "Okay, that would be great." Then a huge smile broke out across her face. "Thank you. For everything."

Jules nodded. "You're welcome."

And just like that, she had all the songs she needed for her album.

Chapter Twenty-four

Margo was still regretting getting Dinah an invite to the wedding. She could not stop thinking about how many ways it might go wrong.

None of those thoughts were helping her accomplish anything. She'd been looking through the comments, notes, and suggestions Conrad had sent since she'd moved into the bedroom to work, but so far she'd yet to act on any of them.

Her goal was to have them all incorporated into the new chapter before the wedding, but that was only a couple of hours away now. All she'd done was rewrite most of what she'd done yesterday and write a couple paragraphs of fresh words. Maybe she should take a break and get a small snack. She wasn't doing herself any good by sitting here thinking through every worst-case scenario.

She carried her lidded water tumbler to the kitchen for a refill but stopped a few feet from the island where Kat and Claire were working. Mostly Claire. Kat seemed to be watching, not helping, as Claire placed decorations on the cake.

Margo was impressed with what she saw. Not a reaction she often had to cake. "Claire, that is stunning."

Her daughter straightened. "You really mean that?"

Margo nodded. "I do. That's beautiful."

Kat nodded. "I told her that, but I don't think she believed me."

"I believed you," Claire said. "But I also thought you were just being nice."

"Mom." Kat laughed. "I was being honest."

"Thank you." Claire stepped back from the cake. "It's so hard to be impartial about a thing like this. I've got too much time and effort in it to see it clearly."

Margo walked around the island, looking at the cake from all sides. "It's not done yet, is it?"

"No," Claire said. "I have more decorations to put on, then some piping to do and I have to add the cake topper."

"Which is?"

Claire pointed at the counter behind her. "Those two Adirondack chairs with the blue letters in them."

"Very appropriate," Margo said.

"I painted the letters," Kat said. "And the cake board, which is what the cake is sitting on."

"There's a cardboard round under the cake," Claire explained. "Then the cake board."

"How is it getting downstairs?" Margo asked. "Looks heavy."

"It *is* very heavy," Claire confirmed. "I don't know what it weighs, exactly, but it's a lot. Probably over a hundred pounds by the time it's done. Cash and Danny are going to take it down."

"Too bad you don't have a cart to put it on, but I don't think we have anything that would hold that kind of weight anyway," Margo said. "I hope you take some good pictures of that. You could put it on the bakery's website as an example of what you can do."

Kat made a little noise. "That's a great idea. Let's make sure the wedding photographer gets some good pictures, Mom."

Claire nodded. "That is a good idea. Thanks."

"You're welcome," Margo said. "I don't know what wedding cakes go for these days, but in a place like Diamond Beach where there must be at least one wedding every weekend, you could get a pretty penny for a creation like that."

Claire laughed softly. "Probably. But I'm not sure I want to get into making wedding cakes. It's a lot of work. This one was...a lot."

"Because you'd never made one before," Margo said. "Now you have. Now you know more about what to expect and how to do things and the next one won't be nearly as difficult. And just think—you'll have that big professional kitchen to work in."

"That part is very appealing," Claire said. "It would have made this cake easier, I can tell you that much." She picked up a small glittery blue starfish and added it to a bare spot on the second tier. "And having help, as in a bakery assistant, would have made it easier, too. Plus, a big fridge dedicated to baked goods."

She took a few steps back and studied the cake. "It is good, isn't it?"

"It's very good," Margo assured her.

Kat nodded. "If I was having a beach wedding, I'd go nuts for that cake."

Claire glanced at Kat, then Margo. "You don't think it looks a little amateurish?"

"Not in the slightest." Margo frowned. "Are we looking at the same cake? I can't even imagine the confection you would have created if it was a more traditional, piped wedding cake. This seems more difficult to me. I'm not trying to talk you into doing anything you don't want to do. But if you want to make wedding cakes, you shouldn't let doubt hold you back. You have what it takes."

"Thanks again, Mom." Claire smiled. "I'll give it some serious consideration. For all I know, Danny might not want to take the bakery in that direction."

Kat snorted. "Why not? He have a thing against making money?"

"No, but it might not be what he wants the bakery to be known for."

Margo went to the pantry and found a protein bar. "The best part about wedding cakes is that they'll appeal to tourists and locals alike. Both get married here. If you rely on just the tourist trade alone, you might not do as well."

Claire seemed to consider that. "The popcorn shops rely mostly on the tourists, and they do all right."

"But the bakery won't be selling popcorn. I'd think having steady local sales would be useful, too."

"It would be," Claire said. "There's no doubt about that."

Margo refilled her water tumbler, then took it and her protein bar and headed back toward the bedroom and her book. "I have more work to do. Call me when the cake is done. I'd like to see it."

"I will, Mom," Claire said.

Margo settled in for some real work this time. She sat on the bed, legs out before her, laptop resting on a pillow. The table and chairs on the back porch were more comfortable, but there was too much distraction out there today. Noise from the preparations downstairs and the music from the third floor had gotten to be too much.

Instead, she was making do in the bedroom.

She opened the wrapper of the protein bar and took a bite as she reread the first comment Conrad had left her.

"What are her emotions in this scene? We should see them more," he'd written.

Margo had to think about that. If she herself had just killed someone and was now faced with talking to the police, she'd be terrified. But Margo was an ordinary woman. Something their protagonist was not.

She was a serial killer. A narcissist. And a psychopath.

So what emotions would a woman like that be feeling?

Margo took another bite of her protein bar and thought hard. Pride in her work? Along with a sense of amusement that she knew more than the police? Certainly she would consider the police detectives as less than herself. Not as intelligent. Maybe even bumbling. But she'd also be smart enough not to let those feelings show.

She'd act how she thought she *should* act. She'd be distraught. The dead man had been a colleague. She might even shed a few tears. A psychopath could definitely manage that.

What Margo needed to do was show that dichotomy. The internal thought process versus the external actions. She nodded. That had to be what Conrad was talking about.

She went back to the beginning of the chapter and started to rewrite. She changed a few words, but mostly added in some thoughts and actions that would reflect the dual nature of the woman on the page.

Pleased with how that turned out, she went on to his next comment. Time passed without her realizing it and when her alarm went off, she was surprised by it. She'd only set the alarm in case she lost track of time. She didn't want to be rushed getting ready for the wedding.

"Mom?" Claire's voice called out. "Cake is done if you want to see the final product."

Margo got up. "Coming." She dropped the wrapper from the protein bar in the trash bin and went out.

As pretty as the cake had been before, it was now worthy of a magazine. Claire had added more of the shells and starfish, as well as the two little chairs on top. But there were also small, piped details in white buttercream. The cake seemed to be shinier than before, too. Glittery.

Margo shook her head, amazed at her daughter's work. "It's stunning. It's not my style, but that doesn't matter. It's an incredible piece of confection. You have outdone yourself. How did you make it so shiny? It seems to catch the light."

Claire grinned. "Clear edible glitter."

Margo snorted. "That might be the most 'Willie' thing ever. I am impressed with you, Claire. And if they don't like it, they're fools."

Claire rolled her lips in as if trying not to laugh.

"I'm sure they'll like it, Mom. They wanted some-thing beachy."

"You've given them that. Beachy and beautiful." A new thought slipped into Margo's thoughts. She frowned. If Dinah said one negative word about the cake, Margo might actually lay hands on her.

Margo pursed her lips. Maybe she was more like her protagonist than she'd realized.

Chapter Twenty-five

Trina knew her mom felt bad about agreeing to look after Nico, and while the timing wasn't perfect, Trina thought the impromptu visit was great, even if the circumstances that had caused it weren't so good. He was an absolute doll and she loved having some unexpected time with him.

Although time wasn't something she actually had a lot of at the moment. Thankfully, she'd already set Mimi's hair and had done her own in beachy waves. But she still had her mom's to do. She sat Nico back in his carrier. "Ma, we should do your hair."

Her mom nodded. "I know. It'll be time to get dressed soon. But I'm not doing that until I have one more check on things downstairs. The florist should be here in about half an hour."

"I can at least start on your hair, Ma," Trina said. "I might even have it done in half an hour, depending on what you want done."

Willie settled back in her chair, eyes on the baby. "I can watch him. You two go do what you need to do."

Roxie didn't look like she thought that was such a great idea. "You sure about that, Ma?"

Willie shot her a look. "I've taken care of babies. You were one once, you know."

"I know but…that wasn't exactly yesterday."

Willie rolled her eyes. "Have babies changed since then?"

"No, but that's not what I mean."

Willie shooed them away. "Go. You're wasting time. Besides, this'll be good practice for me for when Trina brings her babies over to my house."

Trina laughed, amused by the interaction. "She's right, Ma. About the wasting time part." As much as she wanted babies, it was going to be a few years before that happened. "We should really get your hair done."

Roxie exhaled. "Okay, let's go. But if you need us, Ma, just yell."

"I will. But I won't."

Trina moved Nico's carrier closer to Mimi's end

of the coffee table, then set his diaper bag next to her chair. "If he gets fussy, he might need to eat. I can come in and make him a bottle. Just yell."

"Thanks, honey."

Trina tipped her head toward the bedrooms. "Come on, Ma. Let's get you done."

They went back to Trina's room. She patted the chair in front of her vanity. "Sit and let's figure out what we should do. Do you have any ideas?"

Roxie shook her head. "I've been too busy to really think about it. Whatever you want to do is fine by me."

Trina stared at her mom in the mirror, mentally rotating through several possible hairstyles. Impulsively, she gathered her mom's hair and twisted it up. "What do you think about an updo? You almost never wear your hair up. Might be really pretty and different. It'll definitely be cooler."

"I don't know," Roxie said. "Do you really think that will look all right on me?"

"Let's give it a shot and see."

"Okay," Roxie said. "You're the professional."

Trina got to work, brushing out her mom's hair, which had been washed and airdried earlier and left free of styling products. "The color still looks good."

Her mom nodded. "This is going to be a lot

easier to maintain than that intense red. I really love this color a lot. I'm glad I did it."

Trina spritzed her mom's hair with heat protectant, then flat ironed her hair to smooth it, but used the iron to put a soft wave in the hair as well. The texture would help the updo hold. Trina listened as she worked. The soft sounds of the TV came through, but nothing else. "I don't hear any crying. That's a good thing."

"Neither do I," Roxie said. "Not yet, anyway."

"Maybe Nico fell asleep."

"Or your grandmother did."

Trina laughed. "Also possible. Maybe they're both napping."

"That works, too." Roxie sighed. "I hope Paulina's mom is okay."

"Me, too. That had to be so scary for both of them. It was really nice of you to take Nico."

"Thanks. I didn't feel like I had much of a choice. Not that she was pressuring me, just that I knew she didn't have any other options."

Trina pulled the flat iron over another section of hair, turning the iron to set in a wave. "It was the right thing to do."

"Not a great day for it, though."

"There's never a great time for an emergency, is there?"

Her mom smiled. "No, there's not. You're right about that."

Trina's stomach growled, making her flatten her hand over her belly. "Sorry about that. I don't really feel that hungry, but maybe I better eat a little something when we're done."

"There's lasagna left over." Her mom glanced at her through the mirror. "I'm excited we're finally going to get to meet Miles today."

Trina grinned. "So am I. I like him so much. I hope you guys do, too."

"I'm sure we will."

"Mimi can be pretty judgmental."

"True," Roxie said. "But she knows how you feel about him and that will sway her a bit. Plus, she's going to be in a good mood because of what today is. I think it'll go fine. I already know I'm going to like him. Any man who can make you as happy as you've been lately is all right with me."

"Thanks, Ma." Trina got some hairpins out so they'd be handy, then started brushing her mother's hair into place. She was going for a twist but with some volume on top and a few loose pieces at the sides to soften the look and keep it beachy.

She concentrated as she worked, smoothing and spraying on more heat protector. Florida humidity was no joke, even in the spring, so when she was done, she'd have to seal the look with a good dousing of hairspray.

Her mom reached out to grab her phone, checking the screen. "The florist is running a little late but will be here in twenty minutes."

"I'll have you done by then," Trina said. She pinned everything into place, using a few more than necessary just to keep things secure, then worked out a few pieces around the hairline. She used the flat iron again to give them a beachy wave. Finally, she dug through her hair accessories, found a few rhinestone pins, and tucked them along the interior side of the twist for a little extra pizazz.

She held off on setting the whole thing with hairspray until her mom gave her approval. "All right," Trina said. "What do you think?"

She grabbed her hand mirror and held it so her mom could see the back.

Her mom turned her head from side to side, studying the work that Trina had done. She smiled. "It looks amazing. So much better than I thought it would. I didn't think I could wear a style like this. Thank you! I love it."

"I'm so glad. I think it's very sophisticated. Now, close your eyes." Trina grinned and gave her mom a good dousing of hairspray.

When that was over, her mom laughed. "I'm not sure 'sophisticated' is a word anyone's ever used in relation to me. Maybe this is my new look? Although I'm not sure how it would go with leopard-print shorts and wedge sandals."

Trina grinned as she pointed toward the living room. "Do you mind if I run out and check on Nico and Mimi?"

"Of course not," her mom answered. "I think I might take a selfie of my new look, just in case it doesn't survive the night."

Trina went out to the living room. Mimi and Nico were both sound asleep. Trina smiled. There was something very sweet about the two of them napping like that, even if Mimi was in curlers.

Trina pulled out her phone and snapped a picture. This was a moment she wanted to remember.

Chapter Twenty-six

Claire was in her bedroom getting ready, but she could tell the house was a hive of activity with everyone prepping for the wedding. Of course, Cash wouldn't need a lot of time. Men never did. But her mom and sister were undoubtedly taking their time to look their best.

Claire was no different. She took extra care with her hair, blow-drying it with her rounded brush the way Trina had showed her. She carefully applied her makeup, going a little heavier than she did for every-day. Finally, she put on the sundress she'd chosen. There would be a lot of pictures taken, not necessarily of her, but she would definitely be in some of them, and she wanted to look as good as she could.

Having the cake done was a huge relief. Getting her mom's approval on it had been a nice bonus. Now, all that remained was for Willie and Miguel to like it as well. And Danny, too, naturally. She really wanted to impress him.

Hopefully, she would.

The nice thing about having a wedding at the house was that she didn't need to bring a purse. Her sundress had pockets and those were sufficient. She tucked her lipstick into one pocket and a couple of folded tissues in the other. She wasn't sure this wedding was going to make her cry, but she wasn't taking any chances on messing up the makeup she'd so meticulously applied.

She slipped on her strappy black sandals and took a look at herself in the mirrored closet doors. Not bad. Certainly better than she'd looked in a long time.

The few pounds she'd lost seemed most visible in her face. It was almost as if she had cheekbones again. That was a nice thing to see. How had she not noticed it before? Maybe the blush she had used had really brought them out. The new cut and color Trina had given her helped a lot, too.

Smiling, she grabbed her phone and went out to the kitchen. There was a young woman she'd never seen before sitting on the couch. "Hello, there."

The young woman smiled at her. "Hi. I'm Sierra. I'm playing with Jules and Cash for the wedding. I've been working with Jules on her new song, too. I sing and play the keyboard."

Claire gave her a little wave. "Nice to meet you, Sierra. I'm Claire. I'm Jules's sister and Cash's aunt."

"Are you the one who made that cake?"

Claire nodded. "That would be me."

"Wow." Sierra breathed the word out in obvious admiration. "That thing is crazy good."

Claire couldn't help but nod. "Thanks. I appreciate that."

"It must have taken you forever. What flavor is it?"

"As requested by the bride and groom, pina colada."

"For real? I can't wait to taste it."

"Me, too." Claire took a few pictures of the cake, getting it from all angles. Then she did a video, doing the same thing. She walked around slowly, making sure to capture the entire thing. She knew there would be professional pictures, but she wanted these for herself. For the memory of what she'd accomplished.

Sierra came over. "You want me to take one of you next to the cake?"

"Good idea. Thanks," Claire said. She handed over her phone.

As Sierra snapped the pic, Margo came out of the bedroom.

She wore a pretty dress of turquoise and pink flowers with fluttery sleeves. It was one of the most tropical things Claire had ever seen her mother wear. And it made her waist look tiny. "Mom, this is Sierra. She's playing with Jules and Cash for the wedding."

"How nice. Lovely to meet you, Sierra."

Claire gestured at Margo. "This is my mom, Margo Bloom, which also makes her Cash's grandmother."

"Nice to meet you, Mrs. Bloom."

"Thank you, Sierra." Margo gave Claire a smile. "You look wonderful."

Claire appreciated the approval. "Thanks, Mom. So do you. Is that new?"

"Actually, it's old. I bought it on a cruise with your father. An impulse buy and one I never wore again after that cruise. It was just too loud for me. But it seemed appropriate for Willie's beach wedding."

Claire narrowed her eyes. "I don't think it's too loud. The colors look great on you. Maybe you should wear brights more often."

"I'm not so sure about that. This still feels a bit

much. But it is a beach wedding. And Willie does have a penchant for bright, outrageous combinations."

Claire thought that her mom must know how good she looked in the dress, or she wouldn't have had it on. Not with Conrad's sister coming to the wedding. Unless that had changed. "Is Dinah still coming?"

Margo nodded. "As far as I know. Conrad hasn't texted to say differently."

"Are you nervous about that?"

"The only thing that makes me nervous is that Dinah might cause a scene." Margo shook her head. "That woman is a bit of a loose cannon. Hopefully she understands today is not about her or her opinions."

"If there's anything I can do, or if you need me to step in and create a distraction, just give me a look."

"That's very kind of you to offer, but I'm sure Conrad will be keeping a close eye on her."

"Well, just in case."

Her mom nodded. "Just in case."

Kat joined them, her blue and white sundress and white sandals looking breezy and perfect.

Jules came out next in gauzy, wide-legged black pants and a black top with pink and red flowers accented with a little white and green. Toby trotted alongside her. He was wearing a floral bandana around his neck and looked very festive. "Cash isn't down yet?"

Sierra, who'd gone back to sitting on the couch, shook her head. "I haven't seen him yet. Do you want me to text him?"

"Yeah, please do," Jules said. She came into the kitchen and smiled at the cake. "Claire, you really outdid yourself. This is beautiful."

"I helped," Kat said, giggling. "I provided artistic direction."

Claire rolled her eyes as Jules looked confused. "She helped me line up the layers."

Jules studied the cake a little more. "Well, it worked out."

Just then, the elevator doors opened, and Cash walked out in pale-washed blue jeans and a Hawaiian shirt. He held his phone up and grinned at Sierra. "I'm right here."

"I see that," she said laughing. "Your family didn't know where you were."

He shifted his gaze to look at them. "I was taking the guitars and keyboard downstairs and making sure we were all set up with the mics and speakers down there."

"Thanks," Jules said. "I'm glad you took care of that."

"Yeah, no problem." He suddenly let out a low whistle. "Aunt Claire, did you seriously make that thing?"

She nodded. "I did."

"That is epic."

Sierra came over and joined them. She waved at Kat. "Hi, I'm Sierra."

Kat waved back. "I'm Kat. Cash's cousin."

Cash hooked his thumb in Sierra's direction. "She's playing with us tonight."

"Cool," Kat said.

Cash pointed at the cake next. "Does that need to go downstairs now, too?"

Claire shook her head. "Not until after dinner, otherwise the buttercream could melt, and it will be a mess."

"Right." He looked at his mom. "You want to go down and do a quick soundcheck?"

"Sure."

Claire shrugged. "We can all go down. I'd like to have a look at that cake table myself. Just to be sure it's going to support this thing."

"You all go on," Margo said. "I'll be along shortly. I just thought of something I need to do."

"All right, Mom. See you down there." Jules glanced at her dog. "Toby could probably use a bathroom break, too. Let me grab his leash."

"I'll get it," Kat said. She retrieved it from the laundry room, then came back and clipped it to his collar. "Okay, we're all set."

"There's too many of us to take the elevator," Cash said. "Sierra and I can take the steps."

"It's still going to be tight," Jules said.

Cash picked Toby up. "You can have him back when you get downstairs, Kat."

Kat gave him a thumb- up. "Cool."

He and Sierra went out the sliding doors and down the spiral steps while the rest of them waited for the elevator.

Once it arrived, Claire, Jules, and Kat got into the car. As the doors closed, Jules said, "You know that's Cash's new girlfriend."

Kat let out a little gasp. "So *that's* who he's been moony-eyed over. She's very pretty."

"And very talented," Jules said.

Claire just smiled. All these new, blossoming relationships had her wondering who she might be making the next wedding cake for.

Chapter Twenty-seven

*W*rapped in her robe, Willie was back in front of Trina's vanity so that Trina could take out the curlers and put the final touches on her hair. Thankfully, Willie's nap hadn't done any damage. She hadn't meant to fall asleep, but she must have needed it.

The nap had worked, because she felt full of energy now. A little nervous, but that was more about her concern that everything went right than her part in things. She wasn't exactly a blushing bride. She had been through this a few times before. But this was her last marriage. Her last husband. There was a finality to that realization that gave her a great sense of peace.

Maybe that came from the feeling that this was the absolute right thing for her to be doing. Or maybe it came from the strength that having Miguel at her side gave her. He was one of the best men she'd ever known. It felt like a privilege to be marrying him. She knew she was blessed to have him in her life. His family was wonderful, too, although she'd yet to meet his grandson, but she would today.

If she was worried about anything, it was *her* family. Roxie and Trina. She couldn't help but be concerned about her girls and what their future might hold.

Looking at the big picture of life, she knew they'd be all right. They were both smart, strong women. They were hard workers, and they knew how to survive in just about any situation. How to be self-reliant.

But sitting across from that little baby had gotten Willie to thinking. What if Paulina decided to make trouble? Decided the share of Bryan's life insurance money she'd gotten wasn't enough?

That was always a possibility, wasn't it?

What if Paulina mistook Roxie's kindness for weakness? Willie didn't know anything about Paulina, or about what kind of woman she was. She might be a real snake, for all Willie knew. What if she had known Bryan was married? What if getting pregnant had been her way of trapping Bryan? There was no way of knowing. Not really.

That bothered Willie more than she could say. It had also spurred her into action, flipping the switch inside of her that made her feel protective of her girls.

While Trina had been busy doing Roxie's hair, Willie had gotten a Q-tip and gently rubbed it on the inside of Nico's cheek. She wasn't sure that was the right way to collect DNA, but she'd seen it done like that on television. Fortunately, the kid hadn't fussed. Afterwards, she'd stored the Q-tip in a plastic baggie. Now all she had to do was get someone to analyze it.

How hard could that be? Miguel knew people. Maybe he knew someone who could do it. Or maybe she could find a place online that could do it. From what she understood, you could get just about anything done online these days.

As a backup to the Q-tip, which might not work at all, Willie had brushed the little boy's hair and collected the loose strands. She had put those in a separate baggie. One way or another, she was going to find out if Bryan Thompson was really this boy's father.

Of course, she didn't have any DNA from Bryan and he'd been cremated. She was pretty sure you couldn't get DNA from ashes. Even if you could, she wasn't going to sneak upstairs and take a sample from the urn.

But she could definitely have Nico matched against Trina. All that would take would be a couple of strands of Trina's hair, and that was easy to get.

If the test didn't show that Trina and Nico were related, that would be proof enough that Paulina was up to something.

"You okay, Mimi?" Trina put her hand on Willie's shoulder. "You're awfully quiet."

Willie smiled and patted Trina's hand. "All good, my girl. Just thinking about all the wonderful things our futures hold." And what she was going to do to protect her family from the not-so-wonderful bits.

One of those bits was Liz Stewart, but thankfully, she hadn't shown her face again. At least not that Trina had mentioned. Would she keep that from Willie?

Trina might, because of the wedding. She wouldn't want to upset Willie with everything else going on. Trina was thoughtful like that.

But Willie wanted to know. She had to know. "Trina?"

"Yes, Mimi?"

Willie watched her granddaughter's face in the

mirror. She didn't think Trina would lie to her, but she might try to hide the truth. "Has that ex of your boyfriend's bothered you at all lately?"

Trina pursed her lips and shook her head as she kept working on Willie's hair. "Not since I saw her at the grocery store."

"Good. She sounded like trouble. Hopefully, she's figured out she made a fool of herself and that she should leave you alone."

"Yeah, maybe. I hope so, anyway," Trina said as she applied a little more hairspray. She stepped back and put the can down. "All right, Mimi. What do you think? Looks pretty good to me but I want you to be happy."

Willie turned her head from side to side. Her hair was perfect. The decorative clip was just over her right ear and Trina had arranged it so it looked like it was holding some of Willie's curls back. "I think it's wonderful, sweetheart. Best you've ever done. Thank you for all your hard work."

"I'm happy to do it, Mimi. No problem at all. Let me touch up your makeup, too."

"Go right ahead.

That only took Trina a few minutes. "All right, you look like a movie star. We'll put lipstick on you after you get your dress on, which we both need to do right now."

Willie looked at the time. "Holy cow, yeah. We'd better get moving." She went out into the reading nook and looked into the living room where Roxie was watching the baby. Roxie was on her phone. "Trina fixed my hair and we're going to get dressed now. You'd better get dressed, yourself."

"I'm about to. I was just texting Kat to see if she could watch the baby during the ceremony, since Trina and I are walking you down the aisle. She said that would be fine."

Willie nodded. "That's nice of her." That Kat was growing on her. She was a good girl, just like Trina.

Willie went into her room. Her dress was on a hanger and hooked on the standing mirror in the corner of her room. It looked so pretty. Roxie had steamed it for her earlier, so it was as perfect as could be.

She gazed at it for a moment, then got to work. And it *was* work. Getting herself into a pair of shapewear bike shorts and her long-line bra ought to count as cardio. Neither of those garments she liked but for today she'd make an exception. She got hot struggling into them, so she sat on the bed when she was done. She probably should have had a gin and tonic first.

A little drink always seemed to make the hard tasks easier.

After she'd cooled off, she put her silver sandals on. She'd be careful stepping into her dress, but this way she wouldn't have to bend over and risk wrinkling up her dress.

The dress was easy. She just stepped in and put her arms through the little sleeves. She didn't bother zipping it up, just called for help. "Can someone zip me?"

Trina showed up. "Ma already took Nico and all his stuff and went downstairs. She wanted to make sure Kat was all set up to take care of him."

"Already? I know we're getting close but there's still a little time.

Trina shrugged. "She also wanted to have a final look around and make sure everything was perfect. She's going to text us when it's time for us to come down, then she'll meet us at the elevator with your bouquet, and the three of us will walk down the aisle together." She smiled. "Thanks for including me in that, Mimi. That was just..."

Trina's words trailed off and she sniffed.

"Oh, no, you don't," Willie said. Nothing got her

going faster than Roxie or Trina getting emotional. "Don't you start crying. Then I'll start and my makeup will be a big mess. You don't wanna have to redo it all at this hour, do you? It'll take forever and Miguel will think I'm not coming!"

Trina laughed and wiped carefully at her eyes. "No crying. I'm just really touched you wanted me with you. That's all."

"Trina, you are the most precious child to me. I always want you with me. Why do you think I made sure there's a guest room at my new house for you?"

Trina threw her arms around Willie. "I love you so much, Mimi."

"I love you, too, honey." Willie wasn't sure what she'd done in her life to be this blessed, but she was grateful. More than grateful, she was at peace with her life in a way she'd never been before.

It was a wonderful feeling. Especially on her wedding day.

Chapter Twenty-eight

Kat was glad she'd come downstairs early. She'd taken Toby for a walk to pee, then handed him off to her mom when Roxie had texted Kat about looking after Nico. Toby was mostly interested in sniffing the flowers he could reach. She was pretty sure he'd already eaten at least one rose petal.

She smiled at Nico in his carrier. "You're not going to eat any flowers, are you?"

He smiled and made happy noises. Then he stuck his hands out.

Did he want to be picked up? She'd spent almost no time around babies, so she didn't really have a grasp on their wants and needs or how to interpret their body language. Roxie had told Kat to put a cloth over her shoulder if she held him, just in case he threw up.

Good advice, since she was in nice clothes, but it wasn't something she really wanted to think about. She dug a cloth from the diaper bag, put it on her shoulder, then picked Nico up and placed him against her. She patted his back gently. "How's that, kiddo? Hmm?"

"Whoa. Something you want to tell me about, Kat?"

She turned to see Alex and Miles walking around the screens. She smiled. "This is mine and Trina's half-brother, Nico. His mom had a family emergency, so we're looking after him today."

Alex grinned. "Hey, little man. How's it going?"

Miles looked around. "The place looks great. Really good."

Kat nodded in agreement. "They did a fantastic job."

Underneath the house had been transformed into a gorgeous dining venue with linens, blue and lavender painted roses along with other flowers and greenery, potted palms, and electric candles inside glass lanterns. Just beyond the pool, down on the beach, were several rows of white-draped chairs with an ivory runner down the center aisle that separated them.

At the end of that runner was a golden metal

arch swathed in more flowers, greenery, and tulle. Rose petals had been strewn over the runner and lanterns lined the aisle. At the four corners of the seating area were golden tiki torches wrapped with more flowers.

It was very pretty. The perfect fairy tale beach wedding setup. Kat was impressed. She turned back to the guys. "You both look great, by the way."

Alex glanced at Miles. "I only look this way thanks to him."

They were in very similar outfits of tan pants and Hawaiian shirts.

"Thanks, Miles," Kat said.

"No problem."

Danny came over with a younger woman. Older than Kat, but not by much. "Kat, this is my daughter, Ivelisse. Her husband is still at my house with the kids. He'll be over shortly."

"Hi," Kat said. "Nice to meet you."

"Nice to meet you," Ivelisse replied. "Especially since I've already met your mom, the amazing baker."

Kat laughed. "She is pretty good, isn't she?"

"She's incredible," Ivelisse said. "Is that your son? He's precious. Sometimes I wish mine were still that small."

Kat shook her head. "Half-brother. It's a long story. I promise to explain before the night is over." She used her elbow to gesture to the guys. "This is my boyfriend, Alex, and his friend, Miles."

They all shook hands, then Ivelisse motioned toward a young man who was walking over from the Rojas property. He looked a lot like Danny. She waved him over. "This is my brother, Oscar. Oscar, come meet everyone."

Oscar was good-looking. Not Alex, but handsome enough.

He lifted his hand in greeting as he came over. "Hello."

Introductions were made. The guys seemed to hit it off right away.

Good thing, too, because Nico suddenly got fussy. Based on the odor drifting up from his diaper, Kat had a sinking suspicion she knew why. He needed to be changed. "If you'll excuse me, I'd better take him upstairs for a minute. Be right back."

She grabbed his diaper bag and took him up in the elevator. It didn't seem like a thing she'd want to do in front of Willie's guests. Kat had never actually changed a diaper before, but how hard could it be?

She wasn't sure where to change him. They didn't have a changing table. Maybe she ought to just do it on the living room rug. "Come on, Nico. We'll get you cleaned up."

He was crying now, soft little hiccupy sobs that felt like the precursor to some serious wailing.

Kat set the diaper bag down on the floor. Changing a diaper in her nice sundress probably wasn't an optimal situation, but she didn't have a choice. As she started to kneel, her grandmother came out of the bedroom.

"Someone needs to be changed, I take it?"

Kat nodded. "Yes."

"Have you ever changed a diaper before?"

"No, but how hard can it be?"

"It's not hard, but it can be a little tricky." Her grandmother's brows lifted slightly. "You're going to want to put a blanket or something down before you put him on that rug. Trust me. This can be a messy business. No pun intended."

Kat set Nico down, then got a blanket out of the diaper bag and laid it out on the rug. She put him on it and started to get him out of his clothing. The smell was...not great. She wrinkled her nose. "Does it always smell this bad??"

"No. Sometimes it smells worse." Her grand-mother laughed. "Do you want me to do that? I don't mind. I've changed more diapers in my time than I can count."

"I've got it," Kat said. "It'll be good practice for when I have my own kids someday."

She got the wipes out and cleaned Nico up. Then she looked up at her grandmother. "Do I need to do anything after I have him all cleaned? Put anything else on him?"

Her grandmother shook her head. "It doesn't look like he's got any diaper rash or anything like that going on. If he's all clean, then just put the new diaper on him and you can get him dressed again."

"Okay." Kat got him into the new diaper, which, thankfully, had sticky tabs that made securing it pretty easy.

Nico wasn't crying anymore. That was good.

"Nice job," her grandmother said.

"Thanks." Kat put the dirty wipes inside the dirty diaper and took the whole thing to the trash.

"You might want to rethink that," her grandmother said. "That'll stink up the whole house. I'd put it in a grocery bag, tie it up and then throw it away."

Kat nodded. "Thanks, that's a good idea. I'm learning all kinds of stuff." She went into the laundry room and got an old plastic grocery bag. She used it to secure the dirty diaper, then she put it in the trash. After that, she went straight to the sink and scrubbed her hands with hot water and soap. Nico seemed pretty happy to lie on the floor and wave his hands around.

Her grandmother was watching him with a strange, almost wistful look on her face.

Kat dried her hands on a towel and walked back over. "You okay, Grandma?"

Her grandmother nodded. "Babies are amazing things, aren't they? I was just thinking about when you were little. It seems like yesterday, but then some days, it seems like a thousand years ago. Time is such a funny thing."

Kat wondered if her grandmother was hoping for great-grandchildren. If so, it was going to be a while. Kat wasn't even close to having babies yet. She did have something else to offer her grandmother, though.

She kneeled down to pack up the diaper bag and pick Nico up. "Alex is here. Would you like to come back down with me and meet him?"

Her grandmother smiled. "I'd like that very much. I think Conrad and his sister will be here shortly as well."

Kat cradled Nico in her arms as she slung the

diaper bag over her shoulder. "It's going to be all right. Dinah will be fine. It's a wedding. I have to think she'll be on her best behavior."

Her grandmother didn't look so convinced. "I hope you're right. I'll get the elevator."

When they stepped off the elevator, most of the people had moved to the seating area on the beach, but Alex was still standing by the tables.

He smiled at her. "I thought I should wait."

He was so good. "Alex, this is my grandmother, Margo Bloom. Grandma, this is Alex Kelley."

"The firefighting hero," her grandmother said. "Nice to meet you, young man."

"The pleasure's all mine," Alex said. "I've never met a real author before."

Her grandmother laughed demurely. "Well, I don't know if I'd call myself an author just yet."

But Kat knew he'd won points with that.

Car doors shut and gravel crunched under footsteps, announcing the arrival of more people. Aunt Jules strummed an easy tune on her guitar. A moment later, Cash and Sierra joined her. But her grandmother had stiffened as she looked toward the parking area.

"You two go on and get seats. I'm sure that's Conrad and Dinah. I'll wait for them."

Kat tipped her head toward the tent. "Come on, Alex." He nodded and walked with her. She glanced back to see Conrad and a petite blonde join her grandmother. Dinah, obviously. And she already looked bothered by something.

She'd better not start anything. Willie and Miguel might not be immediate family, but Kat was going to be around these people for a lot of years to come. She didn't want anything going wrong on their big day.

And since she'd just changed her first diaper, she felt capable of anything. Even shutting down the sister of her grandmother's boyfriend.

Chapter Twenty-nine

*L*ittle nerves tripped through Roxie's body like tiny sparks going off. She felt like she'd had too much coffee but that was only because it was nearly time for the wedding to start and she was jazzed up with anticipation.

Seated on tall stools at the back of the chairs on the beach, Jules and her group were playing softly. They sounded great together. The florist and party rental people had done an amazing job. The space under the beach house had never looked more festive. The caterers had just arrived and were setting up for the reception. Almost everyone was in their seats.

With trembling hands, she texted her mom and Trina. *Get ready.*

Out on the beach, the officiant rang a small bell.

"Ladies and gentlemen, if you could take your places. We're about to begin."

The last few folks standing found seats and sat down. The officiant nodded at Jules and the music changed into the processional.

Roxie sent her second text. *Now*.

Danny, dressed in tan linen pants and pale blue linen shirt, and Miguel, dressed in white linen pants and matching shirt, each with blue and lavender-hued rose boutonnieres, walked over from next door and to the beach setup, where they went down the aisle. Danny was smiling; Miguel looked solemn.

Danny shook the officiant's hand, gave his dad a warm hug, then took a seat in the front row.

Behind Roxie, the elevator opened. Her mom, looking as beautiful as Roxie had ever seen her, stood there holding onto Trina's arm. Roxie handed Willie her lovely bouquet. She held it in front of her and smiled.

"You look just gorgeous, Ma. Ready to get married?" Roxie asked.

Willie nodded. "You bet."

Roxie turned, caught Jules's eye and gave her a nod. Jules nodded back, said something to her son and his friend, and a moment later, they transitioned into the wedding march.

Roxie faced her mom again as she and Trina walked out of the elevator. Roxie offered Willie her arm. Willie took it, then Roxie and Trina escorted Willie to the beach and down the rose petal-covered aisle.

Everyone stood as they approached, big smiles on all the faces.

The photographer shadowed them, snapping away. There were two video cameras set up as well to capture everything from different angles. Ethan gave Roxie a big grin as they went past. He'd already told her how beautiful she looked. He looked pretty handsome himself.

Standing at the end of the aisle, waiting for his bride, Miguel dabbed at his eyes with a hand-kerchief.

The three of them stopped in front of the offi-ciant, Father Norman Green. The crowd sat down.

He greeted them with a nod. "Who gives this woman to be wed?"

Roxie answered, as they'd previously discussed. "Her daughter and her granddaughter do."

Willie let go of them to take her place across from Miguel as Roxie and Trina each kissed him on the cheek. They each hugged and kissed Willie, then they sat in the front row opposite Danny.

Father Green gazed out at the small audience, and it *was* small. The only people who weren't family were the plus ones some had brought. But Roxie thought the small number only added to the intimate feel of the proceedings.

"Marriage is a lifetime commitment," Father Green said with a smile. He adjusted his wire-rimmed frames. He had a clear, comforting voice that matched his grandfatherly appearance. "No matter what age you get married at."

Soft laughter lifted from the group.

"What you're seeing today is proof of that commitment. Willie and Miguel are going to take their vows in front of you, making you a part of their promise to each other as their witnesses. It's a great honor that we all get to share in.

"In many ways, Willie and Miguel's love story is a miracle. To find love at any point in your life is a gift. To find it in your golden years is a revelation. You know who you are at this stage of life. You know what you want. What you don't want. And you understand, perhaps more than most, just how precious life—and love—are."

Someone behind Roxie sniffed.

"Willie and Miguel could have very easily decided they didn't need to be married. That moving in together would be enough. But that wasn't enough. Not for them. They wanted to pledge themselves to each other. To take the biggest step two people can take. That's why we're gathered on this beach. To join them before you and before God." He smiled. "I am honored to perform this ceremony. I hope you understand how solemn this promise is that they're about to make and how special these two people are."

Roxie glanced over her shoulder. Lots of nodding. A few damp gazes.

"Now, if no one has any objections, let's get on with it." He gave everyone a broad smile. "Willie and Miguel, you may join hands."

Roxie got up to take Willie's bouquet, then Willie and Miguel clasped their hands together. The sweet scent of the gorgeous roses drifted up from Roxie's lap as she clutched the flowers.

"Wilhelmina Pasternak, do you take this man to be your lawfully wedded husband from this day forward, in sickness and in health, in good times and in bad, to love and honor for as long as you both shall live?"

Willie smiled, her gaze on Miguel and no one else. "I do."

"Miguel Rojas, do you take this woman to be

your lawfully wedded wife from this day forward, in sickness and in health, in good times and in bad, to love and honor for as long as you both shall live?"

Miguel looked like he was fighting tears as he focused on Willie. "I do."

"Wonderful," Father Green said. He looked toward Danny. "If we could have the rings?"

Danny got up and handed the rings to Father Green.

Father Green lifted them for all to see. Light from the sinking sun glinted off Miguel's gold band and sparkled on the diamonds in Willie's. "We've all probably heard about the symbolic nature of these rings. That the unbroken circle signifies the fidelity Willie and Miguel have pledged to each other. How that circle is a picture of God's love for us without beginning or end. Some say the opening in the center of the ring represents the door to the future that these two are about to enter together."

Roxie thought that was beautiful. She could feel tears welling. She took a deep breath and did her best not to cry.

Father Green smiled and shifted the rings so that he held up Willie's by itself. "Do you know what this style of ring is called when it has diamonds all the way around it as this one does?"

"Expensive," one of the men in the audience volunteered.

That got a laugh.

Father Green grinned and nodded. "True. But it's also called an eternity band. That's the meaning I like. Eternity. These two are promising themselves to each other for always."

He handed Willie's ring to Miguel. "Repeat after me. With this ring, I promise to be your faithful and loving husband, as God is my witness."

Miguel said the words as he slipped the diamond band over Willie's finger.

Then Father Green handed Miguel's gold band to Willie. "Now you. With this ring, I promise to be your faithful and loving wife, as God is my witness."

Willie's voice cracked halfway through. She cleared her throat and finished.

A happy tear slipped down Roxie's cheek. Beside her, Trina's lower lip was quivering. Roxie reached over and took her daughter's hand.

Father Green beamed at the audience. "It is my great pleasure to pronounce these two husband and wife. Miguel, you may now kiss your bride."

Miguel leaned in and planted one on Willie.

Everyone clapped and got to their feet.

"That's it," Roxie said to no one in particular. "They're official."

Her heart was full. Her mom looked as happy as a person could be. Today was a very good day.

Chapter Thirty

Jules thought the ceremony had been perfect. Now she, Cash, and Sierra played as the bride and groom went down the aisle and off to have some more pictures taken.

Father Green held his hands up to get everyone's attention and as the crowd quieted, she and her little band ended their music.

"Thank you so much for attending this evening. As the sun sets, the bride and groom will be having pictures taken. They would very much like all of you to join them for a group photo. Afterwards, they invite you to the reception area that's been prepared under the beach house. Dinner will be served shortly. God bless you all."

The photographer already had Willie and Miguel posing on the beach. As soon as Father

Green was done with his announcement, Thomas turned and waved everyone over.

"That means us, too," Jules said. She set her guitar on her chair. Three bar stools had been set up for them, but Sierra hadn't used hers, preferring to stand in front of her keyboard.

Sierra hesitated. "They don't even know me."

"Maybe not yet," Cash said. "But you are helping with the music. Come on."

"Okay." Sierra turned her keyboard off. It had taken three extension cords to provide power for it down on the beach. If the ceremony site had been closer to the water, the keyboard might not have happened at all.

The three of them joined the gathering crowd, with Miguel and Willie at the center. Immediate family had been placed on either side of them, then everyone else around them. It was a good-looking group, Jules thought.

Jesse slipped in next to her. "You guys sounded great and those two make a very cute couple."

Jules smiled at him. He looked handsome and tropical in his powder blue pants and Hawaiian shirt. "I'm so glad you came, even if I am going to be playing for a bit."

"I don't mind," he said. "I will have to go to the

club later, but not until I've had at least one slow dance with you."

She smiled. She was looking forward to that, too.

Thomas clapped his hands to get everyone's attention. "In a little closer." He pressed his palms toward each other, motioning for people to move together.

"Closer. There we go. Everyone look at me and look happy. Big smiles. I'm going to take a series of photos, so hold those smiles. Here we go!" As he snapped away, he also held up a big flash that went off simultaneously with his camera.

Jules had done several photoshoots in her time. She knew that flash was to help fill any shadowed areas.

Finally, he lowered the flash and the camera. "Great job, everyone. I just need the bride and groom and their immediate family now. Thank you."

"That's our cue to move under the house," Jules said. "Sierra, you take Cash's guitar and let him take your keyboard."

"Okay," Sierra said.

"What can I do to help?" Jesse asked. "What about your chairs?"

Jules shook her head. "There's already another

spot set up for us under the house. There's even another extension cord waiting for Sierra."

"How about I carry the keyboard and Cash can take both guitars?" he offered.

"Works for me," Cash said.

With Jesse's help, they got everything moved to their new spot. They weren't far from the buffet table and the food smelled great.

"Are you guys going to get to eat?" Jesse asked.

Jules nodded. "Miguel and his son made a playlist for the meal and for after we're done. We're only playing for an hour after dinner, then we're guests like everyone else."

His brows went up. "Then we can have our dance?"

She smiled. "I hope so."

Claire came over. "Jules, if you don't mind, I'm going to take Toby upstairs. I think he's a little bored with the wedding."

Jules laughed. "Fine with me. This is Jesse, by the way. He's the man who owns the Dolphin Club."

"Hi," Claire said. "Great to meet you. My sister has said some pretty nice things about you."

Jesse grinned. "I hope I can live up to them."

Jules nudged him. "You already have."

Kat approached them next. She had a young

man with her. Jules knew right away he had to be Alex and not just because he had his arm in a sling. He had a definite cool, surfer dude vibe.

"Hi, there," Jules said. "Where's Nico?"

"Paulina came and got him just a few minutes ago, thankfully. He's a sweetie but I'm not sure what we would have done with him during dinner and the dancing."

"True," Jules said.

"First of all, Aunt Jules, you guys sounded great." Kat smiled. "Secondly, I wanted to officially introduce you to Alex."

Jules shook his free hand. He was a handsome young man. And about the exact opposite of Ray. "It's so nice to meet you, Alex. I've heard a lot about you."

"You, too," he said. "I think you're the most famous person I've ever met, outside of that time the governor toured our firehouse."

Jules laughed. "I'm not that famous."

Jesse leaned in. "Yes, she is and she's about to be even more famous when her new song drops." He stuck his hand out. "Jesse Hamilton, Jules's boyfriend and owner of the Dolphin Club."

"Hey," Alex said, shaking Jesse's hand. "I love

that place. We went to see Blue House there. Great concert, man."

"Thanks. Next time you want tickets to something, call me direct. I like to make sure our first responders are taken care of."

"Sweet."

Jules was impressed with Jesse's offer, but she knew he wasn't doing it to look good in front of her. He was just that kind of guy.

"That's very kind of you," Kat said. "Why don't you guys sit with us for dinner?"

"Thanks," Jules said. She touched Jesse's arm. "Save me a seat?"

"You bet."

She checked the time, then looked at Cash and Sierra. "Okay, we're going to play a few songs to keep everyone occupied while they finish up pictures before dinner." She nodded at Jesse. "I'll join you soon."

"Looking forward to it," Jesse said. He winked at her before going off with Kat and Alex.

Jules picked up her guitar before settling into her chair. Cash and Sierra got ready, too. She looked at them. "Just like we rehearsed."

They both nodded at her. She counted down. "One, two, three..."

They started with Sam Cooke's *You Send Me*. Jules had talked with Danny and Roxie about what kind of music their parents liked and made up a playlist from that. For this brief interlude before dinner, they'd be playing a list of classic love songs.

It helped that Jules had so many of them in her repertoire already, and they were in her range. After dinner, they were going to pick up the tempo so that people could dance. And once their hour was up, the music would be streamed via Danny's phone through some speakers that had been set up.

Jules expected a lot of milling about and drinking while people waited. However, the dance floor soon had two occupants. Her mom and Conrad. Jules smiled as she sang. They moved beautifully together.

It gave Jules a little pang of longing to see them like that. She wanted to dance with Jesse that way. She hoped he'd stay long enough so she'd get a chance. She knew he wanted to, but she also knew that emergencies could arise at the club.

Maybe they'd get lucky and tonight wouldn't be one of those nights.

The next song was *Just The Way You Are* by Billy Joel. Cash sang this one with Jules and Sierra backing him up.

By the fourth song, the wedding party returned. Father Green introduced Willie and Miguel as "Mr. and Mrs. Rojas," to which everyone applauded. Then he said a blessing over the new couple as well as the food. Danny got his playlist going and Jules and her crew were free to mingle and eat.

Jesse was immediately at her side again. They got in line for the buffet after the bride and groom and the wedding party. "It was a nice wedding, don't you think?"

She nodded. "It was. Simple. In the best possible way. But sometimes that's all you need."

He looked at her, his eyes bright with yearning. "Yeah." It seemed like he wanted to say more but wasn't ready.

She smiled up at him.

He took a breath and smiled back, then looked away. "I'm really glad you asked me to go on tour with you. I'm looking forward to that more than I can tell you."

So was she. It would be the true test of their relationship. One they'd either pass or fail. There was no other possible outcome.

Chapter Thirty-one

*B*eing in Conrad's arms, even with Dinah
watching, had been marvelous. Margo
could still feel the strength of his body under her
hands, the command with which he moved. For a
Marine, he danced like a dream, but then, what
didn't Conrad do well? He was a Renaissance man,
adept at so many things.

Dinah, however, was slowly chipping away at
Margo's joy. She stood ahead of Margo in line,
staring at the food that awaited them on the buffet.
"What is all of that?"

"It's from a local restaurant, Papi's," Margo
answered. "They specialize in Puerto Rican cuisine.
Miguel and his family are originally from Puerto
Rico."

Dinah snorted. "Can you really call that food
'cuisine'?"

Margo glanced behind her at Conrad. He was staring at his sister, giving her a look that seemed to imply he was less than pleased. Margo pursed her lips. "Of course you can call it cuisine. Why wouldn't you?"

"It's so...earthy," Dinah said.

"I don't know what that means." Margo wasn't playing dumb, either. She really didn't know what Dinah was trying to say.

"You know," Dinah said.

Margo shook her head. "No, I don't. Have you tried Puerto Rican food before?"

"I can't say that I have," Dinah answered.

Conrad cut in. "Then you don't know if you'll like it or not, do you?"

Dinah smiled sweetly at her brother. "Now, Connie. I know myself well enough to understand what I like and what I don't. Not to mention my system can be a bit delicate when it comes to foreign spices and weird ingredients."

If slapping someone wasn't considered assault, Margo would have given Dinah a flaming red cheek. The woman was utterly unbearable.

They moved closer to the food. It smelled wonderful. Margo quelled her irritation with Dinah and tried to smooth things over.

"Look," she said, pointing. "There's rice and chicken. Surely you can eat those without upsetting your '*delicate system.*'"

Dinah's mouth stretched to a thin line, and she gazed at the chafing dishes. Based on her expression, you'd have thought they held such things as eyeballs in gravy and fricasseed frog legs. "Maybe."

Margo turned away so she could roll her eyes without being seen. Conrad caught her, however.

He smiled. He understood. "I think it looks like an amazing spread and I can't wait to try all of it."

"You'd better be careful, Connie," Dinah said. "You don't want your evening cut short because you ate something bad."

Margo hoped no one had heard that. She glared at Dinah. "Papi's has been in Diamond Beach for years. They have a stellar reputation. None of us has anything to worry about concerning their food."

"If you say so," Dinah said. "I'm not going to take any chances."

Margo ignored her. What Dinah ate or didn't eat was of no concern to her. If the woman wanted to go hungry when this delicious spread was in front of her, for free, that was her own stupidity. She focused on Conrad instead. "I hope we can dance again."

He smiled, moving closer to her. "So do I. That

was very nice. You know, the American Legion holds a dance once a month. They only play the good stuff, too. Maybe we should go to the next one."

She nodded. "I'd like that very much."

"Then it's a date."

"What's a date?" Dinah asked.

Margo didn't answer.

Conrad looked at his sister. "I was talking to Margo."

Dinah let it go as they moved up in the line again. Servers from the restaurant were stationed behind the chaffing dishes, ready to fill everyone's plates. At the very beginning, right after the plates and silverware rolled in napkins, there was a large basket of assorted rolls and an enormous bowl of green salad. Next to it were a few carafes of dressing.

Dinah filled half her plate with salad and drizzled it with a tiny bit of the vinaigrette. The first chaffing dish held fat, fried fingers of something. They reminded Margo of mozzarella sticks, but she doubted that's what they were.

"*Alcapurrias*?" the young woman behind the dish asked.

Dinah squinted. "What are those?"

"A traditional Puerto Rican dish. It's a fritter of yuca stuffed with seasoned ground beef. Very tasty."

"No," Dinah said. "I'll pass."

Margo happily accepted one. She didn't like to eat a lot of fried food, but she wasn't about to turn them down now. Besides, today was a day of celebration. A little loosening of the rules was definitely in order.

Next was a big dish of yellow rice. The server scooped up an industrial-sized spoonful and offered it to Dinah.

She smiled weakly. "Not quite that much, please." She got half a spoonful and moved on.

Things continued that way down the line. Margo made a point of taking at least a tasting portion of everything. Conrad did, too, she noticed. Well, he took more than a taste of most of the dishes.

When they returned to their seats at the table, Dinah and Conrad across from Margo, Dinah's plate looked pitiful. It was mostly salad and a few small mounds of other things. A little rice. A small piece of chicken. Some vegetables.

Conrad filled their plastic cups with sangria from one of the carafes on the table.

"Thank you," Margo said. She tried the fritter first, taking a small bite off one end. It was surprisingly delicious. "This is really good. Conrad, did you get one of these?" She looked at his plate and saw he had two of them.

"I did and I'm going to try it right now." He took a big bite. "Very good. I could eat a basket of those with a beer. They'd be perfect for watching the game."

She smiled at him. "Maybe I should learn how to make them."

He grinned. "Or maybe we should start eating at Papi's on a regular basis."

Dinah rolled her eyes as she picked at her salad.

Another server came around with a tray that held little plastic cocktail cups filled with an orangey-red drink. "Rum punch?"

Conrad nodded. "I'll try one."

"Connie," Dinah scolded. "Not when you're already drinking wine. You'll make yourself sick."

Margo actually agreed with Dinah. Mixing wine with spirits was rarely a good idea, but spite got the best of her. She smiled at the server. "I'd love one, too."

Dinah just sighed and shook her head as if she was surrounded by lunatics.

Margo laughed. The woman was a bitter pill but at a certain point, her behavior was so over the top it was funny.

Conrad lifted his rum punch. "Here's to Willie and Miguel!" He winked at Margo. "And all the other couples here." He clinked his glass against Margo's, then against his sister's, although she barely held her glass of sangria out.

Margo made a point of touching her cup to Dinah's. Then she sipped the punch. It was good. Strong, but good. Maybe it was better Dinah didn't have any.

Dinah stabbed a cherry tomato with her fork. "You two are going to regret that."

Margo shook her head. "I won't. It's a celebration. So what if I overindulge a little. That's what celebrations are for. Having *fun*."

Dinah narrowed her eyes. "You think being sick the next day is fun?"

"I won't be sick. I know how to handle the alcohol and food I consume." Margo felt pity for the woman. "Why do you care what Conrad or I do anyway? We're grown adults. Very grown. We're allowed to make our own decisions, don't you think?"

Dinah stared at Margo, anger in her eyes. Then the anger seemed to morph into something else. Resolution? She put her fork down. "Well, I know when I'm not wanted. Connie, I'm ready to go."

An icy chill came over Margo, and she was instantly furious that Dinah would do such a thing. The evening had only just begun.

The strings of lights overhead flickered to life, casting everything in a warm glow.

Conrad's response to his sister was a laugh and an amused gaze. "The evening's barely under way. I'm not going anywhere. You can either call an Uber or a taxi or you can just sit there and get over whatever mood you're in. I, on the other hand, plan to stay right here, eat my dinner, and dance with my girlfriend. Besides, it would be rude to leave so soon, and you wouldn't want to be rude, would you?"

Dinah didn't answer. Just seethed.

Margo smiled at Conrad and the chill left her. She mouthed the words, "Thank you."

Conrad reached across the table and took her hand.

Margo laced her fingers through his, the warmth of his hand passing into hers. She'd had her doubts about him and his relationship with his sister, but not anymore.

Chapter Thirty-two

*T*rina sat next to Miles with her mom and Ethan across from them. "This food is so good, isn't it?"

Miles nodded. "I love Papi's. Haven't eaten there in a while, so this is great. It was a nice wedding, too."

Trina glanced over at the table where Mimi and Miguel were sitting. They looked so happy. Mimi had loved Miles when she'd met him earlier, which made Trina very glad. It was important to her that her grandmother approve of the guy she was seeing.

The guy she was falling for.

Miles finished the bite of food he'd just taken, a big mound of yellow rice with a bit of pork, then dipped his head almost like he was being shy. "What kind of wedding do you think you'd want to have?"

That was a curious question, she thought. She

shrugged. "I won't lie and say I've never thought about it but until today, I always figured I'd have a church wedding. Seeing the beach wedding might have changed my mind. It was just so nice. And there's something super romantic about being married on the beach."

He nodded. "I'd agree with that. The whole thing was really chill and laidback but super personal, too. I'm kind of surprised your grandmother wanted one, but she's pretty cool, so maybe I shouldn't be surprised."

Trina smiled. "She's the best. And she is *definitely* cool."

"I like her a lot. And Miguel," he said. "Must be nice to still have her around. I haven't had any grandparents in a long time."

"I'm sorry," Trina said.

"It's all right. I had a lot of good years with them. I just miss them sometimes, you know? I wish they could see where I've gotten to in life."

She nodded, filled with sadness at the thought. "I can imagine."

He smiled at her. "I didn't mean to bring you down."

She smiled back. "It's okay. Life is like that, right? Ups and downs. Sad and happy. It's just...life."

"It sure is." He gazed into her eyes for a long moment before turning back to his food. It seemed like he'd been about to kiss her, but probably didn't want to do that in front of so many people.

Ethan and her mom laughed, pulling Trina's attention to them. She hadn't heard what had been so funny, but she was happy they were having a good time. They looked really good together.

Ethan seemed to realize Trina and Miles were watching him and Roxie. He smiled at them. "That's got to be a hard job, being a paramedic."

Miles nodded. "It can be. But it's a pretty rewarding one, too."

"I bet," Ethan said. "Thank you for your service to the community."

"You're welcome," Miles said. "Trina's been telling me about all the great work you're doing at her new salon. I haven't been over to see it yet, but I definitely want to."

"You should come over. It's looking fantastic," Ethan said. "She'll be opening up before you know it."

"Yeah," Miles said. "Then it'll be harder than ever to see her." He grinned at Trina. "I don't see her enough as it is now."

Roxie spoke up. "The good thing is, Trina will be

the boss and, to some extent, she can make her own schedule."

Trina nodded. "True. I'll do my best to make sure we have the same days off. Or at least part of the same days."

"That would be cool," Miles said. "Or maybe I should just learn how to cut hair and come work for you."

Trina laughed. "No way! I'm not hiring you. We need you to take care of us. So do all of the tourists."

"I guess," he said with a twinkle in his eyes.

Ethan picked up the carafe of sangria and refilled Roxie's glass, then topped Trina's off, too. Miles was drinking water and rum punch.

"I can't wait to taste the cake Claire made," Roxie said.

"Me, too," Trina agreed. "Have you seen it?"

Roxie shook her head. "No, but I'm dying for the big reveal."

"I'm sure it'll be good," Ethan said. "She's the one Danny's opening the bakery with, right?"

"Right," Roxie said.

Miles sipped his drink. "That's Kat's mom you're talking about?"

"Yes," Trina said.

He nodded. "I can vouch for her skills as a baker.

She's sent some things to the firehouse for us to try. Every single one was a winner."

"I didn't know that," Roxie said. "That was nice of her. But the more I get to know her, the more I realize I misjudged her when I first met her."

"Given the circumstances," Ethan said. "I think you get a pass."

Trina agreed. The fact that her mom and Claire hadn't ended up in some kind of knock-down fight when they'd found out about each other was amazing. Not that she'd ever really seen her mom fight anyone, but still. Finding out your husband had another wife and child was enough to make someone do something crazy. She looked around. "Hey, speaking of those circumstances, where's Nico?"

Roxie gestured with her fork. "Kat told me when we were in line for food that Paulina came and got him right before dinner."

"Any word about her mom?"

Roxie shook her head. "Not that Kat said. I'll text Paulina later and ask."

"Okay." Maybe it was silly to worry about her dad's third wife, but Nico was her brother, which made Paulina's mom his grandmother. Trina couldn't help but be concerned.

She looked over at her own grandmother and Miguel at their special table again. They were laughing and smiling and seemed to be sharing a secret.

Trina smiled. She wanted that for herself someday. She looked at Miles. She'd be very happy if the man at her special table ended up being Miles. She touched his arm. "I'm so glad you're here with me."

He wiped his mouth with his napkin. "Thanks for inviting me. You look beautiful, by the way."

She laughed. "I think that's the third time you've told me that."

"Well, that's just how pretty you look."

"I'm probably going to wear this dress to the grand opening of the salon." She loved the strapless, flower-covered pink dress her grandmother had bought her.

"You should. You look like a movie star in it. Thankfully, I don't think there are too many other single guys here or I'd have to fight them off of you."

She grinned. "Now you're just being silly."

He shook his head. "No way. I'm being serious. I'm crazy about you, Trina. I don't want to lose you to another guy."

Her heart melted a little. "You're not going to lose me, Miles. I'm crazy about you, too."

"You know what the priest said about finding love being a miracle?"

She nodded.

He took a breath, his voice softening. "That's how I feel about you."

His words made her warm and happy inside. "That's how I feel about you, too."

He slipped his hand into hers. "Maybe someday, we'll have a wedding like this. I don't want to rush you. I know we've only known each other a few weeks, but ever since you asked me if I want kids, I can't stop thinking about the future. I hope that's where we're headed. Is that what you're hoping?"

She nodded. Maybe it was all the happy wedding vibes in the air, but she could have married him right then and there. "With all my heart."

Chapter Thirty-three

*D*inner had gone by way too fast. Now Claire was faced with the task she was dreading most. Moving the cake. And she wasn't even directly involved with it! She hadn't been this nervous in a long time. Good thing Danny and Cash were both strong men. Moving the cake downstairs shouldn't be a big deal. But it was. Anything could happen. She prayed nothing did.

She inspected it one more time. Nothing had moved or slumped or melted or fallen off. It looked as good as when she'd left it, but then, it had done nothing but sit on the kitchen island since she'd gone downstairs. She nodded. "It's ready to move."

Danny came closer. "Maybe we should pick it up once, just to get a feel for how heavy it is."

"Okay," Cash said. "And then do you want to back into the elevator, or do you want me to?"

"You back in, which means I'll back out."

Claire put a hand to her throat. The elevator wasn't wide enough for them to go in sideways. Not without getting really close to the cake. "Please be careful, whatever you do. There's no rush in getting this thing down there."

Both men nodded as they grabbed the corners of the cake board.

Danny counted off. "One, two, three."

They lifted, testing the weight.

"Not bad," Cash said. "Heavy, but nothing we can't handle, right, Danny?"

Danny nodded. "We got this." He looked at Claire. "You want to push the elevator button for us?"

Claire nodded and ran to the elevator. "I should take the steps so I'm there when you get off."

"Go ahead," Danny said. "We're good."

"Okay. Thanks."

He smiled as the doors opened. "Stop worrying. It's going to be fine."

"I hope you're right." She went out the door and down the steps. She was wearing flat sandals, but she was careful all the same. She didn't want to trip on the way down. Although better her than the cake.

She reached the bottom and saw a lot of expectant faces looking at her. "The cake is on its way," she said. She went straight to the elevator. A couple of seconds later, the doors opened.

Danny backed out. Cash kept pace with him. When Cash was clear of the doors, they turned toward the cake table, giving a much better view of the cake to all of the guests.

Claire watched Willie's eyes light up and instantly felt better. Roxie's mouth dropped open. Claire smiled.

Then she snapped back to the moment and directed the men to the table. She went behind it and guided them. "A little more toward me. That's it. Almost. Another inch. Okay, down. Carefully."

"Are we on?" Cash asked.

Danny nodded. "I think so. Let go of your end."

Cash did and nothing happened. Danny took his hands away, too. The cake remained motionless.

Claire exhaled.

Willie stood up and clapped. "That is the prettiest dang cake I've ever seen. How are we supposed to eat that?" She tugged at Miguel's sleeve. "Come on, honey. I want to see it up close."

Claire could breathe now. She'd done her part. The cake was delivered. Sure, it still had to be cut up and served, but her flavors were good. The cake was moist and had a perfect crumb. The fillings were delicious. And her combination of buttercreams were the best she'd ever tasted. If someone didn't like the cake, that was on their tastebuds and not her problem.

She stood by the cake as Willie and Miguel approached.

Willie let out a little gasp of happiness. "I can't believe how pretty it is." She put her hand to her mouth and looked at Claire, tears shining in her eyes. "You made this for us?"

Claire nodded, feeling a bit like she might cry, too. "I did. I hope you like it."

"I never thought I'd have a cake like this in my whole life." Willie nudged Miguel. "Have you ever seen anything like this? It looks like something from a magazine."

He shook his head. "It's not real. It doesn't seem real."

"It is," Claire assured him. "The only parts of it that aren't edible are the chairs and the initials on top."

"Oh, look, Miguel!" Willie gasped again. "I didn't even see those. They're so cute! There's just so much to look at."

Danny came to stand beside Claire. He leaned in. "You really outdid yourself, you know that?"

She smiled. "Thanks."

"My dad is speechless. That doesn't happen often."

Then Miguel came over to them. He took Claire's hands and kissed her cheek. "You've made my bride so happy. Thank you. I cannot imagine how much hard work and long hours you put into this but…"

He shook his head and cleared his throat softly. "Thank you."

Claire definitely felt tears welling up. "You're welcome."

Willie came over next and gave her a big hug. "I love it. I wouldn't even care if it was sawdust inside. It's the best cake I've ever seen."

Claire laughed. "I promise it's not sawdust. It's pina colada, just like you wanted."

The photographer came over. "How about we get a few shots of the bride and groom with their cake? Then we can do the cutting."

Willie held onto Claire's arm. "I want the baker in the photos, too."

"We can do that," the photographer said.

"You don't want me," Claire protested.

"Yes," Willie said. "We do."

Claire stood with them for a few pictures. She would have been lying if she'd said she wasn't proud. Making the cake had felt like climbing a mountain. She was glad she'd done it. It had been a little terrifying at times, but she knew she could do it again.

As she started back to her seat, Danny caught up with her. "Hey, I have to go emcee the cake cutting in a second, but I had to say thank you again. I know my dad already said it, but I wanted to say it, too. That cake is amazing."

Her happiness was hitting new levels. Every ounce of stress she'd endured for that cake had been worth it. "I only did it to impress you."

He laughed. "Well, it worked." His eyes narrowed in curiosity. "Are you going to do wedding cakes at the bakery?"

She hesitated. "The only answer I can give you is...I don't know. Do you want me to?"

"It's not up to me. It's your decision to make."

"In that case, it depends."

"On?"

"How much help I have. And what the demand is like."

"You put up a picture of that cake and I think the demand will be high. I know a beach-themed cake isn't for everyone, but this is Diamond Beach. People come here to get married with their toes in the sand."

"It would have to be on a limited basis. At least in the beginning. I'm still learning this art."

He nodded. "How about if we charge a pretty competitive price? And maybe only do one or two cakes a month? Or whatever you think is reasonable. And if there are months you don't want to do any cakes at all, that would be fine, too."

He clearly wanted to offer wedding cakes at the bakery. She smiled. "I think we can work something out."

"I feel like there should also be some kind of profit-sharing with the cakes. If you're doing all that work, you should get a percentage of the profit. I don't want it just to be part of your job at the bakery." He glanced at the cake. "Something like that is over and above."

"Really?" She hadn't been expecting that, but maybe she should have. Danny had always been generous to her.

He nodded. "Absolutely."

She looked back at the cake. Now that it was done, she could appreciate it. She *had* actually enjoyed making it. Not just the challenge of it, but being able to do something on that scale. That had been fun. Cupcakes and cookies were great, but they didn't allow for the same kind of creativity that a wedding cake did.

Danny spoke again before she could say anything. "I know you need to think about it. That's okay. We have time."

She turned her attention back to him. "I don't need to think about. With the right parameters, we can definitely offer wedding cakes. Not too many and nothing so crazy that it'll require me to get a second degree in decorating, but the cakes I think I can manage, the ones that feel like they're within my capabilities, yes. We can do those."

He smiled. "You're sure?"

She lifted her chin ever so slightly. If she'd made this cake, she could certainly make another. She nodded. "I am."

Chapter Thirty-four

*W*illie stood with Miguel next to the incredible cake Claire had made for them, posing for the photographer.

At last, Thomas motioned that it was okay for them to go ahead and cut the cake.

Danny stepped up. "Ladies and gentlemen, my dad and his bride are about to cut this gorgeous cake. Then the kind servers from Papi's are going to take care of making sure you all get a piece."

Everyone applauded.

Willie and Miguel both took hold of a knife provided by the caterers, then together they carefully made a little notch in the big bottom layer. Seemed a shame to cut into something so pretty, but Willie knew it had to be done.

She *was* eager to taste the cake. It floored her

that Claire, who wasn't even family, had gone to so much work for them. Willie was truly touched.

The little piece they'd cut got placed on a plate, then cut in half again so she could feed Miguel and he could feed her. The knife was handed off to one of the servers. Willie had already told Miguel that if he smeared cake on her face, she'd divorce him right then and there. She'd mostly been joking about the divorce part, but she was serious about not having cake pushed into her face.

Trina had gone to a lot of work doing Willie's makeup just to have it ruined with frosting. Not to mention it would be disrespectful to treat that beautiful cake in such a manner.

But the cake feeding went off without a hitch. Always the gentleman, Miguel was on his best behavior, no surprise there. Willie treated him with the same kindness and respect.

As the buttercream melted on her tongue, new flavors appeared. The tropical smoothness of coconut and the bright tang of pineapple, all against the subtlety of vanilla. The cake was delicious.

Miguel's neatly trimmed brows lifted. "That was very good."

"I agree," Willie said. "I want a big slice of that."

He leaned in and kissed her. "My love gets whatever she wants."

Two of the Papi's servers moved toward the cake, ready to dismantle it and serve it up.

"Come," Miguel said, taking her hand. "They'll bring us some." He looked at Danny. "Right, son?"

Danny nodded. "You two will be the first served. How was it?"

Miguel smiled. "Delicious. You will soon see for yourself."

"I can't wait," Danny said.

Miguel escorted her back to their table and they took their seats. He leaned in. "Are you happy, my love?"

"I'm beyond happy. This turned out perfectly, didn't it?"

He nodded. "Your daughter is to be commended for all her work. We owe her a huge thanks for doing this for us."

"Your son, too," Willie said. "I know he helped."

A server arrived with two generous slices of their wedding cake. Even cut, it was pretty, the layers so neat and precise.

"And Claire," Miguel said. "I had no idea she was going to make something so elaborate."

"Neither did I," Willie said. "Maybe we should get her a gift certificate to someplace nice to eat? She and Danny could go."

Miguel smiled. "That is an excellent idea. Maybe that will be the next wedding we attend, eh?"

Willie looked for Danny and Claire. Danny was back in his seat next to her and their heads were together as they talked. She smiled. "Maybe."

Then she found Roxie, who was deep in conversation with Ethan. Across from them, Trina and her boyfriend, Miles, were gazing into each other's eyes. "There's a lot of new love all around us, isn't there?"

"There is," Miguel said. "And I think it's wonderful."

Just then, Jules and her little band took up their instruments again. "Ladies and gentlemen, as you enjoy your cake, we're going to see if we can't get you onto the dance floor once you've cleaned your plate."

She nodded at her bandmates, and they all started playing.

Willie stuck her fork into her cake and lifted a big bite. "How did we get this lucky, Miguel?"

He put his arm around her. "I don't know, my love. I think when our house is finished, we should have a big party and invite them all over."

Willie nodded. "Yes. That's exactly what I want to do."

"Then we will."

She smiled and ate her cake. It really was delicious. She wondered if the pina colada flavor was something Claire had made before. There was no way she'd just created it for them. Maybe it was something she'd come up with for the bakery? Either way, they should sell it there. People would go crazy for it.

She told Miguel as much. "You should tell Danny to sell this cake at the bakery. It's the best thing I've ever eaten. And there's not even any alcohol in it."

He laughed. "I'll tell him."

Willie polished off her slice in no time at all. She hoped there was going to be cake left over, because she wanted another piece tomorrow.

Claire came over to their table. "If it's all right with you, I'm going to take the little top tier upstairs and package it up for you so you can stick it in your freezer. That way you can have it on your one-year anniversary."

"Thank you." Willie held out her hand. Claire took it. "Listen," Willie said. "That was the best cake I've ever eaten. You need to sell that at the bakery. I'm serious."

Claire smiled. "I'll tell Danny."

"Good." Willie held on to her a moment longer. "I appreciate what you did for us. You had every reason not to want a thing to do with any of us, and yet here you are. You and your sister over there, playing her heart out. Thank you."

Claire nodded, her eyes softening with emotion. "Roxie and I were in the same boat, weren't we? And it was rough seas for a while, but things have gotten smoother. Even with the arrival of Paulina." She laughed. "I can't believe I'm about to say this, but I'm actually no longer mad at Bryan for what he did. Not like I was."

"Really?" Willie would be mad at that man until the day she died. Heck, she'd find him in the afterlife and be mad at him there if she could.

"Really," Claire said. "Kat and Trina have become friends. In fact, they're becoming a lot more like real sisters. Roxie and I are getting along well, too. I'm glad I've gotten to know all of you."

"Thank you," Willie said. "Without you and your family, this day wouldn't have been nearly as special for me and mine."

And if Claire did someday marry Danny, they *would* be family. Wouldn't *that* be something?

"You're so welcome," Claire said. "Congratulations to both of you."

As Claire left, Roxie and Trina approached. Both of them were smiling like they were up to something.

"What's going on?" Willie asked.

Roxie answered. "Trina and I have something for you and Miguel."

Willie shook her head. "I told you, no presents. Your help with the wedding was more than enough. And Trina did my hair and makeup. Seriously, that was plenty."

"Well, tough," Roxie said. "Because when you leave here, you're both going to the honeymoon suite at the Hamilton Arms to spend your first night together as husband and wife."

"What?" Miguel said. "That's too much!"

"No, it's not," Roxie said. "You're not going to have a lot of time alone until your house is finished, so we wanted to do this for you. And your bags are already packed. Danny packed one for you, Miguel, and Ma, Trina and I packed yours."

Willie looked at Miguel and couldn't hold back any longer. Tears spilled. She tried to sniff them back but it was too late. "I can't believe this. I feel like I'm living in a dream."

His eyes went misty, too. He pulled a handkerchief from his pocket and handed it to Willie. Then he looked at Roxie and Trina with great affection. "You girls...you girls are so good to us."

Willie sniffed again as she dabbed at her eyes. She couldn't have agreed more.

Chapter Thirty-five

"Holy cow," Alex said after another bite of wedding cake. "How come your mom never sent this cake to the firehouse?"

Kat laughed. "Probably because it didn't need to be taste-tested. She already knew it was good." She glanced over at his plate. It was almost empty, but then, he was using his fork more as a shovel. "For a guy with one arm, you aren't having any trouble getting that cake down, are you?"

"I might lick the plate."

She shook her head in amusement. "Do you want another piece?"

Hope blazed in his eyes. "Are we allowed?"

"I know the baker," Kat said. "I'm sure I can swing it."

"Cool, yeah, thanks."

She got up and went over to the cake table,

where extra slices had been set out on plates for people to help themselves. She picked the biggest one. Nearby, Aunt Jules, Cash, and Sierra were playing and singing away, making Kat want to dance but she understood Alex might not want to.

Too much movement probably wasn't good for his recovery, and she definitely didn't want him in any pain on her account.

She went back to their seats and put the second slice in front of him.

"Thanks. Man, this is good." He scooped up another bite. "Do you want to dance?"

She gave him a look. "Should you be doing that with your shoulder?"

He shrugged the good one. "I could slow dance."

She smiled. "I'd like that."

"Cool. Maybe it'll help me burn off some of this cake. I hate to say it, but I could eat a third piece."

"Alex!" She laughed again.

"I know. By the time my shoulder is healed, I'm going to need to lose twenty pounds."

"More of you to love." The last word hung in the air between them and there was no taking it back. She smiled, a little embarrassed by what she'd said. She hoped she hadn't freaked him out.

He smiled, too. "Thanks."

"I didn't mean...That is...I like you a lot, but I'm not trying to rush into anything."

"I know what you meant."

She just nodded. It was still weird. And for some reason, she couldn't let it go. "I don't want you to think that I invited you to the wedding because I had some ulterior motive."

His eyes narrowed and she couldn't tell if he was being serious or not. "So you aren't trying to get me to propose?"

His saying it outright like that made her snort. "No!"

"I guess I'll have to return the ring then."

Her jaw dropped. "What?"

He grinned. "Got you." He laughed. "Which isn't to say that day might not be somewhere in our future." His smile faltered. "If you'd be okay with that."

Was he asking her if she was okay with them maybe getting engaged someday? That's what it sounded like. She nodded. "I would be okay with that."

He nodded, staring at his now empty plate. "Cool. You, uh, you mean a lot to me, Kat. I told you I've had other girlfriends who couldn't handle my job, but you stuck with me at the hospital and that's not something I'm ever going to forget. Meant a lot to me."

"I'm so glad you're okay."

"Me, too." He looked at her again. "But I'm kind of glad it happened, because I got to see what a really good person you are. Not that I doubted it before, but you being there with me...for me...that was huge."

"It's just what you do when you care about someone."

"If you ever need me like that, I want you to know I'll be there for you. I swear it."

"Thanks." She was already in love with him. Maybe it was too early to feel that way, but she didn't care. She wasn't going to tell him until he was ready, but she could wait. "You've already been there for me when I needed you."

He made a face. "I have? When?"

She shook her head. "That little confrontation with my ex, Ray?"

"Oh, yeah, right."

"And then there was when we went surfing and I almost chickened out, but you talked me down?"

"I don't know if that really counts."

"It counts," Kat said. "You've changed my life for the better in a lot of ways. You've inspired me to be a better person and do something more meaningful with my life. It's because of you that I'm about to start work at Future Florida."

"You got that job on your own. That had nothing to do with me."

"I wouldn't have looked for that job if not for you."

A slow smile spread across his handsome face and the corners of his eyes crinkled. "I guess we make a pretty good team."

"We make a great team."

"Then maybe it should be a little more official."

She blinked. "Meaning what? Aren't we official now?"

"Yeah, but we haven't really said we weren't going to date anybody else. Unless you're not ready for that commitment."

She swallowed.

He saw her hesitation. "I know you were with Ray a long time and that didn't go so well. I promise it won't be like that."

"I know it won't. You're nothing like him. I wasn't hesitating because of that. I was just giving it a chance to sink in. I am totally ready for it to be just us."

"Yeah?"

She nodded. "Yeah."

"Cool, 'cuz I actually did get you a ring."

Her heart caught in her throat. "What?"

He dug into his pocket, and pulled out a little blue velvet pouch, which he handed to her. "I didn't think it was fair of me to ask you to be exclusive without some kind of symbol that I was serious."

She opened the pouch and emptied it into her hand. A silver ring tumbled out. It was formed in the shape of a wave and the crest was accented with a few tiny diamonds like foam. "It's beautiful."

"Just like you," he said. "I'm glad you like it."

She slipped it onto her ring finger and looked at her hand. The ring sparkled in the overhead lights. "I love it. I'm never taking it off."

He grinned.

"Oh! I have something for you, too."

"You do?" He seemed surprised.

"Yep." She got up. "Don't go anywhere. I'll be right back." In all the excitement, she'd forgotten about the surfboard clock. She went up in the elevator and got off on the second floor. Toby was fast asleep on the couch. One of his front paws was twitching. Probably dreaming about digging in the sand.

She got the clock off the table on the back porch. The paint was now completely dry. She took it inside and went straight to the laundry room to look through the wrapping paper supplies. She found a plain blue gift bag and some white tissue paper. She stuck the clock in and covered it with the tissue, then went back downstairs.

She held the bag down at her side until she reached Alex, not wanting anyone to think it was a wedding gift. She sat down and put it on his lap. "Here you go."

"What is it?"

"Open it and see."

He pulled the tissue paper out and looked inside. His mouth curved as he lifted the clock free of the bag. "Hey, that is so awesome. It looks just like my surfboard. Where did you find it?"

"I made it. I mean, I painted it to look like your board. I didn't make the clock or the board itself. It was a kit from the craft store."

"It's pretty epic. And I love that you made it especially for me. It's going in my living room, right over the TV." He leaned toward her. "Thank you."

She met him halfway for the kiss, whispering,

"Thank *you,*" before they connected. She was happier than she'd ever been, and she had Alex to thank for so much of that.

She'd meant what she'd said about not taking off the ring he'd given her, too. She wasn't going to.

Not until he gave her a different ring to take its place.

Chapter Thirty-six

Roxie woke up and stared at the ceiling of her bedroom. It was weird to wake up and know her mom wasn't in the house. But she smiled. Her mom and Miguel were married. Probably not awake yet, but soon they'd be sharing their first breakfast as husband and wife. Roxie hoped it was a good one.

She stretched and yawned. The wedding had been beautiful and last night had been so much fun. She and Ethan had danced until nearly midnight. Good thing, too, because she'd eaten plenty of Papi's food and a big slice of that delicious cake.

She would have loved to sleep in a little longer, but she'd promised Ethan she'd go to church with him today and she wasn't about to flake on him.

She went out to the kitchen to get coffee started, then got straight into the shower. She was more nervous about today than she'd been about the wedding.

Not because of being with Ethan or going to church, but because his parents were going to be there. And possibly his daughter. She wasn't sure about his son.

Meeting someone's family was a big step in a relationship. Not just that, but what if they didn't like her?

She exhaled. She couldn't think that way. That wasn't an acceptable outcome.

Her shower was quick because she didn't need to wash her hair. After brushing all the hairspray out of it, it was still pretty clean. All it needed was a little touchup on the styling and she'd be good to go.

She got out, dried off, and put on her robe. She left her hair up in the clip she'd put it in to keep it dry. As she headed to the kitchen for coffee, she heard the shower running in Trina's room.

Trina wanted to go with her to church and had said Miles was going to meet them there. That was sweet. Roxie liked Miles a lot. He was kind and respectful and had a great job. He'd been very focused on Trina last night, too. Making sure she was happy and had whatever she needed.

Roxie approved of that. Her daughter deserved a

man who thought she was worth his time and effort. Every woman did. Sadly, so few actually found men like that.

She poured herself a big cup of coffee with plans already in place for a second one. She was going to need it. Yesterday had taken a lot out of her and it had been a late night.

She took her coffee and her phone out to the screened porch. In a few more months, it might be too hot to sit out there some mornings. The nice thing about being this close to the beach was the breeze that made things bearable, but even a breeze wasn't always enough during the heat of the summer.

She relaxed on the couch and put her feet up on the coffee table. This was nice. Today was going to be a good day. She held onto that thought, using it to guide herself away from her fear that Ethan's parents wouldn't think she was good enough for him.

She had a little of that fear herself. He was a really good guy. And he'd been through a *lot*. Losing his wife to his brother? How did you get through a thing like that?

She wasn't sure she could have survived that kind of betrayal. Although she'd survived a pretty heavy dose of it already, finding out her husband had two other wives and two other families, so maybe she'd have been all right.

Betrayal was hard no matter what form it came in.

The sliders opened and Trina came out. "Hey," she said softly. She had a cup of coffee, too.

"Late night, huh?"

Trina nodded as she sat down, hair up in a towel. "Yeah. Thanks for making coffee."

"You still up for church today?"

"Yep. Miles is meeting me there. I can't not go. I'm looking forward to it. I always liked our little church back in Port St. Rosa, even though we didn't go regular."

"Probably time to change that," Roxie said. "I can't be hit or miss if I'm going to go to the church where Ethan and his family go."

Trina sipped her coffee. "Yeah."

Roxie smiled. Trina was tired and not her usual bubbly self, but she'd come around when the caffeine hit. Roxie got her phone out and scrolled through the pictures she'd taken last night. Thomas had promised to have the official photos within a week.

She knew that wasn't standard, but she also knew he was doing everything he could to make them happy, since Willie was about to be his new landlord.

They sat quietly for about twenty minutes, drinking coffee and just being, Roxie looking through her phone and Trina slowly waking up.

Trina stood. "I'm going to get more coffee, then maybe I should start getting ready. What time do we have to leave?"

Roxie looked at her phone. "Service starts at eleven, but I don't want to be late or rushing in. I told Ethan I'd be there by twenty to. So we should leave by ten twenty just to make sure we don't get lost and can find parking." Being late was not an option. That was no way to make a good first impression.

"And I need to find Miles when we get there. But it's only nine o'clock now, so that's plenty of time," Trina said. "Still, I'd rather be ready early and then sit for a while than push it to the last minute."

"Same," Roxie said. She held her cup out. "Would you refill me, too?"

"Sure." Trina took her cup and went inside.

Roxie took the opportunity to send Ethan a quick text. *Morning. Trina is coming with me and Miles is meeting her there. I hope that's okay?*

That's great, he responded. *I had a lot of fun last night.*

Roxie smiled. *So did I. Maybe too much. Lol*

He sent back a smiley face. *It was just the right amount.*

She nodded at her screen. It *had* been just the right amount of fun. And things between them had been so easy. Almost as if they'd been a couple for a very long time. How was that possible?

She stared out at the blue skies and sparkling water. She ought to be still mourning her husband, but instead, she was thinking about the possibility of a future with another man. "Sorry, Bryan, but you brought that on yourself with your inability to be faithful."

She wasn't going to apologize for what her heart wanted.

Trina came out with the coffee and handed Roxie her cup. "I think I'm going to go back in and get ready. I have to dry my hair and everything."

"Okay, honey. No problem. I'm coming in in a few myself. Thanks for the coffee."

"You're welcome." Trina went inside.

Roxie sat a few moments longer, thinking about Bryan and Ethan and how strange life was sometimes. There was no explanation for the way things worked out. She finished her coffee, then went in, did her makeup, freshened up her hair, and figured out what to wear.

That turned out to be a white eyelet skirt with a turquoise flowered blouse and white wedge sandals. She hoped that was all right. Some churches were more casual, some more formal, but she figured being close to the beach that it would be a mix.

She rinsed her coffee cup, which she'd put in the sink earlier, and sat on the couch, looking at wedding pictures again. What a great night.

Trina came out in a buttery yellow flowered sundress and glittery white flipflops. "Is this okay?"

"You look great. I think it's fine. Ready to roll?"

Trina nodded. "Just let me grab my purse."

Twenty minutes later, they were walking toward the entrance to Coastal Community Church. Ethan was standing by the doors, smiling at them. "Morning, ladies. You both look beautiful."

"You look nice, too," Roxie said. He was in tan pants and a short-sleeved striped shirt. Not much different from how he'd looked last night.

Trina looked around. "Have you seen Miles?"

"Not yet," Ethan said. "But it's early still."

"You guys go in," Trina said. "I'll wait for him."

"You sure?" Roxie asked.

She nodded. "Just save us two seats."

"Will do." Roxie looked at Ethan. "Lead the way."

"Ready to meet my folks?"

She took a deep breath and nodded solemnly. "I am. Wait. I thought your daughter was going to be here, too?"

"Unfortunately, she had to work. Both my kids did. I hope you'll get to meet Tara and Jon soon, though." Then he grinned. "As for my parents, they're really nice people. Nothing to be frightened of, I promise. They're going to love you."

She nodded again, trying to smile this time.

He took her hand, and they went inside. The church interior was very pretty, all done in white and shades of blue with touches of weathered wood, right down to the cross over the baptismal that looked like it had been crafted from driftwood. Very beachy. There weren't pews but chairs instead.

About halfway to the pulpit, Ethan stopped and faced an older couple sitting on the right-hand side. "Mom, Dad, this is Roxanne."

The couple stood. He was tall with gray hair, kind eyes, and a trim moustache. She was petite with sandy brown hair and an infectious grin.

"Roxanne, these are my parents, Andy and Brenda Lewis."

"It's a pleasure to meet you," Roxie said, putting her hand out.

"You, too," Brenda said. She grabbed Roxie's hand in both of hers and gave it a squeeze. "We've heard so much about you and your family."

Roxie smiled. Brenda was wearing Scottie dog earrings. No one who wore Scottie dog earrings could be too awful. "I've heard a lot about you guys as well. My daughter, Trina, is here with me. She's outside waiting for her boyfriend."

"That's nice," Andy said. "The whole family is here."

"Almost," Roxie replied. "My mom just got married yesterday. She's at the Hamilton Arms with her new husband."

"Oh, that's right," Brenda said. "Ethan told us about that. How wonderful for her. Was it a nice wedding?"

"It was great," Roxie said.

Ethan nodded. "It really was."

Andy took Roxie's hand next. "Why don't you tell us all about it at lunch? You are coming to lunch with us after church, aren't you?"

Roxie looked at Ethan. He nodded. She smiled at his parents and, this time, she really meant it. "I'd love to."

Chapter Thirty-seven

*J*ules had decided that after all the work she'd been putting in, today was going to be a day off at the beach. Especially with tomorrow being her big day in the studio. It would be good to just sit on the beach and chill.

And it was, as that was exactly what she was doing. She'd used the wagon in the storage closet to haul out all of her stuff, like a chair and the umbrella. Toby had walked on his own, thankfully.

Her plans, besides chilling, included working on the lyrics of her two new songs, spending time with Toby, who was laying in the shade on his own towel next to her chair, and possibly napping.

She'd sent a group text to her family, inviting all of them to join her, but she wasn't sure if any of them would come. She'd invited Jesse, too, and he was on his way. She'd made sure to tell them they needed to bring their own chairs and anything else they might want.

On the other side of her chair, she had a small cooler that held a few bottles of water, a hastily made peanut butter and jelly sandwich, an apple, and a sandwich baggie of pretzels. She had her beach bag with her and in that was a tube of sunscreen, a hat, her ereader, her lyrics notebook and pen, a ChapStick, her earbuds, a bag of kibble for Toby, his pop-up water bowl, and a power pack to charge her phone if need be.

She was pretty set.

Blue skies stretched as far as she could see in both directions and a nice breeze ruffled her hair. Toby started to snore.

She nodded at him. "I think you've got the right idea, Tobes."

One ear twitched but he didn't wake up.

She leaned back and kicked her feet out in front of her, closing her eyes. Maybe she could get a quick nap before Jesse showed up. Naturally, her phone chimed. She peeked at the screen. A text from Claire.

Can I bring Danny with me?

Jules really didn't care who came. If it turned into a whole group thing, so be it. *Sure. Jesse is on his way.*

Thanks. Might be an hour. Not sure.

That's fine. Whatever works for you. Jules closed her eyes again.

When she opened them because someone was calling her name, she realized she actually had drifted off. That someone was Jesse. Shiloh was leashed at his side. She started wagging her tail as soon as she saw Toby.

"Hey, were you sleeping?" Jesse asked. "Sorry."

She smiled and pushed her sunglasses to the top of her head. "Yeah, I was, but it's all right. Just having a really low-key day."

Toby was up, tongue out, anticipating antics with his girlfriend, no doubt.

Jesse nodded as he set up his chair next to Jules, then settled into it with a big sigh. He looped the end of the leash around the arm. "This is nice."

"Yes, it is." Toby and Shiloh were now giving each other some pretty intimate sniffs. Jules shook her head. Dogs were so funny.

"I have some news to share."

"Yeah? Good or bad?"

"Good."

She glanced at him. "What is it?"

He smiled. "I found my new booking agent. A young woman by the name of Enna Sunday. She's amazing. I interviewed her yesterday afternoon and offered her the job on the spot. It'll take me a few weeks to get her trained so that she understands everything, but she's exactly the right kind of person for the job. Full of energy, bright, and fearless. She's just who I've been looking for."

"That's great! You're one step closer to not having to be there all the time."

He nodded. "Now I just need a really good manager and I'll be ready to take off with you when the tour hits the road."

"Any prospects?"

"A few. No one who's really blown the doors off, you know, but it'll happen."

She nodded. "Managing the club is a tremendous responsibility. You've got to have someone you trust and feel good about. You don't want to rush the hiring process."

"Definitely not."

"And you've got time. We're only just recording the song tomorrow. After that, the whole album has to happen. Then it has to be released. There's promo to do, tour dates to book. It's going to be months before we're actually in that bus."

"I know. But I'd like to have a couple months

with whoever I hire so that there's no question they know what they're doing."

"Which is smart." She changed the subject. "How long are you hanging out with me?"

"Couple hours. Then I'll go back, shower and head in. How long are you going to be out here?"

She shrugged, smiling. "Maybe until the sun goes down. No idea."

"All right. Just don't overdo it. Tomorrow's a big day."

"It is." Toby and Shiloh lay down in the sand together. Jules sighed. "I'm kind of trying not to think about that right now."

"You don't have anything to worry about. Everyone sounds great. Even the three of you last night were fantastic. All that practice has definitely paid off."

"I'm not really worrying about it. I just feel like I'll be...fresher if I can actually forget about it for a day. Not that I could really forget about it. I just need a day to rest my brain." She laughed. "Although I did plan on working on some lyrics while I was down here today. I guess that's not totally resting, is it?"

"Not really." He smiled. "But I suppose when you're in this sort of work mode, you can't ever really shut it off, can you?"

She shook her head. Her phone went off again. This time it was Cash.

Are you still at the beach?

She smiled. *Yes. I plan to be here a while. Jesse is here and Aunt Claire is coming.*

K. I might, too. Need coffee first. You need anything?

Just you. I'm straight out from the house. Can't miss me. Toby might find you first.

A smiley face preceded his answer. *See you in a bit.*

Half an hour after that, Danny and Claire arrived. Carrying a sailboat. Or some kind of boat. Okay, it was a small boat, but it was still a boat with a brightly colored pair of sails.

Jesse stood up, hands on hips, to have a better look. "Now *that* is cool."

They set the boat on the sand and Danny grinned. "Seemed like a good day to take the cat out and Claire's game, so why not?"

"What's a thing like that set you back?" Jesse asked. "If you don't mind."

"I've had it for years," Danny answered. "I think I paid around eight hundred for it, but I had to put new sails on it."

"Is it a Hobie Cat?" Jesse asked.

"Aqua Cat," Danny corrected.

Jesse looked at Jules. "Maybe I should get one of those. It would be fun, wouldn't it? Tooling around the Gulf?"

She laughed softly. "You mean during all of our free time?"

His smile bunched to one side. "Yeah, good point."

Danny slapped Jesse on the shoulder. "You can borrow this one anytime you like, my friend. Just so long as you remember my name the next time I need concert tickets."

"That's a deal," Jesse said.

Jules shook her head. He'd better hire that new manager soon. They were going to need a lot more days off.

Chapter Thirty-eight

Margo thought about joining her daughter on the beach. It would be wonderful to spend a few relaxing hours listening to the waves and the gulls while in the company of family.

But she could also stay in and get some more words written. Of course, she could do that anytime. Being with her family was more important.

What she ought to do was reach out to Conrad and see how things were going with Dinah. That option scared her the most.

Perhaps not scared, exactly. But that direction felt like it had the potential to ruin her day the fastest.

She sighed. She should at least text him and see how he was. That would be the polite thing to do. The caring girlfriend thing to do. After Conrad had rebuffed Dinah's demand to leave last night, Dinah had not spoken a word to either of them for the rest of the evening.

Something Margo hadn't minded one bit. It had bothered Conrad, however. Not so much that they hadn't danced to all the slow songs, but he'd checked on her a few times and only gotten a glare or a shrug in response.

No telling what she was like this morning.

Regardless of how mad Dinah still was, she would be going home today, so that would be the end of that problem.

Margo took a breath and texted Conrad. *How are you today? I had a wonderful time last night. Dancing with you was divine.*

She decided to leave Dinah out of it. If he wanted to bring Margo up to date on that situation, he could, but it wasn't really Margo's place to go prying.

She hit Send, then began to gather the necessary essentials into her beach bag. Sunscreen, her ereader, her cooling cucumber and vitamin spritz, a beach towel, rolled to conserve space, and some moisturizing lip balm.

She dug out her favorite tankini and then her big white shirt to wear as a coverup. She'd wear her hat and sunglasses, too. She glanced toward the kitchen.

Wouldn't hurt to put together a little cooler. She'd had coffee but no breakfast. She was a bit peckish. Maybe she should have a quick yogurt or a couple pieces of toast.

She was about to find something to eat when her phone buzzed.

Conrad. *I had a great time, too. I'm serious about going to the American Legion dance. Let's do it.*

I'm in, Margo typed back. *Hope you have a good day.* How could he not with Dinah getting on the road?

Me, too. One hiccup...

She braced herself.

Dinah has decided she doesn't feel well enough to go home today.

Margo rolled her eyes. Of course she didn't. Margo wasn't quite sure what to say to that. She thought a moment. Then she started typing. *I hope it's nothing serious. There's an urgent care on Vine. Should you take her?*

It's not serious. It's her way of staying an extra day and keeping me from seeing you. But I've already told her we have plans.

Margo wracked her brain. Had they talked about doing something last night? Because she honestly couldn't remember. She sighed. She'd known not to mix sangria and rum punch and yet she'd done it anyway.

He sent another text. *I know we don't, but can I come over for a bit anyway? I don't want her to know I lied.*

Margo laughed out loud. *I'm headed to the beach to spend some time with my daughters and grandson. Please come. They all adore you. Bring a chair.*

I can be there in half an hour.

She smiled. *I'll be waiting on you.*

Still chuckling, she went to make toast with peanut butter and honey, which ought to hold her for a little bit. While she ate, she sent a note to the group chat. *Conrad and I will be there within the hour.*

Toast consumed, she went to change into her tankini.

Conrad stepped off the elevator thirty minutes later in swim trunks and a *Gulf Gazette* T-shirt. He was rolling a wheeled cooler. Over one shoulder hung a folding beach chair that had its own carrying strap. His towel was draped around his neck.

"Hello, there," Margo said.

"Hello, gorgeous." He kissed her on the mouth. "Thank you for letting me crash your family day."

"You're very welcome. And it's not just family, so

don't think that." She glanced at the cooler. "You certainly came prepared."

"I stopped by Publix and picked up some fried chicken, potato salad, a fruit bowl and a couple bottles of iced tea. I wanted to contribute."

Margo nodded. "That will be appreciated, I'm sure." She went into the kitchen, grabbed the remaining roll of paper towels and stuck it in her beach bag. If they were going to have a picnic, they'd need napkins. "All right, let's go. I just need to get a chair from the storage closet downstairs."

They took the elevator to the ground floor, and she opened the storage closet to find a chair. There was a second umbrella in there, too. The big one. Margo put her hand on it. "I feel like we should bring this. There might not be enough shade with just the one and I don't want to get burned."

"I can carry it," Conrad said. "If you pull the cooler."

"I can do that," Margo said. "The beach wagon is gone, or we could load that up. Jules must have used it."

In a matter of minutes, they'd located Jules and the umbrella. Jesse was sitting next to Jules, but there were extra towels laid out. Toby and another dog were sleeping on one of them. That had to be Jesse's golden retriever.

"Hello, all," Margo called out. "Is Cash here, too?"

"Hi, Mom," Jules said. "No, he's not here yet but Danny and Claire are." She pointed toward the water. "That's them on that little catamaran."

Margo looked at the Gulf, shading her eyes. She located the small craft. It looked like a toy from this distance. "Oh, my. Is that safe?"

Jules laughed. "Danny knows what he's doing. He's had that thing for years."

"Looks like fun to me," Conrad said. "Mind if I set up this other umbrella? Didn't want your mom to get scorched."

"That would be great," Jules said.

Jesse got up. "Let me give you a hand. We've got the hole digger."

The two men worked at setting the umbrella up so that the shade would overlap with the one already erected.

"Beautiful day," Margo said.

Jules nodded. "Really nice. I'm glad you and Conrad came."

"He stopped at Publix on the way. Brought a

whole picnic with him." Margo was proud of Conrad's thoughtfulness.

"That was sweet," Jules said. "I kind of only brought snacks. I should have planned it better."

"I thought maybe Kat would be here."

Jules shook her head. "Today's her last day before she starts her new job. She's spending it with Alex."

"I can understand that."

"She'll be back for dinner, though."

With the umbrella up, Conrad unfolded his chair, then Margo's and set them in a line out from where Jules was. He laid his towel over the chair, then kicked off his sandals next to it before bringing the cooler around to act as a side table.

Margo retrieved her ereader from her beach bag before hanging it on the back of her chair, then she settled in. The breeze was lovely. The day really did seem perfect. Especially now that she was with her daughters and Conrad.

He sat next to her and let out a contented sigh.

She nodded. "I feel the same way."

He smiled, gaze directed at the blue water, voice soft and meant just for her. "Dinah was still in a mood this morning."

"That couldn't have been easy for you to deal with."

"Last night was a turning point. She knows she's not going to come between us. She's not happy about that."

"She wasn't happy about it before, so I don't see how that's much of a change."

"True, but I know her. I guarantee you she's not done with her scheming to break us apart."

A subtle smile bent the corners of Margo's mouth as she glanced at him. Handsome, kind, intelligent Conrad. The man who'd made her realize there was so much life left to be lived. "Let her try. I have no intention of giving you up."

Chapter Thirty-nine

Church was so nice. Trina had enjoyed the sermon, a reminder to love your neighbor, something she wholeheartedly believed in. The pastor, Tim Davis, was a youngish middle-aged man with a great sense of humor and a plain way of talking that made him easy to listen to. Trina liked him a lot.

She'd caught Miles nodding at the pastor's words a few times. That had made her smile.

Church was over now, and they were making their way out.

Roxie leaned in. "Ethan's parents have invited us to lunch with them. Are you guys going to come?"

Trina glanced at Miles.

He nodded. "Sure, that would be fine with me. You don't mind, do you, Ms. Thompson?"

Roxie smiled. "I don't mind at all and, please, call me Roxie."

Trina loved how polite Miles was. She slipped her hand into his.

He looked at her. "You want to ride to the restaurant with me?"

"Yeah, definitely."

On the way out, they shook the pastor's hand. When they reached the parking lot, Trina turned to her mom. "What restaurant?"

"Clipper's. You know where that is?"

Miles answered. "I do."

Trina tipped her head in his direction. "I'm riding with Miles. I'll see you there."

"Okay."

Clipper's was a big, older restaurant, well known for its seafood. Trina had never had lunch there, although in years past they'd eaten dinner there a few times.

Trina waited until they were pulling out of the church parking lot to ask her question. "What did you think of the service?"

"I liked it," Miles said. "How about you?"

"I liked it, too. The pastor seems nice."

"He does," Miles agreed. "I used to go to Safe Harbor Baptist when I was kid. Got out of the habit when I was getting my degree and working on my training."

"Would you want to start going again? With me?"

He nodded. "Yeah. That would be good. I mean, it would be good planning for the future, too."

She squinted at him. "What do you mean?"

"You know," he said. "In case you change your mind about a beach wedding."

She smiled and felt her cheeks warm, which she had no explanation for. Hearing him talk about their future like that, like it was a sure thing, filled her with a kind of dizzy happiness that made her as light as a balloon inside. "Yeah," she said softly. "You never know."

"What he was saying today, about loving your neighbor? You're really good at that, Trina."

"So are you. Look at what you do for a job."

"Yeah, but it is my job. I *have* to do it. You treat people with such kindness all the time. Regardless of the situation or who they are." He shook his head. "I'd be a fool not to marry a woman like you."

Her mouth came open, but no sound came out.

Before she could say anything, he clarified. "I'm not asking. Not just yet. Just stating a fact."

Her smile returned. "Well, I'd be a fool not to say yes to a man like you."

He grinned. "You know, that's right."

She laughed, happy and amused and totally falling in love.

They walked into Clipper's hand in hand and waited in the restaurant's foyer until her mom and Ethan and his parents showed up. Even though they were a party of six, they were seated pretty quickly at a big round table.

Trina sat between Miles and Ethan's dad, Andy. He was a nice man. Very happy and full of questions, which Trina didn't mind at all, because they kept the conversation going.

After their drink orders were taken, Trina scanned her menu for something that wasn't too expensive, wouldn't be messy to eat, and also sounded good.

She decided pretty quickly on the grouper sandwich. She hoped that wasn't messy. She looked over at Miles. "What are you getting?"

"Fried shrimp basket."

That was probably less messy than the sandwich, but she'd already settled on the sandwich.

Their server arrived with the drinks, took their orders, and left them with two baskets of cornbread and honey butter. Miles offered one of the baskets to Trina. She took a square of cornbread, then helped herself to some of the butter.

She'd just taken her first bite when another server passing through the dining room caught her eye. The cornbread turned to sawdust in her mouth. She took a drink of her diet soda to wash it down.

"What's wrong?" Miles asked.

Trina swallowed. She didn't want to cause a scene, but she wasn't going to keep this from him, either. She leaned toward him and whispered, "I just saw Liz."

His eyes went steely as they swept the room. "I don't see her."

Trina shook her head. "She went into the kitchen."

"She won't do anything," Miles said. "She must have just gotten this job. She won't want to lose it by being dumb."

"What if she does something to my food?"

Miles was watching the kitchen door. "She's not our server. She won't know what you ordered. It'll be fine."

Trina exhaled.

Her mom was looking at her funny. "You okay?"

Trina nodded and made herself smile.

Roxie pushed her chair back suddenly. "I'm going to run to the ladies room and wash my hands." She looked at Trina. "Why don't you come with me, Trina?"

"Okay." She pulled her cloth napkin off her lap and set it at her place. "Be right back," she told Miles.

Her mom only waited until they were a few steps away from the table. "You didn't look okay."

Trina explained. "I saw Liz walk through the dining room. She was in a server's uniform, so she must have gotten a job here. I mean, obviously, if she was in uniform."

Roxie was looking around. "Do you see her now?"

Trina glanced in both directions. "No. Thankfully. Miles doesn't think it's a big deal, since she's not our server."

"He's probably right," her mom said. "But if you see her again, and she sees you, text me. I want to be prepared. Just in case."

"Okay." Trina really hoped that didn't happen.

They went into the ladies room and washed their hands so they wouldn't be liars. While Trina rinsed off the soap, she wondered if maybe she'd just *thought* she'd seen Liz. It could have been another pretty blonde with blindingly white teeth and a golden tan.

She sighed. Probably not. But there was always a chance.

They went back to the table and took their seats.

"Did you see her again?" Miles whispered.

"Not a sign of her," Trina said. "Maybe I just imagined it was Liz."

"Maybe."

The food came and they all started to eat. Ethan's parents kept them all laughing with stories from his childhood. Trina mostly forgot she'd seen Liz. Until they were walking out. She watched carefully as they made their way through the restaurant.

Then she came face to face with the woman in question.

"Excuse me," Liz said. Then her eyes focused on Trina, and she realized who she was looking at. Her eyes darted to Miles, then back to Trina. Her expression turned haughty. "Boy, you two just can't leave me alone, can you?"

"We were here with friends," Miles said, taking Trina's hand. "It had nothing to do with you."

Liz grinned and fluttered her lashes at him. "Is that what you're trying to make yourself believe? I know you want me back, Miles. But you need to give up that dream, honey, because it's not going to happen. I've moved on."

"I couldn't be happier." Miles rolled his eyes. "We're doing the same thing. Come on, Trina."

"Yeah," Liz said with a sneer. "Follow your boyfriend, Trina."

Trina smiled, because she felt sorry for Liz. She was a small, petty person who would probably never know real joy. "Congratulations on your job. And I hope someday you find the kind of happiness I have with Miles. Maybe you won't be so angry at the world then."

Mouth slightly ajar, Liz just stared at them as they left.

Trina had never been so glad to be outside in the sun again. "Not sure that was exactly loving my neighbor the way Pastor Tim said to."

Miles laughed. "Well, you didn't slug her, so I think you get points regardless. She really is a miserable person, isn't she?"

Trina nodded, still feeling sorry for Liz. "Whatever happened to her, she needs to let it go."

She just hoped Liz could do that, because this was a small town and Trina wasn't going anywhere.

Chapter Forty

The breeze whipped past Claire, carrying a little spray from the water as the catamaran cut through the waves. She turned her face into it, blinking even though she had her sunglasses on. It was refreshing, despite the saltiness of the water.

"What do you think?" Danny asked as he expertly maneuvered the small craft across the surface.

"This is a lot of fun," Claire said. "I wasn't sure I'd like it, but I do. It's like flying across the water."

He grinned. "It is." He did something with the sail, then the rudder, and the boat slowed and changed course. He was turning them. "Me and my brother used to go fishing off a little sailboat when we were kids."

"I didn't know you had a brother. Why didn't he come to the wedding?"

Danny's smile flattened. "Nesto and my dad had a falling out a few years ago. They haven't spoken since then. He hasn't spoken to me either, since I took my dad's side. I got mad at him. Told him to grow up and get over himself and…"

He shrugged. "That was the end of that. I'm not sure why I even mentioned him other than the boat made me think of him. Better times."

"That's sad."

"Yeah, it is."

"Does he know your dad got married?"

"I emailed him. If he read it, he knows." Danny adjusted the sails again, moved the rudder slightly, and they cruised parallel to the shore. "I didn't mean to bring things down. I shouldn't have said anything."

"No, it's okay." She smiled. "Family can be hard. That's just how life is sometimes."

"Yep." He shifted position on the trampoline, the large square of mesh fabric that stretched between the two hulls and formed the deck of the catamaran. Danny had given her a little tour of the parts of the sailboat before they'd taken off in it.

She changed the subject, moving it further away

from talk of Danny's estranged brother. "You said it's been a while since you've been out on this. How come?"

"Busy," Danny answered. "And since we're only about to get even busier, I thought I might not get the chance again for a while."

She nodded. "I hope we're busy. *Really* busy."

"Having doubts?"

"No." She shook her head quickly. "I've just never been a part of anything like this. I don't know what to expect." She leaned down to trail her hand through the water.

"Having that article in the *Gazette* about the sour orange pies will help a lot, but even without that, I think we'll be swamped. Mrs. Butter's is a pretty well-known name in the area. People will initially be curious to see what we're offering." He grinned. "But once they taste all of your amazing recipes, they'll be hooked. They'll have no choice but to come back."

She smiled. She prayed he was right.

"That's one of the reasons I want to offer wedding cakes," he said. "Not just because what you made last night was unbelievable."

"What do you mean about the reason you want to offer wedding cakes?"

"Well, it's definitely more of a service for locals

and it'll show that we aren't just about the tourist trade."

"Tourists come here to get married, too. But I like that way of looking at it." She scooted closer to him. "I am definitely willing to do the cakes."

"But?" The wind was pushing the hair off his forehead, making him look like a movie star in an action picture. "I think I hear some hesitation in your voice."

"I just don't want to get so busy I lose touch with the rest of what's going on in the bakery. It's really important to me that the quality stays the same and that the flavors remain true."

"I agree, but there's an easy solution to that."

"There is?"

He nodded. "We hire a dedicated decorator. You don't have to be the only one working on the wedding cakes. As long as you're overseeing things, and your recipes are what the cakes are being made from, especially that buttercream, we'll be fine."

She exhaled. "That would help. But then, I'm not taking a cut of the profits. Also, no one can know my buttercream recipe. It's my secret."

He smiled. "I promise, we'll keep it locked in the safe."

"Good." She was only joking. It wasn't that much

of a secret, but she didn't know many people who made their buttercream the way she made hers.

"So we'll bring in a decorator specifically for cakes. When they're not working on wedding cakes, they can decorate other things. It'll be fine. We need to start hiring soon anyway. We'll be ready to open in a matter of weeks, the way things are coming together. Ethan and his guys have really been working hard."

"You want me to help with the hiring, right?"

"I would, absolutely."

She made a face. "I don't know how much help I'll be. I've never hired anyone in my life."

"You talk to them, get a feel for what kind of person they are. Look at their resume, check a few references. It's not too hard. Plus, I already know that you're a good judge of character."

Claire laughed. "You mean like how I thought you were the landscaper when I first met you?" She was still a little embarrassed about that.

He chuckled. "Yeah, but then look how quickly you realized I was irresistible."

"That's true." She leaned toward him for a quick kiss. She was blissfully happy. Who would have thought this could be her life?

As the kiss ended, he let out a little gasp and

straightened, lifting up slightly so he could point straight ahead of them. "Claire, look."

She turned in the same direction and followed the line of his finger. She immediately saw what he was talking about. Dolphins, just off to the left of the catamaran. Three of them—no, four. Sleek and perfect, swimming alongside and having no trouble keeping up. They sliced through the water with such ease and power. "Oh...wow. They're so beautiful."

"It's a sign of good things to come," he said.

She nodded. Maybe it was, but good things had already come to her in the form of this man and his generosity. "I wish I had my phone so I could take a picture."

"Next time," Danny said. "And after we get you a waterproof case for it."

"Will they come again?"

"They might. They're pretty common out here and they seem to love to swim along with the boats."

The dolphins were faster than the catamaran and were soon out of sight. Claire leaned against Danny. "As my daughter would say, that was cool."

"Yes, it was."

"Now I want to make a dolphin sugar cookie."

He laughed. "I love how things inspire you. Will it be fish-flavored, too? Dolphins love their fish."

"Ew, no." She chuckled. "No one would want that. But now that I know about edible glitter, it might get some of that sprinkled on it."

He put one arm around her, keeping the other on the rudder. "Kids will go crazy for it."

She thought about the cookie for a minute, but then her mind went straight to how important it was for this business to be successful. Not only because Claire needed this new direction in her life to be something she could do for a long time, or because she had her own money invested in it, or because she didn't want Danny to think he'd made a mistake by bringing her in. Those things were all true.

But Claire needed the bakery to thrive because she needed to know she was capable of doing a thing like this. Of taking a big risk and having it pay off. That she was able to be more than just a wife and mother.

She didn't need to be businesswoman of the year or anything like that. She just wanted to feel like a success to herself.

That wasn't something she'd ever really felt before.

"Think we should head back in?" Danny asked. "Get some lunch?"

She looked at him. "We didn't bring any lunch."

"No, but I can run up to the house and make some sandwiches. Grab a couple of ginger beers. Maybe some chips. Whatever you want."

She nodded. "That sounds great. I'm ready." She kissed his cheek. "You take such good care of me."

"I enjoy it." He hesitated. "And I like having someone to look after. You don't mind, do you?"

"Being taken care of?" She shook her head and smiled. "Not by a man like you."

Chapter Forty-one

The bubbles were up to Willie's ears, but she sank lower into the tub anyway. It was not only the biggest tub she'd ever been in, it was the biggest one she'd ever seen, and she wanted to enjoy every inch of the enormous thing. Wasn't every day she got to spend time in a honeymoon suite.

Miguel came into the bathroom, which was a gorgeous room with tons of white marble and gleaming brass fixtures. He carried two glasses of champagne. He handed one to her, the little bubbles catching the light as they drifted up through the golden liquid. "It's all taken care of, my love. We are staying another night."

Willie clinked her glass against his, then sipped. "Thank you. I love that Roxie and Kat did this for us, but one night in this beautiful suite just wasn't enough."

He sat on the edge of the tub. "I agree. Are you enjoying your bath?"

"I am." She grinned and drank a little more champagne. It was good stuff, and the bubbles were going straight to her head. That was just fine, because they didn't have any big plans, although later they were going to take a little walk on the beach. She lifted one leg and poked at him with her toes. "You wanna join me?"

He laughed. "Not until room service brings our lunch. It wouldn't do to have them walk in on us in the tub together."

"Eh, who cares? We're married now." She set her glass down and looked at her fingertips. She'd already been in the tub awhile. She probably should get out. Her stomach had grumbled twice. "You know what the best part about being old is?"

His eyes narrowed. "What's that?"

"It doesn't matter if you wrinkle in the tub, because you're already wrinkled."

A laugh rumbled out of him. "Oh, Willie. I love you and your way of looking at life." He tipped his glass at her. "You like that tub, don't you?"

"I do. It's enormous! All of me fits in it without

having to bend." She stretched her legs out under the water. Her toes didn't touch the end.

Miguel's eyes narrowed in thought. "Maybe we should talk to Rob over at Dunes West and see about adding something like it to our new bathroom."

Willie nodded enthusiastically. "I like that idea. And there *was* a tub in that bathroom, so making it a little bigger shouldn't be a major deal."

"We'll call him tomorrow."

The doorbell rang. Because the honeymoon suite was so fancy, it had a *doorbell*. That tickled Willie for reasons she couldn't really figure out. It just felt silly and special, and she loved that level of extravagance.

Miguel stood. "That must be our lunch."

"I'm getting out," Willie said. "Just give me a minute."

"Be careful. Old people and wet floors don't always mix."

She snorted. "I know, and I will be, I swear."

As he left, shutting the door behind him, Willie lifted the lever to drain the big tub. She was thankful she wasn't paying the water bill. She eased up and sat on the edge, then carefully moved one leg at a time out of the tub. She made sure to keep her feet on the fluffy bathmat that the hotel had provided.

If they put in a big tub like this at their new house, they should probably add some kind of handrail. She'd have to ask Rob about that. She didn't want it to ruin the look but then again, if she couldn't safely get in and out, she'd never use the thing.

Her robe and towel were both nearby. She dried off, then put the robe on. She and Miguel had been living in the robes since they'd arrived. They were soft and thick, and Willie had already done the math as to whether she could fit the thing into her suitcase.

She was pretty sure she could.

The hotel had provided slippers, too, but she preferred her orthopedic ones. They just felt more secure. She put her feet in them, picked up her champagne glass, and went out to join Miguel.

The door was just closing behind the room service attendant.

"Lunch," Miguel said with a flourish of his arm. "Is served."

She smiled. The table in front of their balcony overlooking the beach had been covered with a tablecloth and set with sparkling crystal and gleaming silverware. Next to the table, a stand had been set up to hold their bottle of champagne.

Condensation beaded on the outside of the silver bucket.

In the very center of the table sat a three-tiered tower of seafood, all of it displayed on ice. Peeled shrimp, sliced poached lobster tails, several kinds of raw oysters, cold steamed clams, and cracked crab claws. Here and there were little pots of dipping sauces and fat wedges of lemon. Her stomach rumbled.

At each of their places was a plate with a domed silver lid. Miguel leaned over and took the lid off her plate. "A petite filet mignon, whipped potatoes with butter, and green beans with dill sauce."

Willie took her seat. "This might be the best lunch I've ever had. You did good, honey."

He grinned as he sat across from her. Under his lid was the same meal. "Thank you, my love. I hope you enjoy it."

"I have no doubt I will. These are a lot of my favorite things." It might also be the most expensive lunch she'd ever had, but she didn't care. There would never be another first day as husband and wife, and she wanted to make a big memory of it.

"Good," he said. "But tonight, we're dining in the restaurant. I've already made us a reservation."

"I'm not sure I have anything nice to wear. I'll have to see what Roxie and Trina packed for me."

He shrugged as he cut into his steak. "The hotel has a boutique. Maybe you can find something."

"Maybe." She took a shrimp from the tower and dipped it in cocktail sauce. The shrimp was sweet and tender, the sauce just the right amount of spicy. She smiled as she chewed, unable to help herself.

He glanced up, saw her expression, and smiled back. "You are happy?"

"Deliriously so. You?"

He nodded. "I think this is what heaven must be like, don't you?"

She glanced out toward the water. "You might be right."

"How about we go down to the pool after lunch? Take a little sun, maybe have a swim, see if this place can make a decent pina colada."

"That sounds perfect, but I have no idea if I have a swimsuit or not." She laughed. "I've never been anywhere with a suitcase I didn't pack myself."

"Neither have I and now that you say that, I don't know if I have a suit, either. We shall see."

After lunch, which really was one of the best meals she'd ever had, they dug into their suitcases.

As it turned out, Willie had a swimsuit. Miguel
did not.

"They must have some men's trunks in the
boutique," Willie said. "I'll call down and ask. If they
don't, there must be a shop close by." She went to the
suite's phone, which was by the bed. She sat down
on the white duvet and dialed the front desk.

A young woman answered. "Hello, Mrs. Rojas.
How can I help?"

Willie grinned at the sound of her married
name. "Can you connect me with the boutique? I
need to ask them a question."

"It would be my pleasure. Just a moment."

Two seconds of hold music played. "Treasures
Boutique."

"Hi, there. Do you have men's swimming
trunks?"

"Yes, ma'am, we do."

Willie gave Miguel a thumbs-up. "What size do
you need, honey?"

"Thirty-four waist."

Willie relayed that to the clerk. "Thirty-four
waist."

"Hmm," the woman said. "I think that would be
a medium."

"Sounds about right," Willie said. "Can you charge a pair to the Rojas and have them sent up to the honeymoon suite? Something in blue if you've got it."

"I have blue with palm trees, if that would work?"

"Perfect," Willie said.

"I'll send them on their way shortly."

"Thank you." Willie hung up.

Half an hour later, they were poolside in front of the private cabana that was included with the honeymoon suite. Willie had never felt more like a movie star. She was glad she'd brought her sparkly rhinestone sunglasses. They felt like exactly the kind of thing to wear in her current situation.

Their server brought their drinks over. Two pina coladas made with fresh pineapple juice, real coconut milk, and the best dark rum. A slice of pineapple and a purple orchid decorated the rim.

She and Miguel each took their drinks and did a little toast.

"To us," Willie said.

He nodded, lifting his drink. "To us. And the most wonderful mini honeymoon ever."

She sipped her drink, which was delicious. "It really is. I know Puerto Rico is going to be amazing, and I can't wait for that, but I'm glad we're having this time to ourselves."

"I am, too." He set his drink down before reaching over to take her hand. "You make me happy, Willie."

"You make me happy, too." She took another sip, then put her glass on the side table.

Life was good and she was blessed, and for a woman her age, that felt like a real accomplishment.

Chapter Forty-two

"Here?" Kat asked.

"Over to the right, like half an inch," Alex said.

She moved the surfboard clock, a small nail pinched between her fingers. "Better?"

"Totally."

She marked the spot with the sharp end of the nail, then set the clock down and picked up the hammer. She drove the nail in and hung the clock, stepping back to have a look at her handiwork. "Looks pretty good."

"Looks great," Alex said. "Thanks."

"Thanks for liking it enough to actually hang it in your place."

He laughed. "Why wouldn't I like it? You made it for me. And it looks just like my board. I think it's rad."

Kat kissed his cheek. "You're the world's best boyfriend."

"Cool," he said. "Does that come with a plaque for display purposes?"

Grinning, she shook her head. "I'll see what I can do."

His phone buzzed. He dug it out of his pocket. "Miles," he said absently as he read the message. Then he sighed and looked up. "Miles and Trina went to lunch with her mom, her mom's boyfriend, and his parents after church, and they ran into Liz."

"Seriously? She's like a rash they can't get rid of." Kat felt bad for Trina. She was such a nice person. Miles's crazy ex was getting to be a serious issue. That girl needed to get over herself and leave Trina alone.

Alex nodded. "Agreed. Help me put a decent shirt on, will you? Just pick one that goes with these shorts. I want to go out for lunch."

"Okay." That seemed like an abrupt change of subject. She took a few steps toward his bedroom. "Was that the plan all along or did you just decide that?"

"I just decided. We're going to Clipper's. That's where Liz is working now, apparently."

Kat stopped short. "Hang on. You don't want to go there to cause trouble, do you?"

"No. I want to go there to let her know Trina's got friends who are going to look out for her."

Kat was all for that, but something didn't seem right. "Did something happen more than them running into her?" It sounded that way to Kat.

"There were some words exchanged," Alex said. "That's all Miles told me. But he said he was tired of Trina getting harassed."

"Harassed doesn't sound good." Kat sighed. "I'll get your shirt."

They arrived at Clipper's about twenty minutes later. Alex had insisted on driving, which Kat had offered to do, but she understood that all the restrictions because of his shoulder were wearing thin. She didn't mind him driving. He was still very conscientious. Her only concern was that he might hurt himself if he forgot he wasn't supposed to be using his arm and grabbed the wheel with the hand on that side.

That didn't happen, thankfully. They went inside and got a table for two. Alex asked for Liz's section.

Kat wasn't sure how well that was going to go, but she admired how insistent he was to make sure Liz knew he and Miles had Trina's back.

The hostess seated them at a table by the window, which was nice, and gave them menus. "Your server will be right with you."

"Thanks," Kat said. She looked around, nodding. "Been a while since I've been here. Last time was a couple years ago with my family, I think. Yeah, it had to be. My dad was with us."

Alex spoke from behind his menu. "Definitely not my usual spot, but they do have good food."

Kat was hungry and in the mood to be a little decadent. She studied the list of seafood baskets. Hmm. Fried seafood with French fries and hushpuppies and a side of coleslaw. That really did sound good. Now she just had to decide what kind of seafood she wanted. Shrimp or clam strips? Or the mixed basket? She didn't want oysters, she knew that.

Two glasses of water were dropped off at the table. "Hello, there. I'm Liz and I'll be—"

Kat looked up at her, but Liz was staring at Alex.

His menu was flat on the table as he nodded at her. "Liz."

She swallowed. "Alex." Her mouth twitched nervously. Not quite a smile but not quite a grimace, either. "Hi."

"Hi," Alex said.

Liz cocked her jaw to one side and a hard gleam filled her narrowing eyes. "You being here isn't just a coincidence, is it."

"No," Alex answered. "Miles told me what happened. I thought Kat and I should stop by and see for ourselves where you were working."

Liz glanced at Kat. "Well, you've seen it. Are you actually going to eat or was this just some attempt to mess with me? I know you and Miles are tight. But *he* came *here*. I didn't seek him out. He wants me back, not the other way around."

"He came here because he was invited to come. Not because of you. He didn't know you were working here. None of us did." Alex shook his head. "And I promise you, he is very happy with Trina."

"Not just happy," Kat said. "He's devoted to her. You should know that." She said it in the nicest way possible, not wanting to upset Liz.

Liz made a face. "I find that hard to believe. She's not the classiest girl to ever—"

"Hey," Kat said sharply. "That's my sister you're talking about. She also happens to be one of the nicest human beings you could ever hope to meet."

Liz sneered. "She's not that nice. She wouldn't hire me when she knew I needed a job."

"Because you weren't qualified," Kat said.

Alex sat back slightly. "Why are you even working? Your parents are loaded. I've never known you to have a job."

Liz lifted her chin. "You're awfully interested in me all of a sudden."

"Because you're harassing my best friend's girl." Alex's eyes narrowed. "I don't know what's going on with you, Liz, but this whole thing needs to stop. You need to forget about Miles and concentrate on your own life."

Liz's mouth set in a hard line, and she popped one hip to the side. "Do you want something to drink besides water? I have other tables I need to take care of."

"I'm fine with water," Kat said. She stared at the wave ring Alex had given her last night, feeling odd about the whole situation.

Alex nodded. "We're good for now."

"Great," Liz said sarcastically. "I'll be back in a few." She stalked off.

Kat leaned forward. "I'm sorry, but I'm not eating here. I don't really want spit in my coleslaw."

Alex nodded. "Yeah, I was just thinking that, too. Come on. We're not far from Coconuts."

Another twenty minutes later and they were at an outside table at Coconuts, enjoying the breeze and the island tunes being played through the speaker system. They already had drinks in front of them. A diet cola for Kat, a regular cola for Alex.

He was looking at his menu, but Kat didn't need to. She already knew she was getting coconut shrimp with sweet potato fries.

"This is better," Alex said, lifting his gaze from the menu. "Sorry. Going to Clipper's was a dumb idea."

Kat shook her head, smiling. "Doing something because you want to support a friend isn't something I'd call dumb. Besides, you left ten dollars on the table. That was way more than she deserved for being so salty."

"Something's up with her. When I asked her why she needed a job, she changed the subject pretty fast."

"I think it's obvious." Kat shrugged. "Her parents have cut her off for one reason or another and she's not happy about it. I mean, I get it. Not many people would be happy about that."

"Okay, that makes sense, except for the part where she seems to actually believe Miles wants her back."

Kat thought a minute. "Jealousy? That he moved on so quickly and seems to have found a real connection while she's still single? And not doing that great in life?"

"Maybe." He sighed and adjusted the strap of the sling around his neck. He gazed off toward the water.

"You'd rather be surfing, wouldn't you?"

A little smile curved his mouth. "Always." The smile didn't last long. "I'm worried we made things worse. Well, that *I* made things worse. You were just along for the ride."

"Not true," Kat said. "I knew where we were going and why and I went along willingly. I talked to her, too. We're in this together."

The smile returned. "Thanks. But I do worry she's not going to leave either of them alone."

"Yeah. Unfortunately, I think you're right." She thought a second. "Did Miles know you were going to Clipper's?"

Alex shook his head. "I should probably fill him in, huh?"

Kat gave him a slow nod. "Then maybe the four of us should get together and come up with a game plan."

Alex gave her a long look. "Does that mean you have an idea about how to calm Liz down?"

Kat snorted. "No. But maybe all four of us working together can figure something out."

"I'll send a group text," Alex said. He lifted the phone closer to speak into it.

Kat sipped her soda and tried to think of what they could do to get Liz to leave Trina alone, but she hadn't had a lot of interaction with people like Liz. Nothing came to mind. She twisted her ring around, thinking hard.

Hopefully, inspiration would strike soon.

Chapter Forty-three

Roxie lounged by the pool at the beach house, absorbing the sun. The warmth was making her drowsy, which was just fine. She had every intention of napping. Not for too long. She didn't want to end up crispy. But a half an hour or so wouldn't hurt. She'd even set her alarm.

She'd yet to fall asleep, however, because she couldn't stop thinking about Trina's run-in with Liz.

Roxie adjusted her sunglasses. She'd known girls like Liz in her day. Girls who'd grown up with too much money and no real problems, so that when one actually did come along, they didn't know how to handle it. Or themselves.

Whatever was going on with Liz, for some reason, she was taking it out on Trina. That made Roxie mad. There was no way Liz could actually have beef with Trina. That would be like being mad at Mother Teresa. Trina was no one's enemy.

So what did that mean? Was Liz really mad that Miles was no longer hers? Did she want him back now that he belonged to another woman? That was possible.

As a woman who'd only just come to realize that she'd been sharing her husband with two other women, Roxie could empathize. Her feelings hadn't turned her into a raving lunatic, though.

Then again, she'd grown up without a silver spoon in her mouth. She expected nothing from life that she hadn't worked for, because she knew how hard real life could be. What it meant to labor for everything she had. The struggle of bills and respon-sibilities and raising a child almost on her own.

She wasn't mad about any of it, either. That life had made her who she was today, and she was good with that. She liked who she was.

Liz didn't seem to like herself much at all.

Roxie let out a sigh and wondered if she should step in and have a chat with this young woman's parents. There was no way Trina wouldn't see that as an intrusion, though. Trina probably wouldn't say anything. That wasn't her way.

Roxie didn't want to step on her daughter's toes. If Trina wanted help, she'd ask.

Didn't make Roxie feel any better, though. She hated the thought that Liz might confront Trina again. Or, worse, do something against the salon.

She wished Willie were home to talk all of this through with. She sat up, shielded her phone from the sun, and checked her messages. Nothing from Willie. She would have thought her mom would be back by now.

Roxie sent her a text. *What time do you think you'll be home?*

Didn't take long for Willie's answer to come through. *Not until tomorrow. We booked another night. Having too much fun!*

Roxie smiled. Good for them. They should have fun. *Great news*, she typed back. *I'm so glad. Love you both. Enjoy.*

Willie didn't need her little getaway spoiled by real life. There'd be plenty of time for that later.

There was one other person she could talk to. She called Ethan.

"Hey. Didn't get enough of me today, huh?"

She grinned. "Nope. I did not."

"Always nice to hear." He chuckled. "What's up?"

"I need someone to talk to."

"You okay?" The change in his tone was immediate. Concern edged his voice.

"I'm fine. Just upset about this whole thing with Trina and Liz and I don't know what to do about it. If anything."

"You're going to have to give me the background on this, so I understand what's going on."

She'd promised to do that as they were saying goodbye at the restaurant. It was too much to explain there and Roxie hadn't wanted to do it in front of his parents. Trina had gone back with Miles to his place, which Roxie thought was a good idea. He made Trina happy, and she needed to be happy after how lunch had ended.

Roxie explained to Ethan everything that had gone down between Liz and Trina.

"Wow. That's...a lot. I had no idea."

"You see why I'm concerned?"

"I do," he said. "And I would be, too. I am. Trina's too nice of a young woman to be the target of anyone's frustration. Do you want me to talk to Liz's parents?"

Roxie hadn't been expecting that. "You know them?"

"Not as well as my parents do, but yes, I know them. They're decent people. They might be able to shed some light on what's going on with Liz. Although part of me worries that if Liz's parents confront her about her behavior, it'll just make things worse."

Roxie nodded. "I thought about that, too. I don't know what the right thing to do is." She let out a frustrated groan. "Not that Bryan would have been much help in a situation like this, but I think things would be different for Trina if she'd had a more present father."

"In what way?" Ethan asked.

"Well...This is nothing against Trina. Nothing at all. I love that girl with my whole being."

"I know you do. And she loves you."

Roxie smiled. "But she's a pleaser. She likes everyone to like her. For the people around her to be happy. That's Bryan's doing. He wasn't around much, so when he was, she wanted everything to be wonderful and for him to be happy."

"And you think if she was okay with things *not* being okay, she'd, what, confront Liz? Tell her to leave her alone?"

"Yeah. Maybe. I don't know." It was easy to blame Bryan for anything that went wrong.

"You might be right. But I don't think Trina did such a bad job of handling herself or the situation."

"You don't?"

"No. She stayed calm. She was kind. She defused things, really. It could have escalated, and it didn't. That was Trina's doing."

Roxie blinked. "I guess I hadn't thought about it like that."

"Because you would have handled it differently, am I right?"

Roxie chuckled softly. "Yes, you're right. I probably would have made a mess of things. A bigger mess." She adored Ethan for not immediately telling her how wrong she was about making a mess just to make her feel better. "You think I should just let things be, then?"

"I'm guessing that if Trina wants help, she'll ask. Now, if something changes, if Liz does something physical toward Trina or the shop or her car, something like that, then obviously we don't let that slide. But right now, Trina's doing just fine."

"Okay. You're right. I'm not going to stop worrying, though."

"Nor should you. You're her mom. That's your job."

Talking to him had helped. "I really enjoyed meeting your folks today."

He laughed. "I think you also enjoyed hearing about what a terrible child I was."

"That, too. I can't believe you really picked all of your mom's prize-winning roses to give to your girlfriend in second grade." She snickered just thinking about it.

"Which is why I always send my mother roses on her birthday to this day."

"Your parents really are great."

"Yeah, they are. I'm blessed to have them."

"For sure."

"They loved you, by the way. And Trina."

"Really?" She almost held her breath. "You're not just saying that to make me feel good?"

"I'm not just saying that. My mom thought you were a breath of fresh air—that's a quote—and my dad said you were the best-looking woman in my age group that he's seen in years."

Roxie laughed. "That was sweet of both of them."

Ethan cleared his throat softly. "My mother also said I should put a ring on it before someone else does. I promised her you weren't seeing anyone else, but she said that didn't matter." He sighed. "I don't know where she gets these ideas."

"Blame Beyoncé," Roxie said.

He chuckled softly. "Figures. Anyway, I sort of

promised my mother I'd get you a ring. Not an engagement ring. I told her it was too soon for that. But a ring of intent. That's what I'm calling it, anyway. Seemed to satisfy her. I mostly think they're afraid I'm going to end up a sad, lonely old man."

She rolled her lips in to keep from laughing but it didn't work. "That's kind of sweet, though."

"Maybe. Mostly seems pushy to me. So what kind of ring do you want?"

"Uh-uh," Roxie said. "This has to be your decision. The only help I'm going to give you is that I don't want you to spend a lot of money on it. Sometimes, the thought really is what matters."

"Hmm. My mom might be right about you being the one for me after all."

She grinned, amused by the whole thing but also growing fonder of his mom by the second. "Oh, she definitely is."

Chapter Forty-four

*J*esse had taken off to get ready for work at the club. Toby watched Shiloh go with sadness in his little eyes, but Jules and Jesse had agreed to take them for walks together more often.

Danny and Claire had hauled the catamaran back up to his house and then gone to shower and, in Claire's case, go grocery shopping so they had food in the house again. Mom and Conrad had said goodbye as well, Conrad to check on his sister and Margo to see if she could write a page or two before dinner. That left Jules with Cash and Toby.

Toby was snoozing. Cash was in the water, perfecting his skim board technique.

Jules had played around with the lyrics for her two new songs, but she hadn't worked on them as much as she'd thought she would. Doing nothing had just been too enjoyable, but now, as the day was coming to a close, she'd begun to get antsy about tomorrow's big recording session.

The only reason for that was how much pressure she felt for the song to do well when it was released. Everyone had hyped it up to her, making her feel like anything less than a runaway success would be a failure.

She blew out a breath. That wasn't true, of course. Regardless of what happened with the song, she was still a very successful singer and musician.

Obviously, she wanted the song to be successful. If it wasn't, that wouldn't bode well for how her new album would do.

Sure, her fan base would probably buy it, but *Dixie's Got Her Boots On* was such a different kind of music from what Jules usually did that there was always a chance her fans wouldn't like it. That was part of her worry.

And if that happened, then the only hope for the song was to find a new audience. Harder than it sounded. In this day and age, where there were so many independent artists forging their own paths on social media, discoverability wasn't easy.

If the song died on the vine, the album probably wouldn't do much, either. There would be no tour.

Maybe a very small one, but most likely none at all. That would mean disappointing Cash and Jesse. Sierra, too.

Jules wouldn't exactly be thrilled about it, either. She tipped her head back to stare at the supports of the umbrella. Suddenly, the weight of the world was upon her shoulders.

"Hey, what's the plan for dinner?"

She looked straight ahead and saw Cash ducking under the umbrella, still dripping wet from being in the water. The skim board lay on the sand nearby.

She smiled, happy to be pulled back to reality. "I have no idea. Your Aunt Claire said she'd take care of it. She's probably figuring it out at the grocery store."

"Well, I'm starving now. Got anything to eat?" He wrapped himself in his towel and sat down on the empty chair.

"There might be some snacks left in my cooler. You can have those if you want." There was no point in telling him not to spoil his appetite. He would still be hungry for dinner. Cash was never not hungry.

"Cool." He dug into the cooler immediately.

"You and Sierra ready for tomorrow?"

He already had a handful of pretzels in his mouth. He nodded and chewed faster, swallowing them down with a big gulp of water from one of the bottles she'd brought. "We are so ready." He grinned. "I can't wait."

She smiled back.

"Oh, boy," he said. "I know that look. You're nervous, huh?"

"I don't know if 'nervous' is the right word, but there's a lot riding on this song."

"On how it's received, sure, I get that. But when it comes to what's going to happen in the studio tomorrow, you have nothing to worry about there."

"No?" That wasn't really her concern, but she was happy to hear her son out.

"No way." Cash shook his head with enthusiasm, as if to underline the statement. "Mom, we are *killing* it in the studio. Everybody sounds so good together. And we've done the song a thousand times now. Everybody knows it. Now they're not playing to learn it, they're playing to have fun."

She nodded. "You're absolutely right. And it makes me feel good to hear you say that, because I agree." It was the response to the song she was most concerned about. What her core audience would think of something so different.

"Cool," he said. "I can't wait for tomorrow."

"It's going to be great," she said. It was the days to

follow that would tell her what was really going to happen.

"So, is Jesse going to master the final version?" Cash asked.

Jules nodded. "He said he and Bobby can do it. If not, Billy has someone that can handle it." She was also a little nervous about sending the song to Billy, her agent. He'd heard her and Cash play through the song once and really enjoyed it, but what would he think about the final version? She needed him to love it. She needed him to work his magic and get the song some airtime.

If the radio stations wouldn't play her song, her only hope then was social media. If she could get the song to go viral, it should sell itself. Again, this was all hope and speculation but that was all she had right now.

Her other shot was to send a sample of the song out to her fan base. She'd put it up on her website, too. But again, the song was so different from what her fans were used to she really didn't know how they'd respond.

And then there was the video that Jesse wanted to do. They hadn't talked about it much lately, so maybe he'd lost interest in the idea. She wasn't sure.

She was willing to invest the money in the video,

because she knew a good one could really do a lot to push the song. And if the video got a lot of views and became popular on YouTube, that alone could drive sales.

She groaned at how much there was still to do.

"What now?" Cash asked through another mouthful of pretzels.

She laughed softly. "Sorry, I didn't realize that was out loud. I was just thinking about how much I have to do. And about whether or not to pursue the idea of making a video to go along with the song."

"You know what I think. You need to do it."

"I know."

"You scared about the money?"

"No. I know it's going to be expensive. I'm okay with that. You get what you pay for."

"Then what are we waiting for? Let's do it."

She sat forward, twisting a bit to see her son better. "It's going to take some work, Cash. You can't just decide you want to make a music video and then the next day you're shooting. Besides all the technical stuff, there's a script to be written."

He shrugged. "Jesse said he had contacts. I guarantee if you tell him tomorrow that you're ready to start on the video, it will only be a matter of days before things get underway. You know how he is. You say jump and he asks how high."

She rolled her eyes. "It's not quite like that."

He laughed. "I didn't mean it in a bad way. The guy loves you, Mom. He'll do anything for you. Why not let him help you when he wants to so bad?"

She sighed and sat back. "We'd still need a script."

"You could look at what Sierra and I have been working on." He said it so nonchalantly that she wasn't sure she'd heard him right.

She turned her head. "You and Sierra have been working on what now?"

"An idea for the music video." He grinned like he'd been caught at something. "You might think it's silly."

"Why?"

"Well...we thought because the subject matter of the song is so serious that the video should be lighter. Kind of campy. We were playing around with the idea of setting it in the environment of the rodeo circuit and pushing the stereotype envelope. Buckle bunnies with big hair, a lot of makeup, and skimpy clothes. Guys with big hats, big buckles, and bigger attitudes. You get what I'm saying?"

She narrowed her eyes as she thought. "I do. And

that does sound fun. Rodeos are always popular subject matter when it comes to country music."

"Instead of houses, we'd show RVs," Cash elaborated. "That's what the rodeo people live in."

She nodded. "Makes sense." The more she thought about it, the more she could see the whole thing. "How about tomorrow, after we record, we talk to Jesse about it? See what he thinks about how easy it would be to film a thing like that and what ideas he might have."

Cash smiled. "Okay. I'll text Sierra when we get back to house so she knows what's going on. She can bring the script tomorrow, too."

He stood up, then frowned down at her in her chair. "Were you not ready to go back yet? Aunt Claire might need help with dinner."

She laughed. It was like he had a second brain that did nothing but think about food. "No, I'm ready."

Her day of doing nothing had come to an end.

Chapter Forty-five

The words came to Margo with relative ease. She knew where the story was going even without Conrad's help, because they'd talked about it on the beach today. She'd incorporated his most recent changes, which she'd sent to him, and he'd loved what she'd done.

She plowed forward, partially driven by his praise, and partially driven by her frustration that Dinah had not yet gone home. That woman. Honestly.

Margo tapped away at the keyboard, layering in description along with the narration, making sure to use as many of the five senses as she could so that the reader got a well-rounded picture of what was going on.

"Mom?" Claire's voice rang out.

Margo looked up from where she was working at

the dining room table, headphones on so she wouldn't be distracted. She moved the headphones off her ears. There were grocery bags all over the kitchen island. She hadn't even heard Claire bring them in. "Do you need me to help bring more bags up? Are do you want me to move?"

"I've already brought everything up," Claire said. "I need to put all of this away and then I was going to make a stir-fry for dinner. I just wanted to ask if you thought we should have chicken or beef. I can make either."

"Beef sounds wonderful. As does the stir-fry."

Claire nodded. "Beef it is. Thanks." She glanced at her mother's laptop. "How's the writing going?"

"Very well, I'd say."

"Good. Because I've never heard such angry typing." Claire laughed.

"Angry typing?"

Claire nodded as she unpacked a grocery bag sitting on the counter. "You're hitting those keys like you're trying to drive them through the tabletop."

"Oh." Margo hadn't been aware she'd been doing that. "Sorry."

"No, it's no problem. Just as observation."

"I am a little...bothered, I suppose."

"About what?"

Margo sighed and shook her head. "Dinah. She hasn't gone home yet like she was supposed to. She told Conrad she wasn't feeling well enough today."

Claire frowned as she carried things to the pantry to put them away. "Did she overindulge at the wedding?"

"Not that I saw. She was complaining about the food being too strange for her. The truth is, she got her feelings hurt. She got mad at me because I stood up to her, so she told Conrad she wanted to go home. That was approximately five minutes into dinner. He flat-out told her he wasn't leaving and if she wanted to go, she could call an Uber. Which she didn't. Instead, she refused to talk to either one of us for the rest of the night."

"Wow. That's some serious high school-level behavior."

"I've learned Dinah likes to control every situation she's in. If she can't, she pouts."

"Again, super mature."

Margo nodded, one corner of her mouth lifting in a lopsided smile. "She's really something."

"I wish I'd known," Claire said. "I would have gone out of my way to engage her in conversation last night."

"Be glad you didn't. She would have ended up

insulting you or belittling you once she realized you were my daughter." Margo hit Save on her Word document. She'd done enough for the day. She turned the laptop off and closed it, then got up. "What can I do to help?"

"I thought you were working on your book?"

"I was, but I've done what I needed to do."

"Okay." Claire looked around. "I was just about to start the rice. Hopefully, that will help fill some of the bottomless pit that is Cash's stomach." She smiled. "But there are plenty of vegetables to be cut up."

"I'd be happy to take care of that," Margo said. "Using a knifc might feel good right now."

Claire laughed. "Mom!"

Margo made no apology, just smiled and picked up her laptop. "Let me put this in the bedroom."

As she came back out, Jules was coming in through the sliding doors from the back porch. "Hey, gang, we're back from the beach. Cash is going up to shower, then he'll be down. I'm about to do the same thing myself."

Claire was looking at her phone. "Kat just texted to say she's on her way back from Alex's, so we'll have a full house for dinner."

Jules stopped at the bedroom door. "You need help?"

"Nope," Claire said. "I have Mom as my sous chef."

Margo nodded. "Take your shower, Jules. We've got it."

"Okay," Jules said. "I'll set the table when I'm done."

"Perfect," Claire said.

Margo took a knife from the block and then selected a cutting board from the cabinet where they were kept. "All right. What do you want done?"

"Peppers and onions sliced into strips, broccoli into small florets, and carrots into thin coins, maybe on the diagonal? Or however you feel like doing it." Claire shrugged. "Doesn't matter to me and they taste the same regardless."

Margo reached for the peppers. "I'm on it."

She went to work, pleased to have something to concentrate on that wasn't related to Dinah. The woman just knew how to push Margo's buttons and Margo didn't care for that. To her, it was a weakness. One that Dinah knew about and was happy to exploit.

Thankfully, she would eventually go home. Hopefully tomorrow. And while the possibility existed that Dinah would visit again, Margo prayed it wouldn't be for a while, even if that was a selfish thing to pray for. Maybe Dinah would stay away for at least a year. Now, that would be a blessing.

By then, Margo and Conrad would be in a different place. They'd be neighbors, for one thing. In a year, Margo would be living in her new house, when most of the work there would be done. Maybe not the secondary bathroom. She saw no pressing need to make that a priority when it would only be used by the occasional guest.

Her relationship with Conrad would be stronger, too. If it wasn't, then they might not be together at all, but that didn't feel like how things were going. They were so good together. Why wouldn't that continue?

She moved on to the onions, dreading the tears that would undoubtedly form as soon as she started cutting them. She squinted in anticipation.

In a year, their book would be done, and maybe even on its way to publication. She didn't want to dream about something that was such an improbability, but she couldn't help herself. It was exciting to think about.

With the writing pace they were keeping, she imagined they'd have it finished in about three months. Amazing, really, but they were dedicated. Granted, Dinah being here had put a crimp in their usual workday, but they'd be back on schedule soon. The work Margo had been doing, along with Conrad's feedback, meant they weren't completely behind, either.

She didn't mind keeping that up for another day, but she'd learned she liked writing with Conrad a great deal better than writing alone. Mostly because she enjoyed his company so much. Being with him was just such a pleasure.

"Mom, your phone is buzzing."

Margo turned to look at her phone where she'd left it on the dining room table. "Thank you. I was lost in thought." She put the knife down, wiped her hands on a towel, and went to see who was calling.

It was Conrad. "Hello?"

"Hi, there. How was your day?"

"Good. I'm helping Claire make dinner."

"Am I interrupting? I can call back."

"No, it's fine. I was just slicing onions. I can chat for a moment. How was *your* day?" That was an answer she was eager for.

He sighed. Not a good sign.

"Uh-oh," Margo said. "What's she done now?" Because it had to be Dinah. It had to be.

She heard him inhale, like he was gearing up to tell her something she wasn't going to like.

"There's no easy way to say this, so I'm just going to come out with it," Conrad said.

Margo closed her eyes and braced herself.

"Dinah's decided to move to Diamond Beach."

Chapter Forty-six

*T*rina waved goodbye to Miles, who'd been sweet enough to drop her off on his way to work. She headed up the steps to the beach house's first floor. Despite the run-in with Liz, she'd had a good day. First church, which had been so nice, then the lunch with everyone, then a quiet afternoon with Miles.

They'd taken a long walk on the beach and talked about all sorts of thing. It had really helped to clear Liz out of Trina's head. Thoughts of her were still there, of course, but not like they'd been before the walk.

Even though Trina hadn't said anything and hadn't had doubts, Miles had reassured her that he had no interest in Liz or getting back with her or anything to do with her, really. He'd confessed that since she'd started bothering Trina, he'd begun to actively despise Liz.

He'd talked about how upset he was over what she was doing and had expressed his desire to find a way to end it.

Trina had talked him out of doing anything. She didn't believe there was anyone who could stop Liz's crazy behavior except for Liz.

Despite that belief, Trina wished Liz would forget about her and Miles. Or maybe just disappear altogether. Not in, like, a bad way. Trina didn't wish ill on her. She just wanted Liz to work on her own life and not be so concerned with what Trina and Miles were doing.

Maybe she'd find a new boyfriend and that would be the distraction she needed. Trina could only hope.

She used her key to unlock the door and went inside. "Ma? Mimi? I'm home."

Something smelled good.

"In the kitchen, Trina," her mom called out.

Trina went in to say hi. She was in her church clothes and wanted to change as soon as she could, but not before she said hello to her family. "Hey, there. Making dinner?"

Her mom nodded. "I wasn't sure if you'd want to

eat or not but I'm making a casserole, so it doesn't really matter, because it'll keep. How was your afternoon?"

"Good and I'm starved, so I'll eat. Is that tuna noodle casserole with peas?"

Her mom smiled. "Yep."

"Awesome." One of Trina's favorites. She looked around. "Where's Mimi? She's not in bed already, is she?"

"Nope. She's still at the Hamilton Arms."

"What?"

Roxie nodded. "She and Miguel liked it so much they decided to stay another night."

Trina grinned. "Good for them. I'm glad they're having fun. I'm going to go change, then I'll be back."

"Okay," Roxie said.

Trina went off to her room, where she shed her sundress in favor of soft leggings and an oversized tee. It was nice to get dressed up, but comfortable clothing had its place, too. She returned to the living room and stood at the breakfast bar that separated the kitchen from the rest of the room. "What can I help with, Ma?"

"Nothing. All I have to do is finish sprinkling on

the cracker crumbs and put it in the oven. You want a drink?"

"Sure, but I can get it. I just want water."

Trina went around the breakfast bar and slipped past her mom to get to the cabinet where they kept the big tumbler cups.

Roxie opened the oven. "How are you doing with the whole Liz thing? Or would you rather not talk about it?"

"I'm okay to talk about it." Trina filled a big stainless-steel tumbler with ice from the fridge dispenser. "I don't like what she's doing, obviously, but I don't think there's anything I can do to change her, either. Eventually, something else will distract her and she'll move on. That's my hope."

"Mine, too," Roxie said. She slid the glass casserole dish onto the middle rack. "And I hope it happens soon."

"So do I." Trina ran water into the tumbler, put the straw in, then stuck the top on before going out to the couch.

"You know," her mom started. "If you wanted help with the situation, I'd be happy to do whatever I can."

Trina looked at her mom. "Thanks. I'm not sure what anyone could do, though."

Her mom set the oven timer, then came over and took a seat in her chair. "Well...Ethan knows her parents. He could have a word with them. If you wanted."

Trina frowned and shook her head. "That's kind of him, but no. I think that would only spin Liz up more. It's not high school, Ma. We can't have our parents interfering. We're adults. Even if she's not acting like one."

"You can say that again." Her mom picked up the remote and turned on the TV. "I just want you to know it's an option. If you ever think you need it."

"Thanks." Trina sipped her water. She gave a little more thought to Ethan's kind offer but decided against it. "I'm not sure talking to her parents would do anything anyway. Pretty sure she's already mad at them. I don't see how making her more mad at them would change her attitude toward me."

"I'm sure you're right. Ethan told me pretty much the same thing." Roxie smiled at her. "I just hate that I can't help you or protect you."

Trina grinned. "Just being able to talk to you about stuff is helping."

"That's good. You want to watch a movie? Or something else?"

"Anything is fine with me. I might not stay awake

for the end of a movie, though. Today kind of wore me out. I don't know how Miles had the energy to go to work. Hopefully, they all have a quiet night with no fires and no emergencies."

Her mom was looking through the available movies on one of the streaming services. "Look, *Private Benjamin*! Classic Goldie Hawn."

Trina shook her head. "Never seen it."

"What?" Her mom looked horrified. "I have failed you as a mother. You'll stay awake for this one, I promise."

"Okay," Trina said. "I have to stay awake long enough to eat anyway."

They watched the movie, which was very funny, and ate tuna noodle casserole, after which they each had another piece of wedding cake, since there was some left over. It was just as good as Trina remembered.

The next thing Trina knew, she was waking up on the couch. She'd been covered with the throw that was usually draped on the back of it. Light filtered in through the blinds, so it had to be morning.

She blinked as she realized she *had* fallen asleep, and her mom had covered her up and let her be. She picked up her phone from the coffee table and checked the time. Quarter to eight. Wow, she'd really slept.

She sat up, mouth dry. Her water was nearby, so she took a big sip. The stainless-steel tumbler had not only kept it cold, but there was still ice in it. She drank more, quenching her thirst and helping herself wake up.

What she needed now was coffee.

She went over to the kitchen and made some. Mimi might not be here to drink it, but Trina knew her mom would. As she was pressing the Brew button, her mom came out of her room.

Trina smiled at her. "Morning. I must have crashed pretty hard last night, huh?"

Her mom nodded. "You were out. I hope you don't mind that I left you on the couch. I didn't have the heart to wake you."

"No, that was fine." Her mom was in her exercise gear. "Going out to walk?"

"Yep. You want to come with me?"

Trina would have rather had coffee first, but spending time with her mom was important. And not just because soon she'd be headed off to work every morning. "Sure. Just let me get changed. Don't expect me to go too fast, either. I think I'm still half asleep."

Her mom laughed. "That's all right."

They hit the beach a few minutes later.

"What did you think of Ethan's church?"

"I liked it," Trina answered. "So did Miles. Why? Are you going to start attending?"

"I think so," her mom said. "It might not have been the one I'd have chosen on my own, but I like it and Ethan's there, so I'm happy. And it'll give me a place to get involved with. I can volunteer for some of the outreach programs they do."

"Plus, you want his parents to like you."

Her mom gave her a look. "They already like me, according to Ethan. His mother told him to put a ring on it."

Trina laughed. "Now that's funny. So is he?"

Her mom shook her head. "I told him it's okay if he gets me a commitment ring, but we're not about to get engaged."

"Why not?"

"Trina, your dad only just passed away."

"I know. But it wasn't like he was exactly faithful. I love him and miss him, don't get me wrong, but I see how happy Ethan makes you. That's a big deal. I don't remember you being like this with Dad."

"It's still too soon."

Trina understood, she did, but at the same time,

she hated to see her mom delay happiness because of what society might think was right. "Just know that I don't care about what the proper amount of time is to be single. And neither will Mimi."

Her mom snorted. "I know that much." Then she smiled at Trina. "I appreciate your support. Thanks."

"You're welcome."

Her mom's brows furrowed. "Hey, you're not saying all that because there's something you need to tell me about you and Miles, is there?"

Trina grinned and shook her head. "No. I mean, we're headed in a good direction. We're committed to each other, and we've talked about what the future might hold, but neither of us wants to rush things. He knows I've got a lot going on with the salon, too."

"Not to change the subject, but are you headed over there today?"

"Yep. I have a couple more interviews and I want to see the progress. There might be a shipment of supplies to put away this afternoon, which I won't be able to do unless the shelving and cabinets are all done."

"You want help?"

Trina was about to say no, but then stopped, remembering what Ethan had said about her mom wanting to be needed. "Sure, if you want to come. I'm not sure how exciting it'll be, though."

"That's okay. I want to be useful."

Trina understood. Her mom was in an odd place in her life. No job, no husband, her own mother soon to move out, and her daughter about to be completely immersed in a new business. She needed to find a spot for herself.

If Trina could help with that, then why not?

Chapter Forty-seven

In between sips of her coffee, Claire dressed in a pair of old shorts, a second-best T-shirt, and sneakers. She was headed to the bakery with Danny today to work. She hadn't been there in a while because she'd been occupied with moving things from the house in Landry and working on the wedding cake.

With both of those things behind her, she could now focus on the next big stage of her future. She was ready, too. More than ready. She was eager and excited.

Her phone chimed with a text from Danny. *Meet you at the car?*

On my way, she texted back. She tucked her phone into her purse, pulled the strap over her head so it lay across her body, then grabbed her laptop with all of her bakery notes, recipes, lists, and ideas on it and went out to the kitchen. She refilled her travel mug with coffee before going downstairs. She was so keyed up she took the steps, but of course, going down wasn't nearly the workout that going up was.

She strolled across the property toward Danny's driveway. He was just coming out his front door.

"Morning," she called out.

"Morning." He glanced at her cup. "Is that coffee?"

She nodded. "I thought I'd need it."

"I was going to stop on the way and get some. I need to get gas anyway."

"That's fine with me. Whatever you need to do."

"Okay." He unlocked the truck, and they got in. He started the engine and adjusted the A/C. It wasn't that hot yet, but the truck was warm inside from the morning sun.

"I can't wait to see how things are going."

He smiled. "You're going to be surprised, I think."

"I'm sure I will be." She put her travel cup in the holder, then got her seatbelt on.

They stopped at the local convenience store for gas and coffee for Danny, then made their way to the shopping center. There were a few trucks in the parking lot, proof that Ethan and his guys were there and working.

Danny parked by the bakery.

Claire peered out the window. "The sign is up!"

"I used our regular sign people, and they did me a favor by putting a rush on it. But there's more inside. Which reminds me..." He turned off the truck and reached over to open the glove box. He pulled something out, then dangled it from his fingers. It was a cupcake keychain with a key on it. "For you. A key to the shop. I meant to give it to you sooner, but I kept forgetting. Sorry."

"No problem." She took the key. "I like the keychain."

"I thought you might." He opened his door. "Come on. Let's go see how things are progressing."

She got out and followed him to the door. She could already see through the windows how different the place looked.

He opened the door and stood back so she could go in first. The sharp scent of fresh paint greeted her. She turned slowly, taking it all in. The paint scheme was mainly black, white, and yellow with touches of bright, happy pink. "It looks incredible. I can't get over how much work has been done."

He stood beside her. "Honestly, a lot of it was just that it needed cleaning and painting."

Not only had the interior been painted, but a new black and white checkerboard floor had been installed and the rough carpentry for the counters was already in place. Against one wall were four round black tables, stacked in twos, and eight matching black chairs. All of them were wrapped in plastic.

Danny started pointing things out. He spread his hands in front of one of the big picture windows that flanked the front door. "This is where those small round tables are going to go. Two on each side. We might be able to add two more, but I want to live with four initially and see how they go. If they don't impede traffic and we get enough dine-in business, we'll add more."

"I like that. That's smart. But I think we'll need them. I hope we need them. I'd love to see us become a sort of neighborhood meeting place."

"So would I." He moved to the far wall. "Over here will be a large glass-fronted upright fridge that will primarily showcase the sour orange pies. I'm having a sign made to go over it, too."

"I love that," Claire said. It was just like what a lot of places did to house their key lime pies, but her sour orange was better. And, hopefully, after the article that Conrad was going to write, those pies would be in high demand.

He took a few steps toward the middle of the space. "Coming out from the wall will be the main display case with the register at the end. That display case is already in the back. It'll be moved into place today."

"Great."

"The bathrooms have been remodeled a little, too." He grinned. "Go look."

She went down the hall and into the one marked Women. The black and white checkerboard floor extended inside. The walls were alternating yellow and pink with a black and white checkerboard trim around the ceiling.

Danny appeared behind her at the open door. "What do you think? The men's room looks the same. And once the menu is finalized, which we need to do ASAP, I'm going to have it reprinted in a poster-sized version and hung in both bathrooms."

"I like that idea." She nodded. "I can probably have that menu done today if you have time to sit down with me and go over it. It really needs to be a joint decision. I know you put me in charge, but I've never done anything like this before. I want to make sure what I've envisioned is actually doable."

"Let's do it at lunch then."

"Okay." It was a good thing she'd brought her laptop.

"Now, for the really exciting part, follow me." He started toward the back.

Smiling, she went after him. They pushed through the swinging door into the kitchen and Claire let out a little gasp.

The space had been transformed since she'd last seen it. Gone were all traces of the previous Italian restaurant. Instead, gleaming stainless-steel industrial ovens, mixers, a dough sheeter, and a dishwasher had been put in place. Long, stainless-steel worktables and tall racks provided all kinds of room for production.

Giant stainless-steel sinks and drainboards lined one wall. But what really caught Claire's eye was that the kitchen had been stocked with every imaginable baking accessory she might need. Stacks of sheet pans and cake pans, rows of whisks, spatulas, spoons, large measuring cups, dough cutters and scrapers, scales, and a pile of bowls.

There were also large wheeled bins for ingredients such as sugar, flour, and cocoa, massive refrigerators for perishables and cake storage. Several rolling racks would make moving goods to the sales-floor an easy task.

At the moment, those racks were blocked by the big glass display case that was waiting to be moved out front.

Claire was overwhelmed. "I can't believe you did all of this."

"I had help. Ethan's crew moved most of this into place. The ovens will be hooked up tomorrow, but the refrigerators are running and keeping temp, so we're ready to start stocking ingredients. We'll be baking in here before you know it. Or at least, you will."

"I can't wait. It's incredible."

"Well, keep an eye out for anything else you might need. I did my best, but you're the baker. If you run across something that's lacking, just let me know."

She couldn't imagine what that might be. It seemed like he'd thought of everything, but all the same she nodded. "I will, I promise."

"Great. Let's start organizing this place the way you want it. All of the baking stuff needs to be sanitized, too, so we should give that dishwasher a test run."

"I've never used a dishwasher like that, so I'm going to need a lesson."

"No worries. We use the same kind at the popcorn stores, though this one is bigger. I'll show you."

They got to work, but before long, a trio of workmen showed up. While Claire continued in the kitchen, Danny went out front with them to show them where the display case needed to be placed.

Claire paused for a moment to look around at her new domain. She bit her lip and shook her head. Crazy that this was hers. Danny's, too, of course, but this was essentially her new headquarters. Where she would establish herself as a real, professional baker.

It was a little daunting, but also very inspiring. She couldn't wait to bake her first batch of something in here. That would probably be cookies. They'd need a lot of them for the Grand Opening and her plan was to freeze some as backup.

Wouldn't it be something when this place was filled with all the delicious scents of sweet treats? She couldn't wait.

Danny had really outdone himself.

Now it was her turn to shine.

Chapter Forty-eight

*W*illie told Miguel what she wanted for breakfast, then he placed the order with room service for their last morning in the honeymoon suite. Their stay at the Hamilton Arms had been just perfect and they wanted to enjoy their last few hours in the suite, soaking it all in.

Also, Willie didn't feel like getting out of her robe just yet. Frankly, she'd thought about just wearing it home, but Miguel might think she'd tipped over into the deep end of the crazy pool if she did that. She still planned on stuffing it into her suitcase. If they charged her for it, that was fine. She was willing to pay to bring that souvenir home.

Order placed, Miguel was out on the balcony, chatting on the phone. He'd said he was going to call Rob to see about making the tub in the master bath bigger on account of Willie's experience with the giant tub here, and she imagined that was what he was doing.

She finished brushing her teeth, then grabbed her phone and joined him. The fresh air was nice, and it was a beautiful day in Diamond Beach. More sparkling water, more blue skies, more salty breezes drifting by. Hard not to be happy in a place like this, but there could have been a hurricane on the horizon, and she still would have been filled with bliss.

She settled into the other padded chair and put her feet up on the little ottoman that matched it. Miguel had the same setup. Between them was a pretty white metal table with a glass top. The Hamilton Arms really understood how to make their guests comfortable, although she wasn't sure all the rooms had this level of accommodation. Maybe it was just how the suites were. She glanced over the railing. They were on the fifth floor, which was also the top floor. From her vantage point, she could see down onto the other balconies.

They had chairs and tables, but they didn't look this nice.

She sat back and inhaled, filling her lungs with the air. She loved the smell of the beach and saltwater. It really gave her an appetite. Which only intensified her hope that breakfast didn't take too long to arrive.

She was hungry but more than that, she was ready for coffee. There was a coffee maker in the room, but that stuff never came out as good as what they could make in the kitchen, so she'd decided to wait.

For her meal, she'd ordered the vanilla Belgian waffles with mixed berries, fresh whipped cream, and a side of bacon.

Miguel had ordered the Spanish frittata with chorizo and vegetables, topped with avocado and sour cream. He'd also asked for a big pot of coffee.

After they'd had their meal, which they had no plans to rush, they'd pack up their few things and he'd order a car to take them back. In a matter of hours, they'd say goodbye to this lovely little getaway.

It would be strange to be away from Miguel after this time together, but they'd decided they'd go back to their own houses during the day to spend some time with their families. At night, they were going to split their time between the two places so they didn't have to sleep apart.

Tonight, she'd be at Miguel's. Tomorrow, he'd be at the beach house with her. She just needed to make sure that was all right with Trina and Roxie. Willie figured it would be, but she also understood it meant having a man around. Not something they were used to. Even if it was Miguel, she didn't want to make them feel uncomfortable in their own home.

She took out her phone and sent them a group text. *Morning, my girls! Headed home after breakfast, which hasn't been delivered yet. It's been wonderful. What a great present. Would either of you mind if Miguel spent tomorrow night at the house with me?*

Their answers came quickly and were pretty much what she'd expected.

Not at all, was Trina's response. *He's your husband! You should be together!*

Willie smiled.

Roxie sent a thumbs-up along with, *What Trina said. It's your house, too. Miguel is always welcome.*

Then another text came in, this time from Roxie alone outside the group text. *Trina ran into Liz again. She's working at Clipper's. We had lunch there after church and Liz was mean to her.*

Willie glared at the screen, having nowhere else to direct her anger. That snippety thing needed to leave her granddaughter alone.

More from Roxie. *I offered to help, but Trina didn't*

want me to do anything. I'm so frustrated. Just needed to vent.

Willie nodded as she typed. *Makes me mad, too.*

Well, say a prayer that crazy girl gets tired of bothering T. See you soon.

Will do, Willie replied. But she couldn't stop thinking about it. Even when breakfast came.

"This looks very delicious," Miguel said. He tipped the man after breakfast was set up on the balcony table.

"Thank you, sir. Have a good day."

"You, too," Miguel said.

Willie spread her napkin over her lap as Miguel took his seat. The next thing she did was fix her coffee with cream and sugar. "It's going to be hard to leave this behind. Being pampered is a lot of fun."

Miguel grinned. "It is, but a spoiled life makes a person soft."

"Does that mean you're not going to keep spoiling me?"

He laughed. "No, I don't mind if you're soft. But we can't both be."

She chuckled. "Glad we cleared that up."

Her waffles were so good she made Miguel taste them so he understood what he'd missed out on. The berries were juicy and plump, and the fresh whipped cream, which had been served in its own silver bowl, was light and just the right amount of sweet. He seemed plenty happy with his frittata, however.

As the meal wound down, Willie's mind was still on Trina. Honestly, it was on Trina a lot these days, mostly because of the salon, but all of this nonsense with Liz didn't help. Hard not to think about her granddaughter, really.

She sighed. "I didn't want to say anything earlier, because I didn't want to ruin our meal, but I have a little situation."

He'd just been refilling both their cups from the carafe. He set the coffee down as his forehead wrinkled in concern. "What is it, my love?"

"It's Trina. Remember I told you about that girl, Liz, who was bothering her?"

He nodded. "Liz Stewart."

"That's right. Well, there was another incident." She told him what Roxie had just told her.

He blew out a long breath as he sat back. "That's unacceptable. No step-granddaughter of mine deserves to be treated that way. I know she said she didn't want help, but this is not my way, my love. I cannot stand idly by."

Willie smiled in appreciation. "I don't want to, either."

"Then there's only one thing we can do," Miguel said. "On the way home, we need to stop by the Stewarts and have a talk with them."

"I like that idea. But I don't wanna make things worse for Trina, either. I also don't want her to get mad at me for interfering. I couldn't stand it if my girl was upset with me."

Miguel smiled as he nodded thoughtfully. "Don't worry, my love. I have an idea about just how to handle that."

Chapter Forty-nine

Kat walked into Future Florida full of the same kind of nerves she'd experienced on her first day of college. It was mostly excitement mixed with a little trepidation over not knowing exactly how things worked.

That was all right, though. She'd soon find out everything she needed to know, and in a couple of months, all of this would be old hat. It was getting through those first couple of weeks that would be the most...interesting.

She went up to the reception desk.

The receptionist, who was just getting herself situated, turned around. She'd been here the first time Kat had come in. "Good morning. How can I help you?"

Kat nodded. "Hi, I'm Kat Thompson. I'm the new hire? The, uh, lead data scientist?" It felt odd giving her new job title. It sounded like it belonged to someone else.

The receptionist, an older woman with copper hair and reading glasses, stood up and gave Kat a big smile. "Of course! I remember you from when you came in to interview. We've been expecting you. Welcome to Future Florida. I'm Arlene." She took something from one of the drawers under the counter, then came around from behind the desk. "Let me show you to your office."

Kat's brows shot up. "I have an office?"

"Of course."

"I just thought I'd be working in a common area."

Arlene shook her head, still smiling. "You're a little higher up the food chain than that."

Kat just blinked. She hadn't realized her position came with its own office. She was glad she'd worn her blue and white print skirt, white blouse, and tan blazer. She felt appropriately dressed for someone with her own office.

What a cool surprise that was. She couldn't wait to take a picture and send it to Alex and her family.

She followed Arlene back through the big door at the side of the reception desk, then down a cool, dark corridor lit with soft recessed lighting. They went past the conference room where she'd done her interview.

Arlene stopped at the second door on the right and tapped a fingernail on the surface. "See? Already has your name on it."

Kat's mouth fell open. It actually did. A little slide-in plaque had been stamped with the name "Katrina Thompson." She was taking a picture of that, too.

Arlene used the key she'd gotten out of her desk to unlock the door, then she handed it to Kat. "That's yours to keep. We have a master key that unlocks all the doors but do your best not to lose it all the same."

Kat nodded solemnly. "I won't lose it." She'd get a copy made immediately and tuck it away somewhere safe at home. Maybe she'd get two copies made and keep one in her car. Just in case.

Arlene pushed the door open and flipped on the light, but there was already some coming in through the window on the back wall. The office had pale gray walls and sturdy, industrial carpet in charcoal.

Behind a brushed nickel and black metal desk with a smoked glass top was a black leather chair with a high back. Behind that was a low bookcase that ran the length of the window above it. The blinds were tilted halfway open to let light in. On the right-hand side of the office were three tall black filing cabinets. In front of the desk sat a pair of slim chrome and black leather chairs.

The desk held a laptop with a folder on top of it, a Future Florida notebook, a pen, and a black phone that looked capable of handling several lines. Next to the phone was a long, narrow box. Kat would investigate that later.

Not a fancy office, but not the most utilitarian, either.

Arlene stepped to one side so Kat could come in further. "It's a little plain, I know, but you're welcome to add your own touches to it. Plants, pictures, whatever you like. There's no policy forbidding any of that. In fact, the company really encourages making your space your own. They're great about wanting everyone to be happy in their environment."

"Good to know." She knew exactly where her surfboard clock was going now. She definitely wanted a plant or two as well. And a picture of her and Alex. She smiled. "I think it's a great space."

"I'm so glad. That folder on the laptop has all of your intake paperwork in it, but you'll have plenty of time to do that today. If you want, I can give you a quick tour of the rest of the headquarters. Unless you want to get started on the paperwork now. There's not that much more to see."

"I'd love to see the rest first." Kat followed Arlene out.

Arlene pointed back the way they'd come. "You already know where the conference room is. These other doors are more offices, as you can see by the nameplates. The rest is this way."

They went all the way to the end of the hall and through the middle door into a big multi-purpose room that smelled of vanilla and coffee. On one side was a large leather couch with four matching leather chairs arranged in a seating area. At the end of that seating area was a large-screen TV mounted on the wall. At the other end were two treadmills and another large-screen TV.

One side of the room featured a full-size black fridge and a black granite countertop with maple cabinets above and below. On the counter was a microwave, a toaster oven, and a heavy-duty coffee maker that looked capable of more than just coffee, although there was a fairly full pot of it on the burner.

In front of that setup was a long dining table with eight chairs. The wall perpendicular to the table held framed certificates, plaques, photographs, and letters of thanks for the charity.

Arlene gestured to the space in general. "This is the employee lounge and breakroom, as I'm sure you've figured out. Feel free to use it at any time you need a break, or even if you want to meet with someone in a more informal way than the conference room. Of course, you're welcome to bring your lunch and put it in the fridge. I make coffee every morning. If you're not a coffee drinker, there are teabags in that little wooden caddy."

Kat smiled. "I am definitely a coffee drinker."

"Excellent news," Arlene said. "I like you even more now."

Kat laughed. "I just realized that I didn't bring a lunch. How long of a break do we get? Will I have time to run out and get something?"

"Of course. Lunch is forty-five minutes, but sometimes we have lunch meetings with all of the staff. On those days, which you'll know about ahead of time, lunch is usually catered. For today, there are a few fast-food places nearby, as well as some nicer spots if you want something a little healthier. There's also a Publix just down the road."

Arlene wrinkled her nose like she was sharing a

secret. "That's where I usually go. They have so much to choose from."

"Good suggestion," Kat said. "That is exactly what I'm going to do today."

"Unfortunately, you won't have too much else to do today, because Tom and Molly were both called away yesterday to meet with a potential donor. I don't know if they'll be back today or not."

Tom Philips and Molly Hargrove had interviewed Kat. She hadn't really known if she'd see them in the office, since they were both on the board of Future Florida, but she had seen their names on two of the offices she'd passed on her way to the employee lounge. "Are they usually here?"

"Yes. When they aren't traveling or meeting with prospective donors or clients, which is how we refer to those we help."

"Clients," Kat repeated. "I like that. Makes them sound important, which they are."

Arlene nodded. "I agree."

Kat had seen another name on one of the offices. "Who else works out of the office here?"

"Eloise French. She handles public relations, promotional events, fundraisers, social media, things of that nature. She works Tuesday through Saturday, though, because so much of what she does happens over the weekend."

"So just you and me today?"

"Yep," Arlene said. "I'll help you as much as I can, but I'm not sure how much help that'll actually be. The folder on your desk should get you started, I think. Tom and Molly both said they'd written some things up for you."

"Then I'll get started." Kat hooked a thumb over her shoulder. "After I get some coffee."

Arlene smiled. "You help yourself to as much as you want. I'll be happy to make more. Cups are in the cabinet above, sugar is in the canister next to it and there's creamer in the fridge. Several kinds, because Tom's allergic to dairy." She frowned. "Do you have any special dietary requirements I need to know about? I handle ordering food when lunch is catered, so just tell me and I'll make a note of it."

"Nope," Kat said. "Thanks."

"All right. Holler if you need me. I'd better get back out to the front desk."

"Okay." Kat took a mug down from the cabinet, filled it with coffee, two teaspoons of sugar, then went to the fridge. There was oat milk creamer, almond milk, and regular half-and-half. She picked the half-and-half.

She sipped the coffee while taking a look around. The employee lounge was really nice. She'd never been in one like it. The space made her feel like Future Florida truly cared about its employees. That was a nice feeling.

She carried her mug back to her office and sat at her desk to look at the folder and the box. First, she put her purse in one of the empty drawers in her desk.

She opened the box. It had business cards in it. The cards had the Future Florida logo and information, then her name. Beneath her name was her title. Lead Data Scientist. She smiled and immediately opened the desk drawer to tuck some in her purse.

The folder held the usual startup paperwork: Company policies, forms to be filled out, that sort of thing.

Then there were several pages of instructions from Tom and Molly, mostly about how to log into the company's internal web server so that Kat could access their current data and begin the process of analyzing it.

Kat was looking forward to that. To finding ways to help the company better utilize the funds they had, make better decisions about who to help and how to help them, anything she could do to create a better workflow. And help more people.

On the last page of Tom and Molly's instructions was the login and password for her new laptop.

Kat took another sip of coffee, then opened the computer up. She was eager to dive in and see how much she could accomplish on her first day.

It was probably overambitious, but she'd love to be able to present Tom and Molly with an initial report tomorrow morning. To really show them that she was here to get things done. And to make things happen.

The screen flickered to life and a dialog box appeared. With a smile, she rubbed her hands together, then typed in the password she'd been given.

Chapter Fifty

oxie was grateful her daughter had invited her along to the salon, and now that she was here, she was happy to be busy. She didn't mind cleaning at all. There was something very satisfying about it. Which wasn't to say she'd want to do it full-time, but working in the salon, helping Trina get things perfect and organized, that was soul-fulfilling in a way that made Roxie smile.

She balanced carefully on the stepladder. She felt useful. The same way she'd felt planning her mom's wedding. She wiped down the shelves in the employee breakroom that were soon to be stocked with products and thought about that. She needed to be needed.

Had she always felt that way? She'd been a nurse, still was one, but hadn't worked much the last several years. She'd always thought that had been about helping people. But was she helping them because it made her feel needed? Those who were sick or hurt definitely *needed* help.

When she'd been married to Bryan, she'd had him and Trina to take care of. Trina mostly, because Bryan hadn't been there all that much. When he had been, he'd been more than willing to let her take care of him.

Something she was starting to resent. He'd had three women taking care of him, treating him like a prince because they all thought he worked so hard. Roxie was assuming Claire and Paulina had doted on him the way she had.

She'd put a lot of effort into making that man happy when he'd been with them. She could remember thinking about how hard he worked to take care of them and how he deserved to be waited on and looked after.

She huffed out a short, quick breath. "Boy, was I wrong."

She rinsed her cleaning rag in the breakroom sink, then went back to work on the shelves. There was a lot of dust from all of the construction that had gone on in the shop.

Raising Trina had taken up almost all of Roxie's life. In a good way. Trina had been such an easy child. Happy with whatever she was given, never picky about what Roxie served for dinner, sweet-tempered and smiling. Only once could Roxie remember Trina having a major meltdown, but that had been Bryan's fault.

He'd promised her a dog for her twelfth birthday, but when he'd arrived for her birthday, he'd brought her a stuffed dog, not a real one like Trina had been expecting. Even Roxie had given him the silent treatment over that one.

Roxie climbed up one more rung so she could reach the top shelf. The poor kid had cried herself to sleep that night. Roxie had thought about adopting a dog anyway, but their budget had always been a little tight and she'd been concerned that if the dog got sick, they wouldn't be able to afford it. And Bryan, having vetoed the idea, might not have given her the extra money to take care of it.

So Trina had never gotten her dog. Poor kid.

Roxie swiped at the last little bit of dust, then climbed down the ladder and rinsed her rag again.

There were workers in the salon, doing odds and ends. Trina was at her table in the front of the shop working on her laptop while she waited for her interview to arrive.

Roxie took off her rubber gloves, then laid them

and the rag over the edge of the sink to dry. She went out to see her daughter. "Breakroom is spotless."

Trina looked up. "Holy cow, Ma, that was fast."

Roxie lifted one shoulder. "What can I say? I like cleaning."

"I have boxes of color, bottles of developer, tubs of bleach powder...all kinds of stuff to be unboxed and organized. You feel like tackling that?"

"Sure, if you tell me how you want it set up. Shelves are damp, though, so might be a couple minutes before I can put stuff on them."

"That's all right. Let's go have a look and I'll tell you where I want things to go."

"Okay."

They walked back to the breakroom together. Trina stared up at the shelves, hands on her hips. "You know what we need?"

"What's that?"

"Labels. I'd love to label the shelves so that things stay organized."

"We could get a label maker."

Trina shook her head. "I have that printer that I bought. All I need is a sheet of blank labels the right size and I can print them out myself. I just need to remember to order the labels." She took her phone out and made a voice note.

Roxie was impressed by how much her daughter knew and how easily she managed it all with technology.

"All right," Trina said. "Back to the organization." She tapped the first shelf on the right side. "Color boxes should go here, but I might get an organizer for them. Those little boxes will fall over if they're stacked too high with nothing to support them."

She went over to the left. "Jugs of developer here. Shampoos and conditioners on the next shelf up, then extra retail products and any paper goods overflow."

Roxie nodded. "I can do all of that. When is the furniture coming for the front? And the racks for the retail products?"

"Supposed to be this week," Trina answered. "I'll need some help when that all arrives, too. If you're not busy."

"I'd love to help," Roxie said. "Where are the boxes of products for back here?"

"Up front in the corner. The ones marked Beauty Supply Outlet. They're heavy, though. Get one of the guys to carry them back. And if you get that done, towels need to be washed and folded." She tipped her head toward the cabinet over the washer and dryer. "They'll go up there."

"Any special way you want them folded?" Roxie asked.

"Hmm. Good question. I'm really not sure. Maybe in threes? But however they fit best is fine with me."

"Sounds good. I'll get a batch of towels in the washer, then start unboxing." Roxie looked around. "We don't have any laundry detergent, do we?"

Trina groaned. "I knew I forgot something."

"Don't worry! I'll run out and get some."

"Thanks, Ma."

"That's what I'm here for, honey. I want to make this as easy for you as I can."

Trina smiled. "I appreciate that so much. But I feel a little bad. Mimi's going to be coming home to an empty house."

"She won't care. She'll probably want to take a nap anyway." Roxie held out her hand. "I just need your keys, since you drove, then I'll run to the store."

"Right. Hang on, they're in my purse."

They went back to the front of the shop. Trina dug the keys out of her purse and handed them over. "Here you go."

"You want me to pick up something for lunch, too?" Roxie asked. It was about that time. "I could get some sandwiches or something."

Trina nodded. "That would be great. Would you get me a diet soda with caffeine? I feel like I need it and I can't drink any more coffee."

"You got it." Roxie grabbed her own purse and went out the door. The day was warm and bright. Summer would soon be here for real.

"Hey!"

She turned and saw Ethan two doors down. He waved.

"Hey, yourself." She walked over to see him. "What are you working on today?"

"The photography studio. Trying to get it ready as quickly as possible but I don't want to pull my guys off the bakery or salon, since we're so close on both of those. Speaking of which, everything all right over there?"

She nodded quickly to reassure him. "Everything's fine. I'm just going to get laundry detergent so I can start washing towels. I'm grabbing us some drinks and sandwiches, too. You want something?"

"That would be great. I have so much going on today, I can't afford to leave."

"I'll take care of it." She leaned in to kiss his cheek.

"Thanks, Rox." He turned his head so the kiss landed on his mouth. He sighed happily as it ended. "I don't know how I ever got along without you."

"Ethan Lewis, are you saying you need me?"

He nodded. "More than you know."

She just smiled. "The feeling's mutual. Back in a bit."

She kept smiling as she walked to Trina's car and got in. She adjusted the seat and turned to get another look at Ethan. Her new life in Diamond Beach was turning out to be so much better than she'd expected.

Chapter Fifty-one

The studio reverberated with the ending strains of *Dixie's Got Her Boots On* and Jules closed her eyes as she sang and played, putting her heart and soul into the final notes of their very last rehearsal.

As the music died away, Jesse whooped from inside the control room. He stood up and pressed the intercom button, his face radiating happiness. "That was the best one yet! Great job, everyone. Really outstanding. That was honestly perfect. We just need to do it exactly like that one more time."

"We will," Cash said. Jules noticed he was smiling at Sierra, and she was smiling right back at him.

Jules nodded at them all. "You guys are so good. I cannot thank you enough for stepping up and learning this song on such short notice. I am grateful beyond words."

Frankie Ritter, the banjo player, grinned. "It's been a real honor to play with you, Jules. Kind of a dream come true, really."

"I second that," Bobby Perkins said. He took his fiddle off his shoulder. "Never thought I'd get a chance like this, and yet, here I am."

Jules smiled. "It's all Jesse's doing. He's the one who connected us. We have him to thank, really."

Rita Dean, the slide guitarist, shook her head. "I am very grateful to Jesse, and to you, Jules, but I was late coming into the bridge. Maybe nobody else heard it, but I did. Sorry. Won't happen again."

"I didn't hear it," Jules said. But she knew every musician was their own toughest critic, and the older woman was no exception. Rita was a real professional. If she said she was late, Jules believed her. "I don't think anyone else did, either. But we're going to do it again anyway, so all good."

"Thanks," Rita said. "I know I can do better. I will do better."

Jules smiled. "Rita, even when you come in late, you still sound amazing."

Rita grinned. "Thanks, kid."

Jesse spoke through the intercom again. "As much as I hate to interrupt the love fest, what do you say we record this thing? If everyone's ready?"

Jules took a breath as she nodded. This was it. "I'd say we're as ready as we're ever going to be. Let's do it."

"All right," Jesse said. "Jules, count us down when I give you the sign."

She nodded. Around her, everyone adjusted their positions and resettled themselves in anticipation of the recording. Behind the glass, Jesse flipped some switches, moved some levers, and pressed a button. He held his thumb up.

Jules adjusted her fingers on her guitar strings as she leaned into her mic. "One...two...three..."

Everyone played and music filled the space with the rollicking opening of *Dixie's Got Her Boots On*.

Jules bobbed her head along with the beat and when the time was right, opened her mouth and began to sing the first verse. "He shoulda been home already but it's half past ten. Dixie knows in her gut that he's done it again. He's down at that bar, taking things too far, making some other woman feel like a star."

She went right into the chorus with Sierra's

sweet voice backing her up. "Dixie's got her boots on, and she's headed to town. By the way she's walking, trouble's about to go down. Yeah, trouble's 'bout to go down."

Then came the bridge, a softer, slower break from the fast pace of the rest of the song. Rita and her slide guitar were right on time as the notes dropped lower. When Jules sang it with Cash's lower register accompanying her, she breathed out the words so that they rang with the warning they were meant to be. "You'd better run, boy, run as fast as you can. There's a woman on her way with a gun in her hand."

She sang the next two verses and the chorus again, all with the help of Cash and Sierra, then strummed the last few chords along with the rest of the musicians. They'd sounded just as good as the last run-through, if not better.

As the music faded, she gazed at Jesse, half afraid he was going to say something had gone wrong and they'd have to do it again.

No one said a word as he held up his finger and fiddled with the control board. Then he tapped a key and looked up at them, smiling. "Fantastic. Once again, that sounded great. Let's do it one more time, all right? I'd like to have three good versions recorded."

Jules agreed. That was generally how she did it, too.

They repeated *Dixie's Got Her Boots On* twice more, then Jesse confirmed that they were good. "All right," he said. "Bobby and I are going to get this thing mastered and ready to send. Shouldn't take us more than an hour, it's pretty clean. Why don't the rest of you go eat some lunch or get something to drink? Kitchen's open and waiting."

Jules took her guitar off. "Sounds good to me." She looked at her new band. "Lunch is on me, by the way." She wasn't letting Jesse pay again, even if it was his club.

"Thanks," Frankie said.

"Yeah, thanks," Rita said. "I can't wait to hear the finished song."

"Me, too," Cash said. "It's pretty exciting."

"It's the most exciting thing I've ever done," Rita said. "Outside of that time I jammed with Willie Nelson."

Cash laughed. "That would be exciting."

Jules and the rest of them left their instruments behind and filed out. On her way past Jesse, she smiled at him.

"I'll text you when it's ready," he said.

"I'll be waiting."

Everyone except for Bobby and Jesse went out to the dining room. They grabbed a big table and settled in to eat.

They were on dessert when Jules's phone lit up with a notification from Jesse.

It's done!! And it's good.

Jules blew out a breath. She motioned the server over to get the check. *We're just about finished. Ten minutes.*

Eight minutes later, they were all crammed into the control booth and Jesse was pressing Play.

The song filled the space. Jules closed her eyes to hear it as purely as possible. She didn't want to be influenced by the look on anyone's face.

She opened them when the song ended. She exhaled and nodded as an invisible weight fell off her shoulders. "Okay. It's really good."

"Good? It's dang near perfect," Bobby said with a grin. "That song's gonna light up the charts, I betcha."

Jules smiled. "I hope so."

Jesse hunched over his laptop. "I'm going to send you the file right now, Jules. Then you can get a copy to your agent, and the song can get uploaded and out there."

"It'll take at least a day for Spotify and iTunes to approve it," she said. "But it'll be more like five days before it's in the algorithms and searchable."

"Then there's no time like the present." He tapped another key. "There. Sent."

Her phone vibrated as the email came in. She opened the message, downloaded the file, which took a minute, then composed an email to Billy Grimm, her agent.

She attached the file, then with a few nerves fluttering in her stomach, hit Send. She quickly texted Billy.

Just emailed you the file for Dixie's Got Her Boots On. *I hope you like what we did with it.*

Outstanding, came his fast reply. *I've already been hyping it up, so I've got eager ears waiting. Here we go!*

She smiled, but that did nothing to quell her nerves. Here we go, indeed. She knew Billy would upload it immediately. He was as excited about this as she was. After all, a big hit for her would also be a big hit for him.

"All sent?" Cash asked.

She nodded.

He smiled. "I know you're nervous, but it's going to be huge, Mom. I can feel it."

"It's a great song," Sierra added. "I can't stop singing it."

Jules appreciated their support more than she could say. But there was nothing any of them could do now.

Except wait.

Claire's Buttercream

Ingredients
2 sticks salted butter at room temperature
1 stick Crisco regular shortening
2 pounds powdered sugar (more or less depending on some variables)
2 generous teaspoons of real vanilla extract

Directions
Mix butter, Crisco, and vanilla extract in the bowl of a stand mixer until well combined. Slowly add in powdered sugar a little at a time until the desired consistency is reached. Refrigerate if buttercream is too soft or use immediately.

Want to know when Maggie's next book comes out? Then don't forget to sign up for her newsletter at her website!

Also, if you enjoyed the book, please recommend it to a friend. Even better yet, leave a review and let others know.

About Maggie:

Maggie Miller thinks time off is time best spent at the beach, probably because the beach is her happy place. The sound of the waves is her favorite background music, and the sand between her toes is the best massage she can think of.

When she's not at the beach, she's writing or reading or cooking for her family. All of that stuff called life. She hopes her readers enjoy her books and welcomes them to drop her a line and let her know what they think!

Maggie Online:

www.maggiemillerauthor.com
www.facebook.com/MaggieMillerAuthor